Books by Laurien Berenson

Melanie Travis Mysteries

A PEDIGREE TO DIE FOR
UNDERDOG
DOG EAT DOG
HAIR OF THE DOG
WATCHDOG
HUSH PUPPY
UNLEASHED
ONCE BITTEN
HOT DOG
BEST IN SHOW
JINGLE BELL BARK
RAINING CATS AND DOGS
CHOW DOWN
HOUNDED TO DEATH
DOGGIE DAY CARE MURDER
GONE WITH THE WOOF
DEATH OF A DOG WHISPERER
THE BARK BEFORE CHRISTMAS
LIVE AND LET GROWL
MURDER AT THE PUPPY FEST
WAGGING THROUGH THE SNOW
RUFF JUSTICE
BITE CLUB
HERE COMES SANTA PAWS
GAME OF DOG BONES
HOWLOWEEN MURDER
PUP FICTION
SHOW ME THE BUNNY
KILLER CUPID

A Senior Sleuths Mystery

PEG AND ROSE SOLVE A MURDER
PEG AND ROSE STIR UP TROUBLE

Published by Kensington Publishing Corp.

A
FURRY LITTLE
CHRISTMAS

Laurien
Berenson

Kensington Publishing Corp.
www.kensingtonbooks.com

KENSINGTON BOOKS are published by
Kensington Publishing Corp.
119 West 40th Street
New York, NY 10018

All Kensington titles, imprints, and distributed lines are available at special quantity discounts for bulk purchases for sales promotion, premiums, fund-raising, educational, or institutional use.

Special book excerpts or customized printings can also be created to fit specific needs. For details, write or phone the office of the Kensington Sales Manager: Kensington Publishing Corp., 119 West 40th Street, New York, NY 10018. Attn. Sales Department. Phone: 1-800-221-2647.

The K and Teapot logo is a trademark of Kensington Publishing Corp.

ISBN: 978-1-4967-4525-5 (ebook)

ISBN: 978-1-4967-4207-0

First Kensington Trade Paperback Printing: October 2023

10 9 8 7 6 5 4 3 2 1

Printed in the United States of America

Contents

Wagging Through the Snow

1

Here Comes Santa Paws

147

Wagging Through the Snow

Chapter 1

"Ho! Ho! Ho!"

I was sitting at the kitchen table, working on a project for one of my fellow teachers when the back door to the house flew open. A blast of frigid air hit my papers and sent them scattering across the tabletop. My hasty grab to save them didn't help. Instead, I knocked into my laptop and sent it spinning into my half-full coffee mug.

Five black Standard Poodles had been snoozing on the floor at my feet. Startled by the intrusion, they jumped up and began to bark. Bud, the little spotted mutt who was the latest addition to our canine pack, scuttled over to stand beneath my chair. Quickly I righted the mug and scrambled to gather the papers before they could blow off the table.

Peace and quiet to utter mayhem in under ten seconds. Even for my house, that was a record.

I turned and aimed a withering look at our uninvited guest. My brother, Frank, was standing in the open doorway, grinning like a fool. Unfortunately, that was nothing new.

"Some welcoming committee," he said, gazing at the dogs.

The Poodles were now looking embarrassed by their outburst. Of course they recognized Frank. They just hadn't expected him to come flying through the door on this tranquil Saturday morning.

Any more than I had.

"Be glad they didn't bite you," I told him.

"They wouldn't do that." Frank took a step back. "*Would they?*"

Nope. No way. Not unless they thought there was a dire need.

My dogs were Standard Poodles, the largest of the three Poodle varieties. They were smart, funny, perceptive, and wonderfully affectionate. Poodles are people dogs. They would definitely attempt to think their way through a problem before resorting to violence.

On the other hand, my little brother has often been the bane of my existence. Maybe it wasn't a bad thing he didn't realize that.

"Come inside and close the door," I said. "It's freezing out there."

"It's December," Frank told me. Like we weren't all aware. "Merry Christmas!"

"Oh please. Christmas is a month away. We're still eating leftover turkey from Thanksgiving."

Frank shut the door, then pulled off his parka and draped it over the back of a chair. "It's never too early to embrace the Christmas spirit."

He walked over to the counter, got a mug out of the cabinet, and poured himself some coffee. The Poodles had yet to resettle and were still milling around the room. Faith, the oldest of the group, was keeping an eye on Frank. As he made himself at home in my kitchen, she shot me a look. *Is that allowed?*

I nodded silently. Faith has been part of my life for nearly eight years. I had never had a pet as a child, so she'd introduced me to the joys of dog ownership. I'd immediately fallen in love with Faith's sweet disposition, her empathetic nature, and her goofy sense of humor. My Poodle and I are soul mates. The relationship we share is deeper and more meaningful than I ever imagined was possible.

Faith found a quiet spot on the floor to lie down. I pushed my work stuff aside as my brother sank into a chair on the other side of the table. It looked like he was going to be here awhile.

"Is there any particular reason why we're feeling the need to embrace Christmas already?" I asked.

"As it happens, there is." Frank made a show of looking around the room. "Where is everyone?"

Aside from the six dogs who were very much in evidence, the rest of the family included my husband, Sam, our three-and-a-half-year-old son, Kevin, and Davey, our older son from my first marriage. On weekend mornings, our house is usually a hub of activity. I should have known better than to think I would actually score an uninterrupted hour in which to get some work done.

"Davey spent the night with Bob and Claire." Bob was my ex-husband and Claire was his new wife. Married the previous New Year's Eve, they lived in a house on the other side of Stamford. "He'll be back this afternoon. Sam and Kev are running errands."

I looked pointedly at the cluttered tabletop. "I'm supposed to be working."

Frank leaned forward eagerly. His straight brown hair, the same tawny shade as my own, fell forward over his eyes. Absently, he reached up and brushed it back. My brother and I also shared hazel eyes and a strong, determined, chin—a feature that looked better on him than me.

Beyond the physical similarities, however, Frank and I didn't have a lot in common. Growing up with a four-year age difference, we were always more likely to be squabbling than to have each other's backs. Even now that we're in our thirties—with Frank married to one of my best friends and partner in a thriving business—I still find it hard to think of my little brother as a mature adult.

"What are you working on?" he asked.

"Just school stuff."

"Like what?"

See, this is the problem. I'm pretty sure that Frank didn't show up in my kitchen at ten o'clock on a snowy weekend morning to talk about my job. For the record, I work as a special needs tutor at a private academy in Greenwich, Connecticut. Frank is already well aware of that. Which means that for some reason he's either stalling or trying to butter me up.

Color me skeptical, but neither of those options ever seems to end well. For me, that is. Things often turn out just fine for Frank.

But since I wasn't in any hurry to find out what sort of dilemma he'd found himself in now, I figured I might as well humor him. "Remember the Christmas bazaar last year at Howard Academy?"

"Who could forget it?" Frank smirked. "You were in charge of running the event and your Santa Claus got himself killed."

"Most people wouldn't find that funny," I told him.

"Most people don't have a sister who has a habit of tripping over dead bodies."

Sadly, he did have a point.

"It turns out that Russell Hanover, HA's headmaster, has asked me not to participate in this year's bazaar."

"Gee, I wonder why."

I ignored him and said, "I'm organizing my notes so I can hand them over to the new chairman, in case he wants to see what worked for me and what didn't."

"Big help, Mel. I'm pretty sure he already knows what didn't work." Frank was laughing now.

It was almost enough to make me wish one of the Poodles *had* bitten him. Maybe Tar. He's our older male Standard, a retired specials dog who'd enjoyed an enviable career in the dog show ring. Tar is drop-dead gorgeous. He's also endearing, endlessly amusing, and, well . . . dumb. Tar is the only Poodle I've ever met who's lacking in intelligence. He makes up for that deficiency by trying really hard to get things right.

Tar *wants* to be good. He just doesn't always succeed. And usually he hasn't a clue why. Come to think of it, he and Frank had more than a little in common.

"Very funny," I said. It was time to cut to the chase. "Frank, why are you here?"

"About that. . . ." He gazed at me earnestly across the table. "I need a favor."

Quelle surprise.

Then a sudden thought hit me. "Is everything all right at home? Bertie's doing well? Maggie and Josh are fine?"

Bertie and I had been friends for almost a decade. She'd been married to my brother for half that time. Their daughter, Maggie, was four and their second child, a son named Josh, had been born in September. The pregnancy wasn't an easy one and ten weeks after Josh's arrival, Bertie was still taking time to regain her footing.

"Sure, they're great. Bertie and Mags have everything under control. It's just that Josh, well, he's . . ."

"A baby?"

Frank winced. "I guess I didn't remember this part. Josh cries a lot. I mean, he really wails. Maggie never did that."

"Maggie wasn't colicky," I told him. "You know Bertie had Josh checked out and he's fine. This is just a stage he's going through."

"Yes, but that doesn't make it any easier. I feel like I haven't slept in days."

If Frank was angling for sympathy, he wasn't going to find it here. "Poor you," I said. "Does Bertie need my help?"

"Bertie?" Frank frowned. "Why are we talking about her? *I'm* the one with a problem."

Of course he was. I should have realized that. I settled back in my chair and asked, "What did you do now?"

"It wasn't my fault."

It never is, I thought with a sigh.

"You know The Bean Counter's been doing great, right?"

I nodded.

The Bean Counter was a café situated just north of the Merritt Parkway in Stamford. Originally opened by Frank, the bistro was now owned and operated in partnership with my ex-husband, Bob. The two men worked well together. Frank served as manager while Bob took care of the finances. Over the years, the café's popularity had grown and now it was considered a trendy destination for people who lived and worked in the area.

"Things are going so well that Bob decided we should start looking around at other investments," Frank explained. "Mostly real estate, because here in Fairfield County it's hard to go wrong."

"That sounds like a good idea," I said cautiously.

"I know, right?"

Frank sounded so eager for my approval that I found myself nodding again.

"So here's what happened. Yesterday morning, Josh *would not* stop crying. It was making me crazy. I had to get away, you know? So I figured I'd hop in the car and go for a drive."

It might have been more helpful if he'd taken Josh for a drive, I thought. Apparently that useful idea hadn't occurred to my brother.

"So there I was meandering around Wilton, not going anywhere in particular, when I saw a sign by the side of the road. It said ABSOLUTE AUCTION! ALL BIDS ACCEPTED! It turned out that ten acres of land was being sold to settle an estate. And just my luck, the auction was taking place at noon. I figured I might as well go have a look."

Oh boy. I could guess where this story was heading. Frank never had been able to resist a deal.

"Only a couple of other guys even showed up to bid. Maybe because it was the day after Thanksgiving, and everyone else was busy at the mall. Honest to God, I was only planning to watch and see how it went. But . . ."

"You raised your hand, didn't you?"

"I had to," Frank said earnestly. "Compared to the other lots Bob and I had looked at, this place was a *steal*. Ten acres of forested land in the northeast corner of Wilton. Wait 'til you see it."

I didn't need to see the property to know that if a deal sounded too good to be true, there had to be a catch.

"You know there's probably something wrong with it," I said. "Some zoning issue or easement dispute that needs to be resolved. Maybe the place is all wetlands. And an absolute auction means you own that land now, no matter what the problem is."

"I'm not worried about that." Frank brushed off my concern. "I'm sure Bob will get everything straightened out."

Possibly, I thought, depending on what the difficulty was. But Frank might also be placing too much faith in his partner's abilities. Bob was an accountant, not a magician.

"I'm glad you're happy with your purchase," I told him. "But there's really no need for me to see it."

"Sure there is! You haven't even heard the best part yet."

"There's more?" I asked dubiously.

"This isn't just any old piece of land with trees on it. The old guy who owned the place died over the summer, but through last winter he was running a seasonal business there. You're going to love this. Our new property is a Christmas tree farm!"

It took me a minute to form a suitable reply.

Frank couldn't wait that long. "Isn't it great?" he prompted.

"Um . . . yes?"

"And Christmas is in four weeks. Which makes this whole thing, like, perfect."

No. It was so not *like, perfect.*

"Frank, what are you going to do with a Christmas tree farm?"

"Get it up and running, of course."

"Don't you have to make preparations to do something like that?"

Frank, never one to plan ahead, seemed surprised by the question. "Like what?"

I could think of half-a-dozen answers off the top of my head. I went for the most obvious one. "Maybe grow some trees?"

"That's the beauty of it. The place is already overgrown. It's a veritable wilderness out there." My brother refused to let my misgivings dampen his enthusiasm. "You'll see. That land is going to pay us back in no time."

His phrasing brought me up short.

"Just to be clear," I said. "By *us*, you mean you and Bob, right? Sam and I aren't any part of this scheme."

"Not unless you want to be. But if I were you, I wouldn't make any hasty decisions about that. Wait until you see the place."

At least that was good to know. I was still feeling suspicious, however.

I peered at my brother across the table. "Have we come to the part yet where you ask me for a favor?"

"It's about Bob."

There was a sudden, sinking feeling in my stomach. "You talked to him before buying this place, didn't you?"

"Not exactly," Frank admitted. "Because I never meant to bid. And then it all happened so fast there wasn't time to check with him."

That was bad. Possibly really bad.

"You and Bob are supposed to be partners," I said. "And he has no idea you spent his investment money on a Christmas tree farm?"

"It's my money too." Frank sounded defensive. "And I know he'll be fine with the idea once he has a chance to think about it. That's where you come in. You guys are still friends even though you're not married anymore. I figured you could break the news to him."

Chapter 2

I shot that idea down in a hurry.

Then for my second act, I ushered my brother firmly out the door. After that, I went back to work. That lasted approximately twenty minutes before all you-know-what broke loose again. At least this time the chaos involved people I was happy to see.

"We got kibble!" Kevin announced. Almost four, he has yet to learn how to use his indoor voice. Or maybe he was just trying to make himself heard from within the pack of Poodles—including honorary member Bud—that was now eddying around his short legs.

"Forty pounds." Sam followed Kev through the connecting door from the garage, cradling the first bag in his arms. "That should last us a while."

Sam is tall, and strong, and surprisingly graceful. He has a great smile and the hands of a virtuoso. When he yanked off his wool cap and tossed it on the counter his blond hair, currently cropped short, stood straight up. If he hadn't been carrying twenty pounds of dog food, I'd have reached up and smoothed it back into place. As it was, I jumped up and hurried to open the pantry door.

Inside, the bag landed on the floor with a loud thump. Sam emerged from the pantry and headed back to the garage for the second load. I started to follow, then realized that Kev was peeling off his mittens and down jacket. He dropped them on the floor, then sat down to yank off his red rubber boots.

I quickly nudged aside the Poodles and scooped up Kev's discarded clothing before Bud could beat me to it. That little dog was obsessed with knitwear. Winter had barely begun and we were already on our third pair of mittens.

"Boots and jacket in the closet," I said to Kevin, handing them over.

He ambled toward the front hall and a Poodle escort followed. Kevin has been known to drop cookies, shoes, and the occasional rawhide strip. Tar, Faith's daughter, Eve, and our younger male, Augie, trailed along behind him, no doubt hoping for edible discards.

Bud, meanwhile, had given up on the mittens and gone trotting into the pantry. He was probably checking out the new bag of kibble. Half-starved when he'd been dumped by the side of the road the previous summer, the small dog had gained back all the weight he needed and more. Pretty soon he was going to be on a diet.

"Anything exciting happen while we were gone?" Sam asked when he'd delivered the second bag, shooed Bud out of the pantry, and firmly shut the door behind him.

The question—Sam's customary homecoming query—had become a standing joke. The way my life went, you'd think he would know better than to ask. But apparently not.

"Frank dropped by," I said.

"Just Frank? Not Bertie and the kids? Is everything all right?"

"More or less. My brother made an impulse purchase yesterday. He stopped in to tell me about it."

Sam had crouched down beside our fifth Standard Poodle, Raven. He was ruffling his hands through her coat. "Christmas shopping already? Good for Frank. If he braved the mall on the day after Thanksgiving, he's a better man than I am."

"He didn't go to the mall." I pulled out my chair and sat back down. "Frank bought a Christmas tree farm."

Sam paused to let that sink in. Then he looked up. "You're kidding, right?"

It took ten minutes to tell the whole story. Mostly because Sam alternated between interrupting me for details and laughing so hard that he couldn't hear what I was saying. By the time I was finished, he was shaking his head.

"So did you talk to Bob?"

"No way. Frank's going to have to break the news to Bob himself. I'm staying out of it."

Sam didn't look convinced. "Don't forget, Bob will be coming by later to drop off Davey. Frank's probably counting on you to tell him then."

"Then he's going to be disappointed," I said. "I've spent half my life cleaning up after my little brother. This time he's on his own."

Brave words. I just hoped I could make the resolution stick.

But as it turned out, I needn't have worried. The first thing Bob said upon his arrival was, "Did you hear what your harebrained brother has done now?"

"Hello to you too." I stepped around my ex-husband and gave Davey a quick hug.

Father and son, Bob and Davey were mirror images of one another. Both had sandy colored hair and dark eyes. They also shared the same lean, lanky build. At thirteen, Davey had yet to grow into the length of his limbs. Looking at him standing beside his father, I wondered if he ever would.

Davey gave me two seconds of hug-time, then squirmed out of my grasp. He tossed his backpack onto a nearby bench and said, "What's for dinner?"

"Guess."

"Not turkey again."

"You like turkey."

"Yeah, but not every day."

"Excuse me." Bob inserted himself between us. "Can we get back to what's important here? Your brother—"

"Your business partner," I corrected.

"—has bought himself a Christmas tree farm. What was he *thinking*?"

Davey had been on his way to the kitchen, but that pronouncement stopped him in his tracks. He spun around and stared at the two of us. "A Christmas tree farm? For real? Way to go, Frank!"

Someone growled under his breath. It might have been Bob.

I shooed Davey on his way and turned back to my ex-husband. "Apparently Frank was thinking that the two of you should open a new business selling trees."

Bob looked pained. "It's only four weeks until Christmas."

"Then you'd better hurry up and get started. Have you had a chance to take a look at the new property yet?"

Bob pushed aside Davey's backpack and sank down onto the wooden bench. "All I've seen so far are the few pictures the auction company put online to entice people to come to the sale. Although why anyone would be tempted by what they showed, I have no idea. The place looks pretty run-down. And that's putting it mildly."

"Frank told me that the owner passed away last summer," I said.

"Trust me, that place has been in a state of disrepair for a lot longer than that. Abel Haney was in his nineties when he died.

He'd owned the land for fifty years and it doesn't look as though he'd made a single recent improvement. Who knows if the place is even compliant with current safety standards?"

"Abel Haney?" Sam came walking into the front hall. He was staring down at his phone. "As in Haney's Holiday Home? It says here that your Christmas tree farm has been a seasonal fixture in North Wilton for decades. *Fairfield County Magazine* even named it a 'top holiday attraction.'"

"I'll bet," Bob muttered. "What year was that?"

Sam squinted at the screen. "Nineteen eighty-eight."

"That's a whole different century." Davey laughed from the kitchen doorway. "I wasn't even born then."

"That Frank, he's a dreamer," I said happily. Wasn't it wonderful that this wasn't my problem?

"That's one way of putting it." Bob clearly wasn't amused. "Don't think I'm forgetting it was your fault that I went into business with your brother in the first place."

"Oh no you don't," I said. "You are not blaming this problem on me. Besides, until yesterday the two of you made great partners. Look at The Bean Counter. It's a big success."

"And do you know why?" Bob shot back. "Because each of us has stuck to doing what we're good at. Frank is operations and I'm finance. He's not supposed to wake up one morning and decide to squander *my* money on some holiday pipe dream."

Sam cleared his throat. "It wasn't entirely your money, was it?"

"Like that makes all the difference." Bob braced his hands on either side of the oak bench and pushed himself to his feet. "I suppose there's no point in complaining about something I can't change. The only thing left to do now is go have a look at the place, and see what we've gotten ourselves into." He pulled the edges of his parka together and ran up the zipper. "How's tomorrow? Are you guys free?"

Sam, Davey, and I shared a look.

"What?" Bob stared at the three of us. "Of course you're coming. I'm not checking out Haney's Holiday Home on my own."

"Now that you own the place, it needs a new name," Davey said. "What about Frank's Folly?"

"You're not helping." I pointed toward the kitchen where Davey was supposed to be doing something. Anything. I didn't even care what. He eluded my outstretched hand with a grin.

"Call it whatever you like, but you guys are in on this too," Bob said. "Eleven o'clock. I'll see you there."

Sam watched as Bob left, pulling the door shut behind him. "That must be why you divorced that man," he said thoughtfully.

"What do you mean?"

"You've never been good at taking orders."

I wanted to muster some outrage at that, but I really couldn't. Whatever.

Early Sunday morning my phone rang. A glance at the name on the screen confirmed what I'd already suspected. The only surprise was that it had taken her this long.

Even in a family as contentious as mine, Aunt Peg was notable for her forceful personality, her unending curiosity, and her total inability to ever, under any circumstances, *leave well enough alone*. Which meant that if there was trouble brewing anywhere in the vicinity, Aunt Peg wanted in. And if possible, she'd also like to drag her relatives into the fray too.

So this situation had the potential to be the sum of all good things as far as she was concerned. Christmas. Family troubles. And Bob had a problem. Did I mention that Aunt Peg and my ex-husband don't get along? To say that she would greet his tree farm predicament with gusto was an understatement. I could practically picture her rubbing her hands together with glee.

"I take it you've heard the news," I said into the phone.

"Claire called me," Aunt Peg replied. "Thank goodness I have *one* relative who takes the time to keep me informed."

Claire was a relatively new addition to the family. She was still naïve enough to believe that Aunt Peg used her formidable powers for better, rather than worse. She'd learn.

"I hear you're going to have a look at the place."

"So Bob tells me," I said. "It didn't sound like we had a choice."

"Excellent. Eleven o'clock, right? I'll see you there."

She disconnected before I even had a chance to ask if she'd been invited to accompany us. Which was obviously a moot point. But still.

Faith and Eve were lying on the nearby bed. Both their heads had been inquisitively cocked to one side as I'd spoken on the phone. Two sets of dark eyes watched as I put the device down on my dresser. I was certain they knew who I'd been talking to.

Aunt Peg was a renowned Standard Poodle breeder. She was also a long-time dog show exhibitor and now a Toy and Non-Sporting group judge. Her Cedar Crest Kennel had produced many of the best Standard Poodles bred and shown in the U.S. Dogs were Aunt Peg's vocation and her passion. And no matter how often she and I clashed, I would always be grateful for the fact that Faith had entered my life as a gift from Aunt Peg.

There was no way I could ever repay her for that and we both knew it.

"I'm sorry," I told the two Poodles. "She didn't ask to talk to you."

It was clear they didn't believe me.

"Really," I said. "Would I lie to you?"

Eve hopped down off the bed and left the room. Davey appeared in the doorway a moment later. He was wearing flannel-lined jeans, Bean boots, and a thick Williams College sweatshirt: warm clothes for tramping around a snowy tree farm.

"Blueberry pancakes for breakfast," he told me. "Sam's cooking. If you don't hurry up, Kev and I will eat them all before you get there."

He didn't have to tell me twice.

Chapter 3

From our house in Stamford, the drive to northwest Wilton took twenty-five minutes. Though it was only the last week of November, there was already snow on the ground. We'd had six inches on a school day two weeks earlier, followed by another three inches the day before Thanksgiving. New Englanders are used to dealing with winter weather, however, and even the small roads were clear and easily passable. It occurred to me as we neared our destination that a fresh coat of glistening snow might make the Christmas tree farm look more attractive than it otherwise would have.

Unfortunately, that turned out to be wishful thinking. My first impression of Frank's new acquisition was that it was hardly worth the trip.

Our only indication that we'd arrived at the right address was a faded wooden sign that had fallen off its post and was leaning against a tree by the side of the road. Block lettering that might have once been red, but was now a tacky shade of pink, announced the name of our destination. Beside the empty signpost, a narrow dirt driveway led the way into the densely wooded property. At least the driveway was plowed.

"Well." Sam cleared his throat as he nosed the SUV into the rutted lane. "This looks rustic."

Davey leaned toward his window for a better look. "I was going to say *shabby* myself."

The SUV bounced from side to side as we negotiated the driveway. I reached back to steady Kevin in his seat. "This is only the entrance. Maybe it will look better when we get to the buildings."

"Time to buy a Christmas tree?" Kev asked hopefully.

"Not today," I said. "We're just going to have a look around."

"Ornaments?"

"No ornaments," Davey told him. "But while the grown-ups are talking, you and I can collect pinecones. I bet we'll find lots of them around here."

Kevin clapped his hands. He enjoyed doing anything his big brother suggested.

A few seconds later, we emerged from the trees and got our first look at the portion of the property where Haney's Holiday Home conducted business. Sam lifted his foot off the gas pedal and the SUV rolled to a stop. The driveway had been in a state of disrepair. What we saw before us looked even worse.

Two weathered clapboard buildings had been erected on the far side of a clearing. The smaller building had a corrugated roof and double garage doors. I guessed it was an equipment shed. Hopefully, it was only my imagination that the walls of the decrepit structure appeared to be swaying in the light breeze.

Thankfully, the larger structure looked more secure. A sign, stuck in the ground beside a shoveled walkway, identified that building as the office. Two wooden steps led to a covered porch whose banister was mostly intact. A narrow door, coated with peeling green paint, provided access to the building. It was flanked on either side by small, square windows whose glass was coated with grime.

A parking area on the other side of the clearing had recently been plowed, and I saw that we weren't the first to arrive. A black Jeep Wrangler was already pulled up beside a low drift. As Sam parked the SUV, the Wrangler's door opened and Frank hopped out.

"So . . ." he said, waving a hand expansively. "What do you think?"

I hoped to God he wasn't looking for an honest answer.

"It could do with some *sprucing* up," I told him.

Frank frowned. He didn't get it. "Well, sure. But that's just cosmetic stuff. We can have that fixed in no time."

"Good one, Mom." Davey looked at me and grinned. That boy is a child after my own heart.

The sound of approaching cars had us all turning back to look at the tree-shrouded entrance. After a moment, Aunt Peg's minivan and Bob's dark green Explorer came bouncing into view.

"Your driveway needs some work," Sam commented.

"It's too late now, but we'll get to that next year," Frank told him. "I'll be sure to earmark some of the profits for paving."

"*Some of the profits?*" Sam muttered under his breath.

I looked at him and shrugged.

There'd been plenty of times in the past when Frank's optimism had left me feeling incredulous too. My brother has a tendency to leapfrog over problems, seeing only the desired solution that lies ahead. Sometimes that tunnel vision worked for him. Other times it left him knocked flat on his back and wondering where things had gone wrong.

Davey unloaded Kevin from the SUV. I took a minute to check that his boots were fastened and his mittens were actually on his hands. By the time that was done, Bob and Aunt Peg had parked and joined us.

We all stood and stared at the pair of dilapidated buildings.

"Hey," Frank said suddenly. "There's even a chimney. I bet the office has a fireplace."

I saw Bob's eyes widen fractionally. He turned and looked at his partner. "Don't you *know*?"

"Um . . . not exactly."

"But you must have gone inside the building before you bought it." When Frank didn't reply right away, Bob added, "You *did* look inside the building, didn't you?"

"I would have." Frank's voice edged toward a whine. "But the auction was hectic and there wasn't time."

"*No time to step inside a building that you were planning to buy?*"

"Land!" Frank blurted out. He sounded pleased with himself, as if he'd come up with a particularly clever answer. "I was buying the *land*. Look around. Isn't it beautiful?"

I had to admit, what we could see of the property did possess a certain pastoral charm. Particularly if you were willing to look past the tattered buildings and pothole-filled parking lot and fasten your gaze on the wondrous forest of pine trees that spread out around us in three directions. As I'd suspected it might, the blanket of new snow had freshened everything up. I hated to think what Haney's Holiday Home might look like during spring thaw.

Aunt Peg was already on her way to the steps. "Rather than standing here wondering what's inside, let's go have a look, shall we?"

The porch sagged beneath our collective weight as Frank fished around in his pocket for the key to open the office door. While we waited, Bob stepped to one side and pulled out his phone. He began to record what sounded like a to-do list.

"Replace front step," I heard him say quietly. "Brace banister. Check porch supports."

Davey and Kevin had remained behind on the walk. Davey

took his little brother's hand and said, "Kev and I are going to go explore the woods, okay?"

"I guess that's all right." I looked at Sam, who nodded. "But don't go too far. And don't get lost. And don't let Kevin out of your sight."

"*Mo-o-om.*" Davey stopped just short of rolling his eyes. "It's all good. We'll be fine. They're just trees."

"*Strange* trees," I clarified. Then frowned. Even to my own ears that sounded overly protective. "Don't get into any trouble. And if you do, come right back."

"No trouble," Kevin agreed. "We're going to look for pinecones."

"And grizzly bears," Davey told him.

Kev's mouth opened to form a round O.

"No bears," I said quickly. "No coyotes. No beavers. In fact, no wildlife at all. Got it?"

"Got it," Davey called back over his shoulder as he and his brother went tromping away through the snow.

"Got it!" Frank announced, pulling the key out of his pocket.

It was an ornate skeleton key, at least four inches in length. Bronze in color, it looked heavy. How Frank could have misplaced something that size in his pants pocket, I had no idea. He shoved the key in the lock and turned it hard to the right.

For a moment, nothing happened. Then we heard a small thud as the bolt receded. Frank turned the knob and pushed. The door didn't budge.

"Oil hinges," Bob said into his phone.

Frank turned the knob again. This time he applied his shoulder to the door and pushed harder. There was a sharp squeal as it finally gave way. The door swung open before us and revealed . . . virtually nothing.

The four of us stood on the porch and squinted into the building's dimly-lit interior. The only available light was that filtering through the dirty windowpanes. The bright glare of the sun on snow behind us didn't help. It made the single room appear darker and gloomier.

Frank remained undaunted. "There must be a light switch," he said. Reaching inside, his hand fumbled around the door-frame. A few seconds later, we heard a sharp click. "Found it!"

Nothing happened.

"Turn on electricity," Bob said into his phone.

"Wash windows," I muttered under my breath.

Frank shot us both a look. "Is that really necessary?"

"I should think so," Bob replied. But when Frank continued to glare at him, he made a show of turning off the device and tucking it in his pocket.

While the rest of us stood there wondering what to do next, Aunt Peg was ever prepared. "I thought something like this might happen. I've got a lantern in my van. Be right back."

In no time at all she was leading the way into the building.

The interior room looked to be about twenty feet square. Shelves, now empty, lined one of the unfinished wooden walls. On the other side was a waist-high counter. An old-fashioned cash register sat on top of it. Its drawer was open and also empty. A cane and wooden rocking chair with a well-worn seat had been abandoned in one corner. Frank had been wrong about the fireplace, but there was a wood-burning stove. A box next to it held a pair of fire tongs and a small pile of logs.

Dust motes, stirred up by our footsteps, danced in the stale air around us and I stifled the urge to sneeze. A long, vinyl ban-ner lay curled up on the wood plank floor. Sam picked it up, spread it out on the counter, and read aloud, "After Christmas Sale! Everything Half Off! All Decorations Must Go!"

"It seems kind of sad." My eyes came to rest on the rocking chair. "When Mr. Haney closed up this building last January, he had no idea that he'd never be back."

"Perhaps not," Aunt Peg said tartly. "But he doesn't seem to have left much behind."

"Haney's loss is our gain." Never one to dwell on sentiment, Frank was walking around the room, checking things out. "This place has potential, doesn't it? Okay, so it needs to be cleaned up and aired out. But that's no big deal. Picture the room decorated with holly and pine boughs, and maybe some swags of red ribbon."

My brother's gaze flicked in Bob's direction. "Claire could be in charge. She's great with stuff like that."

Bob didn't even hesitate before shaking his head. "Before you go nominating my wife to be in charge of housekeeping—which, by the way, is something she won't thank you *or* me for—I think we need to discuss the feasibility of getting this business up and running at all. Is that something we even want to tackle? Especially on such short notice."

"Sure it is," Frank replied. "Haney's Holiday Home is a Christmas tradition. It was even profiled in a magazine. You told me Sam said so."

Sam held up his hands in a display of innocence. He wasn't about to assume credit or blame for any part of this project. "All I did was look it up on the internet. Anyone could have done that."

"Think of all the children whose holidays will be ruined if their families aren't able to come here like they've always done and cut down their own special Christmas tree," Frank implored.

"Heaven forbid they have to buy a tree from a nursery," I said.

"Or Walmart," Sam added. It looked like he was trying not to laugh.

"You see?" Frank said to Bob. "Haney's Holiday Home isn't just a business. It's a community service."

Aunt Peg leaned toward Frank and said in a stage whisper, "Don't oversell it. Back off now and give Bob a day or two to think about it. He'll come around."

"I will?" Bob sounded surprised.

"Of course," Aunt Peg told him. "Christmas is coming and you own a Christmas tree farm. If that isn't fate, I don't know what is."

We heard a clatter from outside. Davey came racing up the steps and through the open doorway.

"I thought I told you not to let go of your brother's hand," I said as he skidded to a stop.

"He's right behind me," Davey said breathlessly. Thank goodness he was right. "You guys better come and have a look. There's something weird out here."

"Weird how?" Aunt Peg immediately perked up. While the rest of us were processing that information, she was already on her way to the door.

Davey gulped for air. "Out in the woods. It sounds like someone's crying."

"You're imagining things," Frank said with a snort.

Davey looked at me and shook his head. *Damn.* I had hoped Frank was right.

We all scrambled through the doorway together. As Sam scooped Kevin up in his arms, I shut the door behind us. Davey flew across the porch and hopped down the two steps. "This way."

At first glance, the wooded area behind the building looked as though its trees had been planted in an orderly fashion. Although that might have been the case at one point, once we entered the forest it quickly became clear how overgrown the farm's cash crop had been allowed to become.

The main path leading into the woods was about six feet wide and clogged with snow. Foliage encroached on either side.

Some of the Christmas trees were only waist-high. Others soared way above my head. Most appeared to be Scotch pine, but I also saw some spruces and a batch of balsam firs. Mr. Haney had clearly believed in catering to a variety of tastes.

Aunt Peg was out ahead of us. Moving with assurance, she was retracing the footsteps the boys had left in the almost knee-deep snow. Determined to catch up, I raced ahead of the rest of the group.

We left the main path behind and veered off into the trees. The vegetation was thicker there. Snow-covered boughs hung low over the narrow trail. I'd gone about fifty feet when the sound of a soft, mournful whimpering made me stop abruptly in my tracks.

"See?" Davey came up behind me. "I told you. Something's out there."

"Go back and take Kevin from Sam," I told him. "You two stay behind the adults while we go see what it is."

Reluctantly, Davey did as I'd requested. As soon he reached the three men I took off again, following in Aunt Peg's foot-steps. In the quiet woods, the low, mewling sound seemed to float on the light breeze. It had an almost ghostly quality. I could feel the hair on the back of my neck beginning to rise.

It was hard to travel fast in the wet snow. I was looking down and watching where I was placing my feet, so when Aunt Peg stopped unexpectedly, I almost ran into her.

Aunt Peg is nearly six feet tall and broader than I am. There was no way I could see around her. As I ducked to one side, pushing several heavy branches out of my way, I heard her suck in a sharp breath.

Then the view in front of me cleared and I saw what she had seen.

The body of a man was lying in a drift of snow beneath a lush fir tree. There was a jagged, bloody gash across the top of his head. A thick branch, broken off the tree above, lay on the ground beside him. The man's skin was pale and waxy looking. His eyes were open and staring at the sky.

I flinched and quickly turned away. When I raised my hands and held them in place, Frank, Sam, Bob, and the boys halted immediately. No one needed to come any closer. There was nothing any of us could do to help.

Whatever had made the sound that drew us to this place, it was clear that we'd arrived too late.

Chapter 4

Bob called the police. Sam hustled the kids back down the path and took them home. Under these gruesome circumstances, Aunt Peg definitely wouldn't be going anywhere. I knew I could catch a ride with her later.

My brother has never been the most useful person in an emergency. Now Frank walked into a nearby thicket of trees and threw up. As he finished heaving, I once again heard the soft keening sound that had drawn us to the clearing in the first place.

Aunt Peg and I shared a startled glance.

"That man looks dead," I said. "He *is* dead, right?"

"*He* is," Aunt Peg replied. "But maybe he's not alone."

Davey had said there was something weird going on out here. As I recalled those words, I found my thoughts scattering in all sorts of unwelcome directions. Even in broad daylight. Even though I was accompanied by two strong men—and Aunt Peg, who could probably take them both down in a brawl.

While I was envisioning malevolent forest spirits, Aunt Peg

opted for a more practical approach. Giving the body a wide berth, she trod carefully around to the other side of the clearing. There she knelt down in the snow, removed one of her gloves, and held out her hand.

"What are you doing?" I asked.

"I think there's something burrowed underneath the body. A little animal of some kind. I can see a pair of dark eyes looking out at me."

I took a step back. "Well, don't ask it to come out here. What if it's a wolverine? Or a biting otter?"

Aunt Peg cast me a look. "You don't spend much time in nature, do you?"

"Not in the woods. Not in the middle of winter."

"Trust me, it's not a biting otter. I think it might be a little white dog." She turned her attention back to the task at hand, beckoning as she crooned, "Come on out, little guy. Nobody's going to hurt you. You must be very cold under there. Come to me and I'll take care of you."

Aunt Peg loved dogs completely. She could communicate with them on a level most people didn't even know existed. If there was a dog in the world who could resist her charms, I had yet to meet it.

I heard a rustling sound, followed by scratching and scrambling. A black nose poked out from beneath the body. Then a dirty white head emerged. After a brief hesitation a small, raggedy dog with dark, button eyes crawled out of his hiding place. He walked cautiously across the crusted snow to Aunt Peg's outstretched hand.

Even from afar, I could see that the bedraggled canine was wet and shivering.

Aunt Peg remained still as the dog sniffed her fingers. When he relaxed and pressed his head into her hand, she picked him up and tucked him against her body. "You poor thing. Have you been out here all night?"

"Possibly longer." I glanced at the corpse between us.

"The police are on their way," Bob said, returning to my side. "I sent Frank back to the office to wait for them. When they arrive, he'll show them where we are."

"Good idea." I was sure Frank had been grateful for the assignment.

Bob nodded in Aunt Peg's direction. "What's that?"

"Unless I miss my guess, it's a Maltese," she informed him.

A Maltese. There was a dead body lying on the ground just a few feet away. Somehow, that wasn't enough of a distraction to keep Aunt Peg from identifying the breed of the dog she held cradled in her arms. Amazing.

Bob looked around the clearing. "Where did it come from?"

"It was under the body," I told him. "It must have belonged to that man."

"He was keeping him company." Aunt Peg unzipped her parka and slipped the small dog inside, then closed her jacket again for warmth. "I suspect he was waiting for his owner to wake up."

We'd all been avoiding looking at the body. Now our attention was directed back that way.

"Who do you suppose he is?" asked Bob.

Aunt Peg took a step toward the corpse. "Maybe there's some ID in his coat."

"No. Don't." To my surprise, she stopped when I held up my hand. "You've already appropriated the guy's dog. I think we'd better let the police handle the rest."

"I guess you have a point." Aunt Peg gazed up at the tree above him. "That branch must have broken off and hit him on the head. But what do you suppose was he doing out here in the first place?"

"Walking his dog?" I said.

Bob frowned. "This is private property. The least he could have done was have the decency to die somewhere else."

In the silence that followed that statement, I could hear the sound of approaching sirens. It sounded as though the emergency crews had turned out in force. Wilton was a quiet town. I was guessing the police here didn't receive many reports of unidentified dead bodies.

"That's odd." Bob was still peering at the body on the ground.

"What is?" I asked.

"Look at the guy's clothes. He's got on a ton of layers to stay warm, but everything he's wearing looks old and worn. Even his boots."

I took a peek at the dead man's feet. There was a hole in one of his upturned soles and the toe of his other boot had been mended with duct tape.

"See what I mean?" Bob asked. "This is a nice area. If he lived around here—close enough to be out for a stroll in these woods—you'd think he wouldn't be wearing clothes that looked like they came from the Salvation Army. Or the dump."

"Maybe he's an eccentric recluse." Aunt Peg sounded pleased by the thought. "Or a hobo that hopped off a passing train."

Except there were no passing trains in the vicinity. As Aunt Peg knew perfectly well.

"Just my luck," Bob muttered. "I *knew* there had to be something sketchy about this deal. 'It's just beautiful open land and trees', Frank said. 'Undeveloped property in Wilton. What could possibly go wrong?' And here we are."

I'd expected there would be a catch too. But even I hadn't imagined one of this magnitude.

"I'm sure the police will get everything sorted out," I told him. "They'll remove the body and notify the next of kin. In an hour or two, this unfortunate episode will all be over and your life can go back to normal."

"Normal." Bob shook his head. "Which I suppose means

going back to arguing with Frank about opening a Christmas shop on five minutes' notice."

The next hour passed in a flurry of activity. A pair of policemen were the first to arrive. They were followed by an ambulance and EMTs. The medical examiner rolled in after that. Frank kept busy making trips back and forth from the parking lot, directing each new group to the scene. Bob, who'd identified himself as co-owner of the property, was asked a multitude of questions—most of which he had no answers for.

Aunt Peg and I stood off to one side, trying to stay out of the way as the officers photographed the body, then conducted a brief examination. Mostly that seemed to consist of them pointing at the dead man's head wound, then at the broken tree branch, and nodding in agreement.

The police also searched the body for identification, but I didn't see them remove anything from the man's pockets. So when the officers stood up and stepped away from the body, I was surprised to overhear one of them refer to the man on the ground as Pete.

"Excuse me," I said to the one nearest me. "Do you know who that man is?"

Earlier, Aunt Peg and I had been asked to supply our names and the reason for our presence. The two policemen—busy dealing with Bob—hadn't bothered to introduce themselves to us. In the intervening time they'd neither paid us any further attention, nor commented on the little white dog whose head was clearly visible poking out of the opening of Aunt Peg's parka. Now they seemed surprised to hear me speak at all.

"His name is Pete," the officer replied.

Thanks to my big ears, I already knew that much. "Does he have a last name?"

"I'm sure he does, but I'm not aware of it."

"But you do recognize him?"

"We've seen him around town," the other policeman told

me. "Pete's made his home in Wilton for quite a while now. Four or five years, I'd guess. Usually we'd see more of him in the summer months."

"Did he live around here?" I asked.

"That's the thing. Pete didn't live any one place in particular. He did quite a bit of wandering. Then he'd just set up camp wherever he found a likely spot."

"Are you saying that Mr. Pete here was homeless?" Aunt Peg asked.

"That's about the gist of it. People felt sorry for him and gave him money, most of which he took directly to the liquor store."

The first policeman added, "Pete didn't seem to have anywhere to go. And sometimes he got confused about where he was. But other than that, he was harmless. We made sure that he stayed away from the schools, but beyond that there wasn't much else we could do."

"But—" I sputtered. "Wasn't there a shelter he could go to? Some place safe that would take him in?"

"There are social services that could have helped him. But Pete would have had to do his part too. For one thing, he would have needed to get the drinking under control. For another, he had to want to be helped. Have you ever dealt with the homeless, ma'am?"

I shook my head.

"Many of them don't want to be part of the system. They prefer to make their own choices and look out for themselves. For some, that kind of enforced structure is something they purposely left behind. They'd rather live on the streets and maintain their independence. During the time Pete was here in Wilton, he always seemed to manage tolerably well."

"Until now," Aunt Peg said drily.

"Yes, ma'am," the officer agreed. "Until now."

He stepped away from us and walked over to confer with the

EMTs. The medical examiner had arrived a few minutes earlier and the group of men stood huddled around the body. They spoke quietly among themselves, their voices too soft for me to hear what they were saying.

"What about Pete's dog?" I asked the officer who'd remained with us. "What will happen to him?"

"Dog?" His gaze shifted to Aunt Peg, who was frowning at me mightily. I could see that she was tempted to stuff the little Maltese down out of sight and zip the parka up to her chin. "Is that Snowball in there?"

"Snowball?"

"That's what Pete called him. He and that little dog were just about inseparable. Where'd you find him?"

"He was with the body, shivering and crying," Aunt Peg said. "That's how we came to find his owner."

The policeman frowned. "I suppose this means we'll have to call animal control. Of course, nobody's going to pick up that phone on the Sunday after Thanksgiving. And I suppose we can't leave him here. . . ."

"Certainly not," Aunt Peg said sharply. With effort, she moderated her tone. "If I may offer a solution. Why don't I take Snowball home with me until you're able to make other arrangements for his care? I assume you'll also be contacting Pete's next of kin?"

"We will do so if we're able to," he replied. "Right now, I wouldn't say that's a given. Pete's fingerprints might or might not be in the system. And we can check with social services to see what kind of information they have on him in their records. But we may have trouble making a positive ID."

"Surely his family will want to know what happened to him," I said.

"If he *has* family. Or any people at all who still care about his welfare. I wouldn't say that's a given either. If you'll excuse me?" The officer left us and went to join the group of men beneath the tree.

Bob came over to stand beside us. Even though we'd been divorced for a dozen years, I could still read his moods. Now, for some reason, he looked relieved.

"They're saying there's no indication of foul play," he told us. "The guy appears to have frozen to death in the snow. Apparently he was known around here as a vagrant and an alcoholic. One of the EMTs said the body reeked of gin."

"What about the gash on his head?" I asked.

"They're guessing he was drunk, lost his balance, and grabbed the branch to steady himself. That—added to the weight of the snow on top of it—made the branch break and hit him on the head. The ME will do an autopsy, but he's pretty sure that once the guy was unconscious he died of exposure. It looks like it was just an unfortunate accident. So that's good news."

I turned and stared at him.

Bob's nose was already red from the cold. Now his cheeks grew red to match. "Sorry, I didn't mean that the way it sounded."

"I should hope not," said Aunt Peg. "But surely that can't be the whole story."

"Why not?" asked Bob. "It sounded logical to me."

"Didn't anybody stop to wonder why a homeless man would have been way out here in the middle of nowhere, wandering around in the snow?"

"I didn't hear them say anything about that." Bob looked pained. He wanted answers, not more questions.

"That's what I was afraid of," Aunt Peg said.

Chapter 5

Frank joined our small group and we withdrew to the head of the path. The authorities were wrapping things up.

Once they'd realized who the body in the snow belonged to, it felt as though the mood in the clearing had changed. Any sense of urgency had vanished. Now the authorities' response felt perfunctory.

It was as if the death of a homeless man was less important than the other things I could hear them discussing: an upcoming football game, a traffic accident on Route 7, their holiday vacation schedules. Dealing with the remains of the man we knew only as Pete was just another chore they needed to finish before moving on with the rest of their day.

"That was a good question," Bob said to Aunt Peg. He didn't look nearly as reassured as he had a few minutes earlier.

"Of course it was." She lowered her zipper a few inches, shifted the bundle beneath her parka from side to side, then looked pointedly at me. "Someone should try and figure out the answer."

"What question?" asked Frank.

"Aunt Peg wanted to know why a homeless man would have been out in these woods on a snowy winter night," I said.

"Hmm." Frank considered that. "I wonder if Sean Haney knows anything about him."

We all turned to look at him. Even Snowball popped his head out of the opening at the top of Aunt Peg's jacket.

"Who is Sean Haney and why might he know something?" she inquired.

"He's the former owner's son. I met him the other day at the auction. At the end of the bidding, he came over and shook my hand, and wished me luck with the property. Sean gave me his card, although at the time I couldn't imagine what I'd ever need it for. I think I tossed it in my glove compartment."

We made our way back down the now well-trampled trail. The small parking area was crowded with official vehicles. Frank skirted around them and went to his Jeep. He searched around the car for at least five minutes, but finally emerged holding a lavender-tinted business card.

"What does Sean Haney do?" Bob gazed at the card with a slight smile on his face as Frank tapped out the number on his phone.

"According to this, he's the owner of Sean's Spa and Salon in Weston." My brother glanced up. "That family loves their alliteration, don't they?"

Frank put the phone to his ear, then walked several feet away so he could conduct the call in private. I wasn't having any of that. Bob and Aunt Peg hung back, but I shadowed his steps across the parking lot. I listened as my brother identified himself to Sean and explained what had happened.

Then there was a long period of silence, while Frank listened and frowned. "I see," he said.

"See what?" I mouthed impatiently.

Frank glared at me and angled his body away.

The evasive move annoyed me every bit as much as he'd

known it would. Given the slightest opportunity, my brother and I snap right back into the fractious relationship we'd had as children.

"I see," Frank said again.

I walked around and planted myself in front of him. *Would it kill him to ask a pertinent question or two?*

"Uh-huh." Frank nodded. "I get that." He looked at me and stuck out his tongue.

And there it was. The last straw.

"Give me that." I reached over and snatched the phone out of Frank's hand. "Hello, Sean, this is Melanie Travis. I'm Frank's sister and I'm delighted that you have some information for us."

"Oh, I don't know about that," Sean replied. "But I'm happy to try to help if I can. I was just telling Frank a little bit about my day spa over here in Weston."

Seriously? They'd been talking for several minutes. Thank goodness I had appropriated the phone when I did.

"We offer the best massage therapy in all of Fairfield County," Sean continued happily. "And our mud and avocado wrap is second to none."

Clearly he was a guy who liked to talk. I hoped Sean would feel the same way after a change of subject.

"That sounds wonderful," I said. "But about the man whose body was found here this morning . . . the police told us his name was Pete."

"Yeah, Pete—that's it. I remember him."

"What do you know about him?"

"Truthfully, not a whole lot. The tree farm was my dad's thing, not mine. I haven't spent much time there in years. But Dad used to talk about some spacey dude who hung around the property in the winter. He was always trying to get the guy to stay out of sight during the holidays. Dad didn't want him interfering with customers who were in the woods chopping down Christmas trees."

"If Pete was a problem, why didn't your father tell him to leave?" I asked.

"Dad would never have done that. Pete was okay, just a little too into the sauce, if you know what I mean. Dad believed in paying things forward. He thought Pete was the kind of guy who could use a helping hand."

"Your father sounds like a lovely man," I said.

"He was," Sean agreed. "He was a practical man too. After the holiday season ended the farm just sat empty for the rest of the winter. Come spring, Dad could book events there, or sometimes commercial shoots. But January through March, the place was just a bunch of trees growing. So if Pete wanted to make his home in the woods for the winter, Dad wasn't about to object."

I tried unsuccessfully to picture how that would work. "Was Pete camping out there?"

"Oh, heck no." Sean laughed. "He'd have frozen if he did that. In the back of the property there's an old tumbledown shack. Been there for years. It's hardly much more than a roof, four walls, and a floor, but with a little stove I guess it stays warm enough."

"That sounds pretty Spartan."

"Tell me about it. I'm much too sociable to live like that, but Pete did okay. Dad always said it suited Pete, because the only thing he wanted was for the world to go away and leave him alone."

I exhaled slowly. "What a sad way to live. Did your father know why Pete felt that way?"

"If he did, he never told me. Tell the truth, I don't think Dad spent any time worrying about it. He just accepted Pete for who he was. If I had to hazard a guess, I'd say the drinking had

something to do with it. And now your brother told me the police think that's what caused his death?"

"That's right," I said. "Did your father know Pete's last name?
Or where he'd lived before he came to Wilton?"

"Stuff like that, Pete didn't talk about it and Dad didn't ask.
That's probably why the guy kept coming back. Every year
when the weather got warm again he'd disappear for a while.
Probably found somewhere to hang out that better suited his
needs. But he always seemed to find his way back to the farm in
the fall."

"What about Pete's dog?" I asked.

"That little rug rat that followed him around? What about it?"

"Apparently it's a purebred Maltese. Do you know where it
came from?"

"You're kidding me, right?" Sean snorted. "I don't even
know what a purebred Maltese is, much less where you'd find
one."

Okay, I'd been grasping at straws with that last question.
But Aunt Peg would have been disappointed if I hadn't at least
tried.

"Thank you for taking the time to talk to us," I said. "You've
given us more information than we had."

"So?" Aunt Peg demanded as I handed the phone back to
Frank. While I'd been busy talking to Sean, she'd sidled over to
stand beside me. "What does the younger Haney have to say
for himself?"

Aunt Peg would want hard facts. Unfortunately, I had none
to offer.

"That his day spa offers the best mud and avocado wrap
around?"

"Mud and avocado," she sniffed. "That sounds disgusting.
What else?"

"He didn't have much information about Pete," I admitted.
"But he did point us in the right direction."

"Excellent," said Aunt Peg. "Which way?"

"North." I pointed. "Into the woods."

Frank and Bob both declined to participate in an excursion back into the forest to look for Pete's cabin. Aunt Peg and I were fine with that. Those two would only slow us down anyway.

We deliberately skirted around the clearing where Pete's body had recently lain. While we were in the parking lot, the authorities had transported the corpse out of the woods and placed it in the medical examiner's van. Shortly thereafter, the EMTs had been the first to depart. The police officers had paused to have a few words with Bob, then their cruiser and the ME's van had driven away as well. They were followed by Frank and Bob.

Now Aunt Peg and I were on our own, which was just the way we liked it.

"Ten acres is a lot of land to search," I said. My house was on a two-acre lot and I thought that was spacious. "Especially since these woods are so dense we can't see very far ahead of us. The shack Sean told me about could be anywhere."

"Which is why we're going to let someone who knows where it is lend us a hand. Or a paw, as the case may be."

She unzipped her parka, lifted Snowball out of his snug shelter, and set him gently down on the ground. The Maltese celebrated his freedom by giving a mighty shake that started at his head and ended at the tip of his matted tail. That done, he walked over to the nearest bush and lifted his leg. Then he sniffed the yellow snow and peed again.

"*That's* our guide?" I said with a smirk.

"Give him a minute. He's just getting his bearings. After the night he's had, I'd be very surprised if Snowball doesn't want to return to familiar surroundings. The only home he knows out here is the shack he and Pete have been living in."

Of course Aunt Peg was right. Two minutes later, Snowball was scampering along the top of the crusted snow, moving with a sense of purpose as though he had a specific goal in mind.

Aunt Peg and I slogged along behind him. In the deep woods, some of the drifts were higher than my boots. Dealing with the footing and dodging between tightly packed trees, we struggled to keep the little dog in sight.

Thank goodness for Snowball's unerring sense of direction. Even when he stopped and began to bark, it still took me a moment to pick out the cabin from the low-hanging branches that surrounded it. On my own, I might have walked right by without stopping.

As shelters went, it wasn't much. The shack was barely more than a lean-to with slatted wood sides and a tar-paper roof. I didn't see a single window and the entire structure couldn't have been more than eight feet long. It was hard to imagine that someone had actually been living there in this weather. And that he had chosen to do so. Despite its lack of outward appeal, presumably the shack was snug enough to keep its occupants warm and dry.

Aunt Peg leaned down and scooped Snowball up in her arms. "Poor pup. He probably thinks Pete is waiting for him inside."

"Have you thought about what you're going to do with him?" I asked.

Aunt Peg cast me a glance. "What's to think about?"

That was pretty much what I'd figured.

The door consisted of a single sheet of plywood. Instead of a knob, a simple latch held it closed. Aunt Peg reached for the latch, then withdrew her gloved hand. Snowball whimpered under his breath.

"This feels like an invasion of privacy," she said.

"Unfortunately for Pete, he no longer cares."

"It's still his cabin."

"Technically, it's not." I reached around her and opened the door. "Frank bought the property in its entirety. As is. So we have just as much right to be here as anyone."

The interior of the cabin looked scarcely better than the outside. There was no furniture to be seen. The cramped space held only a tiny woodstove that looked as though it served as both a source of heat and a cooktop, a sleeping bag with a moth-eaten blanket on top of it, some canned goods stacked in a corner, and a pile of assorted junk that was probably the remainder of Pete's worldly goods. It was every bit as cold inside the shack as it was without.

"Now I'm even sadder than I was before," I said.

Aunt Peg, who'd already moved through the doorway, offered not a shred of sympathy. "Buck up, Melanie. We've got work to do."

She started by sifting through the cans until she found one that held dog food. Snowball followed her every movement as she opened it up, found a bowl, and dumped it in. When she placed the bowl on the floor, the Maltese dug in eagerly.

"I suspect he's missed a meal or two," she said. "That should hold him for now. What else is there to see?"

Between us, we dug gingerly through the pile of stuff. Two shirts lay on top. Next we came to a coil of rope and a piece of tarp. Under that was a stack of old newspapers, several paperback books with broken spines, and a baggie filled with rubber bands. When we went to lift the tattered blanket beneath those finds, there was a thump, followed by a clinking noise, and then several empty bottles rolled across the floor.

Aunt Peg prodded one with her foot. "Gin. Probably Pete's last meal."

"I wonder why he went to the trouble of hiding the bottles," I said.

"If I was a psychologist I might posit that he was attempting to hide the evidence of his addiction."

"From who? Snowball?"

Mention of his name made us both look to see how the Maltese was doing. The little dog had finished his meal and disappeared.

"There." I pointed toward the other end of the room. "He's burrowed inside the sleeping bag."

Aunt Peg sighed. "That poor dog knows something is very wrong. He just can't figure out what he needs to do to fix it." She leaned down and slipped her hand into the bedding. "Come out here, you little scamp."

The lump at the foot of the bedroll didn't move. Abruptly, Aunt Peg frowned and withdrew her hand. Her fingers were clenched around a small, rectangular object.

"What do you suppose this is?" she asked.

We walked to the doorway and examined it in the light.

"It looks like an old wooden matchbox."

"Indeed. I think you're right." Aunt Peg gave the box a small shake. "And there's something inside."

She used her thumb to slide the inner compartment open. We both leaned in for a closer look. The box held just two things: a tiny tooth and a ring.

"That's a puppy canine," Aunt Peg said. "Probably one of Snowball's."

I was more interested in the ring. I reached inside with my fingertips and fished it out. The bauble felt heavy in my hand. It was thick and made of silver, with a flat, deep-set reddish stone and engraving around the crown.

"This looks like a high school ring." I examined the initials that circled the gemstone. "What school is SCHS?"

"I haven't the slightest idea," said Aunt Peg. "But I suppose we should take it along and give it to the police. If they locate Pete's family, his relatives might want the ring back."

"I'm not sure the police will even bother to look for Pete's family," I said. "They didn't sound particularly interested."

As I slipped the ring in my pocket, Snowball emerged from the sleeping bag. When he saw us standing in the doorway, his tail began to wag. He scampered across the floor to join us. Even filthy and matted, the Maltese was pretty cute. He certainly deserved better than this.

"That's not the only thing Pete's family might want back," I pointed out.

Aunt Peg frowned. "I'll cross that bridge when I come to it."

Chapter 6

Monday morning I went to school.

After the four-day Thanksgiving holiday, I was dragging a bit when I entered the hallowed halls of Howard Academy, where I worked as a special needs tutor. The school was situated high on a hilltop near downtown Greenwich. I'd always thought its location was fitting, considering that the private academy's lofty objective was the guidance, development, and education of America's future leaders.

Years earlier, when I was new to Howard Academy, that mission statement had sounded boastful to me. I quickly discovered I was wrong. HA numbered congressmen, ambassadors, and a vice president among its illustrious alumni. Not to mention too many titans of industry to count.

A heritage like that was enough to keep all of us teachers on our toes. If we were ever tempted to let standards slip—even for a moment—Headmaster Russell Hanover II was always on hand to ensure that everything remained up to snuff. His words, not mine.

Mr. Hanover was a strict disciplinarian and a stickler for school rules, but he allowed me to bring Faith to work with me.

For that, I would forgive the man just about anything. My Poodle held court on a cedar-filled bed in the corner of my classroom, and the students who arrived for tutoring greeted Faith with a great deal more enthusiasm than they ever lavished upon me.

I wasn't complaining about that. Whatever brought kids through my door with a smile on their faces was fine by me.

The current semester's schedule left my afternoons free on Tuesdays and Thursdays. Bowing to parental pressure, Howard Academy also offered early dismissal on Fridays—a perk that enabled students' families to get a jump on their weekend getaways to Aspen, Wellington, or Fishers Island.

I wasn't aware that Frank was privy to the details of my calendar, but Bertie must have clued him in because Faith and I had barely left the school on Tuesday afternoon when my phone rang. I grimaced when I glanced at the screen. Faith, who was riding shotgun, looked at me and wrinkled her nose. She was clearly counseling me not to pick up.

"It's Frank," I told her. "If I don't talk to him now, he'll just call back."

Faith just sighed. That was easy to understand. I felt much the same way.

"Hey Mel," Frank said cheerfully when I'd put the phone to my ear. "I have a job for you."

"Thanks, but no thanks. I already have a job."

"Yeah, but this one's fun."

Somehow I doubted that. If it was fun, Frank would already be doing it and he wouldn't need me.

"Think about it," he said. "Davey's bus doesn't bring him home until later and Sam's got Kevin until you get back. So you've got a couple free hours that you could spend up here in Wilton. Bob and I are working overtime to get Haney's Holiday Home ready to open for business this weekend. We could really use an extra pair of hands."

"What about Claire?" I asked.

"She was here all morning."

"Bertie?"

"New baby. She already has her hands full."

Now I was getting desperate. "Aunt Peg?"

There was a long pause. Then Frank said, "You're kidding, right?"

Yes, I supposed I was.

"Where's your family spirit?" asked Frank.

Right about then it occurred to me that it would probably take less time to help my brother than it would to win the argument. Half an hour later, Faith and I were approaching the tree farm's driveway. In the forty-eight hours since my previous visit, there had already been at least one improvement. Someone had repainted and rehung the sign. I decided to take that as a good omen.

Faith loved to visit new places. She was standing on her seat, wagging her tail, when I parked next to Frank's Jeep. As soon as I opened the car door, the big Poodle hopped out and began to explore. We were at least a quarter mile from the road, so I let her run around for a few minutes before we went inside.

Like the sign at the end of the driveway, the office building had already seen some repairs. The rotting step had been replaced and the banister beside it now felt solid beneath my hand. The porch was neatly swept and the windows on either side of the door glistened from a recent cleaning. The doorknob turned easily and the door itself swung inward without complaint.

Best of all, the electricity had been turned on and the wood-stove was lit. The room that Faith and I entered was bright and wonderfully warm. I had to give Frank credit. This was an amazing, inviting change from the dark, gloomy space I'd visited just two days earlier.

Speaking of Frank, he had drop cloths spread across the floor and a long-handled paint roller in his hands. Half the back wall was still a dingy shade of gray, but the remainder was already sporting a coat of cheerful yellow paint. Frank set down the roller as I closed the door behind us. He turned and greeted us with a grin.

"So," he said, spreading his hands wide. "What do you think?"

"I'm impressed."

My brother peered at me intently. "Does that mean you're impressed like, *Considering it's Frank, he didn't screw up too badly,* or as in you really like what you see?"

"Definitely the latter." I thought about what he'd said, then added, "Am I really that hard on you?"

Frank didn't even hesitate. "Yes."

"*Still?*"

"I guess you're improving a little," Frank admitted. "Maybe you're mellowing with age."

Not a comforting thought.

"Where's Bob?" I asked. "I thought he'd be here helping too."

"He left a little while ago to go iron out the details on the business license and tax ID number. Then he's going to stop by The Bean Counter and make sure everything's running smoothly there."

Frank crossed the room, crouched down, and greeted Faith with a thumping pat on the head. She preferred a caress with more finesse, but subtlety wasn't Frank's strong suit. Nor has he ever understood my passion for Poodles. As far as Frank was concerned, all my big black dogs were interchangeable. But at least he'd made the effort to acknowledge her presence.

Faith was no dummy. She redirected Frank's energy by sitting down and offering him a paw to shake. Surprised, my brother rocked back on his heels and sputtered a laugh.

"Did you see that?"

"Of course," I told him. "Faith is saying hello to you."

Frank shook her paw gently, then rose to his feet. "I have two kids now, you know."

"Of course I know that." I took off my coat and hung it on a hook by the door. "Bertie's been so busy that I've barely seen her since Josh was born. I am well aware of the addition to your family."

"Aunt Peg thinks that children should grow up with a puppy." No surprise there.

"Aunt Peg thinks that *everyone* should have a puppy," I said.

"We didn't when we were little," Frank pointed out.

"I guess we weren't as lucky as some kids."

His head dipped in a brief nod. "Anyway, I just wanted you to know I'm thinking about it."

"Good for you." If I pushed, Frank would push back. So instead I changed the subject. "I'm here and I'm all yours for the next two hours. What do you want me to do?"

"There's a can of white paint and some smaller brushes behind the counter. How are you with trim? A fresh coat of paint on the window frames would really brighten things up."

Faith lay down on the floor near the stove while Frank and I worked in companionable silence for the next hour and a half. Between applying coats of paint, I sifted through the collection of holiday decorations—delivered that morning by Claire—that were spread across the countertop.

There were giant tinsel garlands, gaudy ornaments, roping made of Christmas ribbons, and even an inflatable life-size Santa Claus. Claire had also managed to find several sets of holiday-themed curtains depicting the flight of Santa's sleigh. The woman was a marvel. I closed my eyes and imagined everything in place. Once the paint was dry and the decorations hung, the office would be totally transformed.

Faith lifted her head and a moment later I felt a draft of cold air as the office door opened behind me. A stocky, middle-aged man with ruddy cheeks and a bristling black moustache came walking inside. His head was entirely bald and the tips of his ears were bright pink. In this weather, I was surprised he wasn't wearing a hat.

Frank looked up. "I'm sorry, we're not open for business yet. Could you come back this weekend? We plan to be up and running by Saturday morning."

"No problem." The man held up a hand. "I don't need a tree. I'm just here looking for a friend of mine. A guy about my age, brown hair, blue eyes? His name is Pete. This is the address he gave me."

Frank and I exchanged a look.

"Who are you?" I asked.

"John Smith." The man stuck out his hand for me to shake. "And yes, that's my real name. My parents had a weird sense of humor. Pete's a bit of a wanderer and he doesn't have a phone. But he told me last month that if I needed to find him, this was the place to come. He missed a meeting we were supposed to go to, so I thought I'd better come and check on him. Have you seen him?"

"I'm afraid I have some bad news for you," I said. "Pete was involved in an accident over the weekend."

"Is he okay?"

"No, he's not. I'm very sorry to have to tell you that Pete was killed."

"Killed?" John Smith shook his head. "I think you're mistaken."

I flipped the tarp off the old rocking chair and dragged it across the room. "I'm sure the news has come as a shock. Maybe you should sit down."

"Hell, no, I don't want to sit down." Smith glared at the chair, then back up at Frank and me. His gaze narrowed. "What I want is to know what happened to Pete. Are you people the Haneys?"

"No, I'm Melanie Travis," I said. "And this is my brother, Frank Turnbull. Frank and his partner are the new owners of this tree farm—"

"Since when?"

"Last week," Frank answered.

"Last week, Pete was alive," Smith said. "I just saw him. And now you're telling me he's dead?"

"Yes, I'm afraid so. There was an accident—"

"Don't tell me he was hit by a car." John Smith, who'd been so certain that he didn't need a seat, now sank down into the rocking chair anyway. It creaked beneath his weight. "Did that little dog of his run out in the road? I told him he needed a leash for that mutt. Heck, I even offered to buy him one if he'd use it."

"It wasn't a car accident," Frank said.

"Then what the hell happened?"

"It appears that Pete had had quite a bit to drink," I told him. "He was out in the woods with Snowball. A tree branch hit him on the head and knocked him unconscious. By the time he was found he had died of exposure."

Smith frowned as he listened to my explanation. At the end he said, "You're sure about that?"

Frank and I both nodded.

"And you're sure the man that was found in the woods was Pete?"

"The police identified him," I said. "They told us Pete was a homeless man who'd been hanging around town for years. Apparently they were quite familiar with him."

"And they told you he was drunk?"

Frank nodded. "The EMTs could smell the gin on him. And the police said Pete's drinking had been out of control for years."

"But not recently," Smith muttered.

"Excuse me?" I said.

"There's something wrong with your story. Things didn't happen the way you're telling me they did."

"We're not making up a story," Frank told him. "We're telling you what happened. If you don't believe us, you can talk to the police. They'll confirm what we've said."

Smith pushed himself up out of the chair. He walked over to a window and stared out into the woods for a minute before turning to face us again. "I'm not accusing you of lying. I'm just telling you that things don't add up."

"In what way?" I asked.

"The Pete you're describing is the man he used to be. Not the man I've gotten to know over these last few months. Sure, he'd had his problems with alcohol. He was the first to admit that the juice brought out the devil in him. But Pete finally realized that his addiction had cost him just about everything that mattered. That was why he decided it was time to turn his life around."

"What are you saying?" I asked.

"Pete joined a substance abuse program in August. That's how we met. I've seen men who join up because they feel obliged to go through the motions. But that wasn't Pete. He was motivated. He really wanted to change. That was why I became his sponsor. And I'm telling you flat out that's why your story doesn't make sense. Pete hadn't had a drop to drink in more than three months."

Chapter 7

"That can't be right." Suddenly it felt as though the room was tilting. I thought I might need that chair myself.

"Trust me. I know what I'm talking about. Last time I saw Pete was three days ago."

"That would have been Saturday," I said.

"The day he died," Frank added.

John Smith nodded. "Saturday afternoon Pete was sharp, sober, and in an optimistic frame of mind about the direction his life was heading. And now you're telling me that a few hours later he was falling-down drunk? Nope. It didn't happen."

"Maybe you didn't know Pete as well as you thought you did," I ventured.

"I'm betting I knew him better than you did."

That wasn't saying much.

"My aunt and I had a look around Pete's cabin after he died," I told him. "We were hoping to find something that would tell us who he was and where he'd come from."

"And did you?"

I shook my head. "But what we did find was a cache of empty alcohol bottles hidden under a blanket."

"Empty," Smith said. "You found *empty* bottles."

"Which means that somebody had drunk their contents," Frank said.

"Somebody." Smith strode across the room toward the door. "But not Pete."

He reached for the knob. Before he could leave, I asked, "What was Pete's last name?"

That made him pause. "I don't know," he admitted. "It's not required. He never told us."

"Where was he from?"

"Pete wasn't big on sharing information of a personal nature with the group. That was his prerogative. We were there to support him in his journey, not to grill him about his past."

"It sounds like maybe you didn't know Pete very well, either," Frank said.

John Smith let himself out and slammed the door behind him.

On the way home from the Christmas tree farm, I stopped at Aunt Peg's house. Yes, strictly speaking, Greenwich isn't located between Wilton and Stamford. But if ever there was a good time for a necessary detour, this seemed like the one.

Aunt Peg and her pack of Standard Poodles—all of whom were related in various ways to the Poodles at my house—were universally delighted to see us. While Faith and that canine crew raced around the fenced backyard renewing their acquaintance, Aunt Peg and I went inside. She led the way to her kitchen.

Together we stepped over the baby gate across the doorway. That was new. Then I realized why it was there. Snowball was lying in a plush dog bed beside the butcher-block table. The little dog jumped up and ran over to greet us.

I reached down and gave him a gentle pat. "If I hadn't known who this was, I wouldn't have recognized him."

The Maltese's formerly tangled and dirty coat was now white, silky, and mat-free. Aunt Peg had also trimmed him, shaping the hair so that it framed Snowball's body. A small barrette on the top of his head held up the topknot hair that had previously fallen forward over his eyes.

"It's amazing what you can accomplish with a good bath and a pair of scissors. Snowball managed it all beautifully. He's very well socialized for a dog who has probably led a mostly solitary life. But there are notable gaps in his training—housebreaking being chief among them. He's confined to one room until we have that figured out, but as you can see, he has adapted to life here quite happily."

"He looks great," I said. The Maltese snatched up a furry toy mouse and began to bounce around the floor, squeaking the toy with each joyful leap. "Has anyone from Wilton called to check on him?"

"I haven't heard a single peep from the police or animal control, which is all to the good. It would be a shame if the authorities decided they wanted to take custody and he had to be uprooted again so quickly. They seem to have forgotten about him and that suits me just fine."

Aunt Peg pulled out a chair at the table and took a seat. "Since you're here, I'm sure you must have something interesting to tell me. Sit down and spit it out."

It didn't take long to relate the conversation Frank and I had had earlier with Pete's sponsor.

"John Smith," she said when I was finished. "What kind of name is that?"

"Plain. Basic?"

"Maybe it's an alias," Aunt Peg mused. She takes great delight in suspecting everyone of everything.

"Only an idiot would choose an alias like John Smith," I pointed out.

Instead of replying, Aunt Peg got up and left the room. While I was awaiting her return, I made myself a cup of coffee. Instant. The only kind Aunt Peg keeps on hand for visitors who won't join her in sipping Earl Grey tea.

"The results of Pete's autopsy aren't available yet," she announced upon her return.

"How do you know that?"

"I called the Wilton medical examiner's office and told them I was a concerned citizen checking up on a recent death."

"And that *worked*?"

"I got the answer, didn't I? Now tell me what else Mr. Smith said."

"I've already told you everything. He said he'd last seen Pete Saturday afternoon, and that there was no way Pete got drunk that night."

"Despite the empty bottles we found?"

"Despite everything apparently. John Smith was quite adamant about what he knew."

"With a name like John Smith, I suppose you'd have to be an adamant sort," Aunt Peg decided. "Otherwise you'd get lost in the crowd."

"What if the gin the EMTs smelled was on Pete's clothing?" I'd been thinking about that on the way there. I paused to let her consider the possibility, then said, "Somebody might have spilled it on him. Maybe on purpose."

"Somebody like who?"

That was the $64,000 question. If indeed it was a question we should be asking at all.

"Pete was homeless," I said. "He had few belongings and not even a fixed address. Who would want to harm a man who had nothing?"

"I have no idea," Aunt Peg replied. "But I'm beginning to think that it might not be a bad idea to find out. An accidental death on a piece of property recently acquired by the family is a misfortune. A murder on that same land has the makings of a catastrophe."

"Pete froze to death in the snow," I pointed out.

"*After* being bonked on the head—by a conveniently falling

tree branch, no less." Aunt Peg frowned. "Why did we ever believe that was an accident?"

"Because the police told us it was?"

"Oh pish. The police don't even know who Pete was or where he came from. Why should we believe everything they say?"

Her eyes lit up with a familiar fervor and I knew what she was thinking. *Especially when the alternative was so intriguing.*

"We don't know anything about Pete either," I said.

"Then clearly we should attempt to remedy that. It seems to me that the only clue we possess is the ring we found in Pete's cabin. What did you do with it?"

"I have it here. I put it in my purse for safekeeping."

"Let's have another look and see what it tells us."

I produced the chunky ring and handed it over. Aunt Peg nestled it briefly in her palm. "SCHS. I would think those are the school's initials. With luck, it will be somewhere in Connecticut. At any rate, that's where I'll begin my search. We'll see what we can discover, shall we?"

There was a laptop sitting on the counter. Aunt Peg brought it over to the table. While she went to work, I reached down and lifted Snowball into my lap. Each of our Standard Poodles weighed more than fifty pounds. And Bud was close to twenty. Though I was accustomed to having dogs in my lap, I wasn't used to handling one who could be cupped between my two hands.

Snowball stood up on my legs, braced his front feet against my chest, and gave my sweater a very thorough sniff. No doubt he was checking out the scents my dogs had left there. When I returned home, I was sure the Poodles would subject me to the same treatment.

On the other side of the table, Aunt Peg was hunched over and frowning at the computer screen. Loathe to break her concentration, I reached around Snowball and picked up the ring. I held it between my thumb and forefinger and lifted it up to the light.

Immediately I saw something neither Aunt Peg nor I had noticed earlier. There was writing on the inside of the band. I lowered the ring and squinted at the tiny print. One side was engraved with a set of initials: PCD. The other had a date, presumably the year of graduation: 1994.

"I've found something," I said.

Aunt Peg looked up. "So have I. There's a good chance that the initials on that ring stand for Stonebridge Central High School."

Stonebridge was a small town located on the Connecticut coast between Fairfield and Bridgeport. I'd seen the Stonebridge exit on the Connecticut Turnpike, but I'd never had a reason to go there. I suspected that was about to change.

I passed the ring back to Aunt Peg. "Look inside."

She did, then smiled with satisfaction. "How did we miss this the first time around?"

"Because we weren't looking. I was planning to give the ring to the police, remember?"

"Well, it's a good thing you didn't. Obviously the *P* is for Peter. The *C*, maybe Charles? D . . . d . . . d . . ." She drummed her fingers on the tabletop. "Dalton? Dreyer? Dunleavy?"

"I bet somebody at Stonebridge Central High School can tell me what those initials stand for. Or if not, I'd imagine they'll let me have a look at their 1994 yearbook. I'll pay the school a visit on Thursday afternoon."

"That's two full days from now!"

I looked at her askance. "What's your point?"

"I should think you'd be more eager to uncover Pete's backstory."

"Yes, but I'm also eager to keep my job. I have classes all day tomorrow at Howard Academy."

"I suppose that's a decent excuse," Aunt Peg grumbled.

Indeed.

*   *   *

Thursday morning, I told Sam that I'd be making a side trip to Stonebridge after school.

My husband was standing at the stove, scrambling eggs. I was checking to make sure that all of Davey's homework was inside his backpack, and looking for Kevin's missing sneaker. Since both the shoe and Bud had disappeared at approximately the same time, I was pretty sure I knew where to start my search.

"What's in Stonebridge?" Sam asked over his shoulder.

"A high school with the same initials as the ones on Pete's ring. It's possible he was a former student there, and I'm hoping I can get information about him."

I had told Sam what John Smith had said during his visit to the tree farm. I'd also mentioned that Aunt Peg and I were troubled by this new information. Then I'd left the rest to Sam's imagination. We've been around this block before. He had to know what would happen next.

Now he simply turned back to the stove and said, "Stonebridge isn't far. I assume you'll be home in time for dinner?"

"Of course."

"Because if not, I can take the boys out for pizza."

"Pizza?" Kevin looked up with interest.

"Not now," I told him. "Later."

"Found it." Davey entered the kitchen, holding Kevin's sneaker. Predictably, Bud was nowhere to be seen. "It needs a new lace."

"I have spares. Where's your math homework?"

Davey handed me a shoe that was wet with slime, but otherwise mostly intact. "I finished it at school yesterday. History was boring. I needed something to do."

"History isn't boring," Sam told him. "It's the foundation upon which civilization is built."

"Says the man with a degree in computer science." I sniffed the air delicately. "Are those eggs burning?"

"No." He leaned in for a closer look. "They could be a little well-done. Who's ready for eggs?"

"Me!" cried Kev.

He jumped in the air and knocked over a wooden bowl that was filled with unshelled walnuts. The bowl went careening off the counter and the nuts hit the hard wood floor with a splatter that sounded like gunfire. Dogs came running from all directions.

Davey and I both dove to the floor. We scooped up nuts as fast as we could. Kevin squealed with laughter. Sam dished out the eggs.

Mealtime is an adventure around here.

Chapter 8

I hated taking a Poodle somewhere with me, then making her wait in the car. Especially Faith. But that afternoon she was out of luck, because when I left Howard Academy, I drove straight up the turnpike to Stonebridge.

GPS directed me to the town's high school and we arrived while classes were still in session. Even though it was December, I chose my parking space with care to ensure that the temperature inside the car would remain comfortable while I was gone.

Then I had to explain to Faith that not all schools were as understanding as Howard Academy about big black dogs roaming through their hallways. She sat and listened in stoic silence. When I locked the car, Faith was lying across the backseat with her head nestled sadly between her front paws. That Poodle knew a dozen different ways to make me feel guilty and she wasn't above exploiting every single one of them.

Stonebridge Central High looked like any number of other public schools I'd seen. The single-story building was long and rectangular. Constructed primarily of brick and concrete, its stern façade was softened only by a long row of classroom windows. A sidewalk that wrapped around the parking lot led me to the portico-covered front door.

I walked through the door into a large lobby. Wide hallways on either side led to classrooms. Directly across from the entrance was a well-lit display case whose shelves were filled with sports trophies, team pictures, and a big red banner reading GO ROCKIES!

Rockies? Stonebridge? I supposed that was cute.

Next to the display case was a door marked OFFICE. Easy peasy. I knocked once, then opened the door and let myself in. A woman seated behind a metal desk popped her head sideways around a computer screen.

"Can I help you?"

I introduced myself and explained that I was seeking information about a possible former student.

"Mrs. LaRue is our assistant principal. She might be able to help you. Let me see if she's busy." The woman got up and went into a side room whose door was sitting partially open.

While a murmured conversation took place in the other office, I surveyed my surroundings. I was pleased to see a long shelf holding a row of SCHS yearbooks that appeared to date back through several decades. If Mrs. LaRue wasn't able to help me, hopefully I could get permission to peruse the yearbooks for clues.

After a minute, both women emerged from the inner office. Sharon LaRue walked straight over to me. We introduced ourselves and sized each other up.

Sharon was a solid woman in her early forties who looked like a former college athlete. She had broad shoulders, a direct gaze, and a grip that was strong enough to make my fingers tingle. Her brown hair was pulled back in a tight ponytail and she had a cardigan sweater draped across her shoulders.

"Carol tells me you're trying to locate one of our former students?" she said.

"Yes. If you have a few minutes free, I'd love to ask you about him."

Sharon nodded, ushered me deftly into her office, and shut the door behind us. Her manner was both stern and approachable, a combination of traits that must have been useful in her current position. She waved me into a seat and walked around behind her desk.

"What's the student's name?" she asked.

"That's part of the problem. I don't know. In fact, I'm not even sure he *was* a student here. His first name was Pete and this ring was found among his belongings." I withdrew the piece of jewelry from my pocket and handed it over. "I'm hoping it's a 1994 class ring from your school. The initials *PCD* are engraved on the inside."

Sharon glanced down at the ring, then back at me. She closed her hand, wrapping her fingers firmly around the heavy bauble.

Something in her expression prompted me to say, "You know who he is, don't you?"

"I might," she allowed. "But before we go any further, I need you to explain why you're interested in this information."

"My brother recently purchased a piece of property in Wilton. After the fact, he discovered that Pete was a squatter who sometimes made use of a cabin there. Last Sunday morning, Pete's body was found on the property. He'd frozen to death in the snow."

Blood drained from the woman's face. She clutched either side of the desk for support, then slowly sank into her seat. "Dead?" she choked out the word. "Pete is *dead*?"

"Yes." I nodded slowly. "I'm sorry to have broken the news to you so bluntly. I'm assuming you knew him?"

"Oh yes, I knew Pete." Sharon's expression was bleak.

"Years ago, I knew him quite well. He and I were high school sweethearts, right here at Central High. As soon as you handed me the ring, I knew it had to be his. Peter Charles Dempsey. We grew up together in Stonebridge. His family still lives here."

She opened her hand and extended it toward me. I took back the ring.

"You're sure it's his?"

"Yes, there's no doubt. This isn't a huge school. I'm quite certain it was the only ring with those initials made that year."

"How long had it been since you'd seen Pete?" I asked.

Sharon thought back. "It must be at least five years since he left town. Nobody seemed to know where he went."

I sat back in my seat. "Why did he leave?"

"For several years before that Pete had been having... problems."

"What kind of problems?"

Sharon didn't answer.

"Professional problems?" I prodded. "Personal?"

After a few seconds, she gave a small shrug. "I suppose under the circumstances, it doesn't matter if I talk to you. Especially since everything I have to say is already common knowledge around town. Stonebridge isn't a large community. There are families who have been here for generations. At times it seems like everybody knows everyone else's business."

"Where did Pete fit in?" I said.

"The Dempseys are one of the older families in town. Pete's parents and grandparents were successful and well-connected. He was raised with the expectation that he would succeed at any endeavor he put his hand to. In high school, Pete played football, he was on the debate team, he got good grades. It seemed like he could do no wrong."

Her eyes became misty. I wondered if she was remembering

her former beau the way he'd been. I gave her a minute, then said gently, "What happened?"

"He grew up. I guess we all did. Even those of us who went away to college, came back." Sharon glanced around her cozy office. "Stonebridge is just that kind of place."

I nodded encouragingly.

"Pete married Penelope and they started a family. He and two of his friends, Larry Potts and Owen Strunk, started an executive search firm. There's plenty of business to be had in Fairfield County and it took off right away. The three of them were flying high."

"That all sounds great," I said. "So what changed?"

"Bit by bit, things began to fall apart. Pete's father passed away and his mother went into a deep depression. Then Pete began quarreling with his business partners. I suspect the dissatisfaction at work affected his home life too. Pete had always enjoyed tossing back a few beers, but over time it became more that that. He'd start drinking and then it was as though he didn't know how to stop."

"Pete became an alcoholic," I said.

"I guess that's what you would call it," Sharon agreed reluctantly. "All I know is that the man he became had little in common with the boy I'd thought I'd known."

"Life changes everyone," I said. "Some people learn to roll with the punches. Others fall down."

"Pete didn't fall down, he just . . . disappeared. One day he was here and the next he was gone."

"Didn't anyone look for him?" I asked curiously.

"Oh sure. I'd imagine Larry and Owen must have. Although by that time I wouldn't be surprised if they were relieved not to have to deal with him anymore."

"What about his wife, Penelope?"

"Ex-wife," Sharon corrected me. "He left shortly after their divorce became final. Penelope said he'd told her he needed a change of scenery."

"What about his friends?" I asked. "Any other family?"

Sharon just shrugged. "It's not like I was keeping tabs. Pete and I were over a long time ago. What he did and where he went wasn't any of my business anymore."

And yet, I thought, she seemed remarkably well-informed about Pete's adult life. Perhaps that was a function of living in such a close-knit community.

"Are you saying you don't care that he ended up as a vagrant, living on the streets in Wilton?"

Sharon frowned. "I'm sorry Pete's dead. He deserved a better end than that. But it's not as though he and I were still close."

"Is Pete's mother still alive?" I asked.

"Yes, although I gather Betty Dempsey is not well. Pete's younger brother, Tyler, has moved back home to take care of her." She stopped and swallowed heavily as a sudden thought struck her. "They must not have heard the news. Otherwise everyone would be talking about it."

"The police might not have been able to identify Pete yet," I said. "On Sunday, all they had to go on was his first name. No one knew who Pete was until you recognized his ring a few minutes ago."

Sharon stared at me across the desk. "Tyler needs to be told about what happened to his brother. You have to go see him and do that. Then he can break the news to his mother."

I was already shaking my head. "The Wilton police—"

"The Wilton police aren't here. *You are.* Nobody asked you to come to Stonebridge but you did. I answered your questions; now you need to do your part. Betty and Tyler are Pete's family. They deserve to hear the news from someone who was there."

Sharon opened a computer that was sitting on the side of her desk. She typed something, waited a minute, then turned the screen in my direction. "Is this the man you found?"

I'd only glanced at Pete's body for a moment before quickly looking away. Even so, I hadn't been able to forget what I'd seen. An image of Pete's face had stayed with me. Now I saw that same face staring out at me from the computer. The man in the picture on the screen was younger, sleeker, healthier looking. But the two were undeniably one and the same.

Sharon didn't wait for me to answer. Instead, she snapped the computer shut and said, "That's what I thought. The Dempseys are at one-eighty-three Meadow Lane. It's just outside of town. I'll call Tyler and tell him to expect you."

Faith was delighted by my return and not at all amused when I drove three miles, then left her behind in the car once again.

The Dempseys lived on a quiet residential street that was lined with mature trees. Their branches, now bare, met to form a canopy across the middle of the road. In another season, the effect must have been shady and welcoming. But now, the tangle of intertwined tree limbs snaking upward toward the stark winter sky made me shiver and wish that I'd tied my scarf more tightly around my neck.

"Don't worry," I told Faith. "This time I won't be gone long."

The Dempsey home was an older colonial with white siding and freshly painted black shutters. A brick walkway led me to the front stairs. As I approached, the door opened. Sharon must have kept her word and called ahead.

The man standing in the doorway—Tyler Dempsey, I assumed—didn't look pleased to see me. The pinched expression on his face was accentuated by his thin lips and high forehead.

Tyler had a slender build and the cashmere pullover he was wearing did nothing to add bulk to his narrow chest. His long, pale fingers rested on the doorknob as if he wanted to be prepared to slam the door shut at a moment's notice.

That wasn't reassuring.

He waited until I'd climbed the three steps and was standing right in front of him before speaking, "You must be Melanie Travis. Sharon LaRue warned me about you."

"Excuse me?" I tipped back my head to look up at him. "She was the one who wanted me to come here. Are you Tyler Dempsey?"

"I am."

"I'm afraid I need to talk to you about your brother." I looked past him into the empty foyer. "Maybe we could step inside for a minute?"

"I don't think that will be necessary. Nothing you could say about Pete would surprise me. What did my brother do now?"

"Are you sure you want to have this conversation outside?" This wasn't at all how I'd pictured delivering the news of Pete's demise.

"Quite sure. Did Pete send you—is that why you're here? What does he need this time? Money? A place to stay? Someone to bail him out of jail? I'm sorry, Ms. Travis, but whatever convincing sob story my brother told you to bring you to my door, I assure we've heard it all before."

They hadn't heard *this* before, I thought meanly. Apparently my only option was to deliver the news standing on his steps.

"Pete Dempsey is dead," I said. "He died of exposure last Saturday night in Wilton."

"Dead?" Tyler cocked an eyebrow disdainfully. Other than that, his face betrayed no emotion. You might have thought I'd told him that the chef at his club was out of caviar.

"I'm sorry to be the bearer of bad news," I added.

"Yes, that is bad news," Tyler agreed in a flat tone. "Where did the unfortunate event take place?"

"At a Christmas tree farm, Haney's Holiday Home, in Wilton."

"What was my brother doing at a Christmas tree farm?"

"There was a cabin in the woods. A small shack, really. He appeared to be living there."

"Well." Tyler frowned. "That part sounds about right."

"The Wilton police can give you more details about your brother's death," I told him. "I'm sure they'll be relieved to hear from his next of kin."

"I'll take care of that. And see what arrangements need to be made."

Once again I gazed into the house. "Perhaps I could offer my condolences to your mother?"

"No, that won't be possible. Mother isn't well. News like this would be upsetting to her and, in her condition, that wouldn't be good at all."

I should hope she'd find the news upsetting, I thought. But frankly, Tyler didn't look terribly undone by the revelation of his brother's death. Pete's descent into alcoholism must have been painful for his family. And perhaps humiliating. Even so, I wasn't sure that excused the lack of emotion with which Tyler had absorbed the news.

"Thank you for doing your duty," he said shortly. "Now you should be on your way."

Tyler stepped back and shut the door between us.

"Wait!" Belatedly I remembered I'd brought something to give to him. "I have your brother's school ring."

The door didn't budge. I heard the lock click into place.

If there had been a mail slot, I might have pushed the ring through. Instead, I shoved it back in my pocket.

It seemed odd that Tyler had never asked for any details

about what had happened. He hadn't even appeared to be curious. The police had dismissed Pete's death as an alcohol-related accident. His friend, John Smith, was sure Pete hadn't had a drop to drink in months. Whichever version was the truth, Pete's only sibling hadn't even wanted to hear about it.

Even after I'd made it clear that Pete no longer wanted anything from him, Tyler had been chiefly concerned with getting rid of me. I wondered what I should make of that.

Chapter 9

When I turned and started down the steps, I saw a tiny woman standing on the sidewalk next to the Volvo. She was bundled up against the cold in a long, puffy coat with a hood trimmed in fake fur. There were thick-soled boots on her feet and her hand, extended toward the car, was encased in a bright red mitten.

Faith was wise in the ways of the world. She knew better than to throw herself against the car window, barking at someone she couldn't reach. Instead, she was sitting upright on the seat, looking at the woman quizzically through the glass. As I drew near, I realized that the two of them appeared to be holding a conversation.

"Her name is Faith," I said when I reached the sidewalk.

The woman turned. Clear blue eyes peered up at me from a face that was wrinkled and covered in age spots. Several wisps of gray hair escaped from beneath the hood and fluttered in the breeze.

She smiled and said, "I'm Stella. Stella Braverman. That's a pretty dog in there. Is she a Poodle?"

"Yes. She's a Standard."

"I used to have a couple of Poodles, Chloe and Pierre. They weren't that big, though. I think they were Mini size. They were great dogs. I wish I could have another but at my age, I don't want to get a pet I might not outlive. Because then what would happen to it when I was gone?"

"Maybe your family—?"

"No, there's just me. Even my friends are dying off now. Old age isn't for weenies. Don't let anyone ever tell you differently. What's your name? I don't think you said."

"Melanie Travis," I told her.

"I saw you were visiting the Dempseys. Are you a friend of Betty's?"

"No, although I was hoping to speak with her for a few minutes."

"And Tyler left you standing on the step." Stella shook her head. "That boy needs to learn some manners. Although in his case, it's probably too late. I've known Betty since before he was born, and some days he tries to keep me away too. Tells me she's feeling too poorly to see me."

"Is she very ill?" I asked.

"Cancer." Stella whispered the word as though it was too awful to say out loud. "Betty doesn't have more than a few months left. Leastwise, that's what the doctors tell her. So if Tyler thinks I'm not going to visit my best friend now, he can think again. I've had a key to the back door of that house for fifty years, same as Betty has one for my house. As soon as Tyler goes off somewhere in his car, I'm in there like a shot."

She looked up and winked. "Kids. They don't know as much as they think they do. So what did you want to see Betty about?"

"I'm afraid it's complicated," I said.

"Good. I like complicated. Let's go inside and get warm and you can tell me all about it. Bring Faith along too. She doesn't look very happy sitting in that car all by herself. Do you like herb tea? If not, you should drink it anyway because it's good for you. How about Fig Newtons? I just got a new box yesterday at the supermarket."

There was something surprisingly comforting about placing myself in Stella's hands and simply following her directions. Plus, she struck me as the kind of woman who wouldn't take no for an answer.

Five minutes later, Faith and I were seated in her front parlor. Stella came in from the kitchen carrying a small tray that held two delicate china cups and a plate of cookies. Now that she'd shed her bulky outerwear, the elderly woman looked even smaller than she had outside. I jumped up to take the tray from her, but Stella waved me away and set it down on the coffee table between two love seats.

"I found a couple of shortbread cookies in the pantry for Faith," she said. "They're pretty stale, but she probably won't mind. I read online that you're not supposed to feed dogs raisins. Did you know that?"

"Yes. No grapes or chocolate either."

"Well, then I guess you're on top of things. Raisins and figs seem kind of similar to me. So I figured better safe than sorry."

Stella handed Faith a shortbread cookie. The Poodle swept it gently out of her hand. Stella watched with satisfaction as Faith chewed and swallowed the cookie. Then she sat down on the other love seat.

She handed me a flower-sprigged cup and saucer, and picked up the other set for herself. "Now then, suppose you tell me what's complicated?"

I started with my brother's purchase of Mr. Haney's Christmas tree farm. I didn't know exactly why, except that Stella seemed like she would enjoy a good story. I wasn't surprised that she made a great audience. Stella concentrated as she listened. Her attention was focused on me like a laser. When I got to the part about finding Pete's body in the snow, she issued an audible gasp.

"I'm sorry," I said with a guilty wince. I'd gotten so caught up in telling the tale that I hadn't thought to soften the news. "You must have known Pete too. I shouldn't have just blurted that out."

"You don't need to apologize on my account. It's poor Betty I'm worried about." Stella sighed. "This will come as a real blow to her. The rest of us . . . well, it's been five years. I guess we all suspected that something had gone terribly wrong. But Betty still held out hope that she would see Pete one more time in this life. When she got the diagnosis, she even sent Tyler out looking for him, hoping he could track him down. But nothing ever came of his efforts."

"I'm very sorry," I said again. The words felt wholly inadequate.

"For pity's sake, don't keep apologizing." Stella waved me off again. Apparently she was good at that. She dropped her hand beneath the table and slipped Faith another cookie. She was good at that too. "To tell the truth, in some ways it was a relief when Pete went away. Of course, at the time nobody suspected that he wouldn't come back. But let's just say that most of us were ready for a break. That boy's life was one big drama."

I finally took a sip of my tea. It tasted like weeds. "I understand he had a drinking problem."

"That's right. Even worse, Pete was a mean drunk. He'd get soused and set his sights on something he thought he ought to have. He didn't give a flip who was standing in his way. Fistfights, car wrecks, marriages falling apart . . . the consequences meant nothing to him."

"That must have been hard on his family," I said.

"Not just his family," Stella said. "It was hard on everyone around him. Stonebridge is a small town and Pete wreaked havoc around here. Plenty of people were just as happy when he disappeared. Excepting Betty, of course. She knew her son had lost his way, but she was always hopeful that Pete would find himself again."

"And Tyler? How did he feel about it? Were he and Pete close?"

"Not really. Not so's you'd notice anyway. It can't have been easy for Tyler, growing up in Peter's shadow. It wasn't his fault he wasn't born the favorite, but it was something he had to deal with. Tyler was a quiet child, the little boy standing in the background that you might not even notice when his brother was around. So I guess that's one good thing that came out of all of Pete's problems."

Faith tapped the toe of my boot with her paw. She was looking for another cookie. Faith wasn't a spoiled dog, but she wanted to be. There was just a single shortbread cookie remaining. Stella looked on approvingly as I handed it over.

"One good thing?" I said.

"After Pete left, Tyler really stepped up. I guess you could say he came into his own. He's a whole new man now. Betty's spent the last five years pining for her lost son. I'd imagine Tyler spent the same amount of time thanking his lucky stars that Pete was gone."

Maybe that explained Tyler's dispassionate response to his older brother's death, I thought. Or maybe it gave him a motive for making sure that Pete never returned home.

"It was very nice to meet you, Stella," I said, rising to my feet. "Thank you for taking the time to talk to me."

"My pleasure. These days I'm happy to talk to anyone who comes by. Otherwise it's just me and the television."

She stood up and walked us to the door. "You want to talk to someone who knows what-all Pete got up to, you should go see his ex-wife, Penny. That woman will give you an earful whether you want one or not."

"Does she live in Stonebridge?"

"Yup. Born and raised here, just like the Dempseys. Her name is Penelope Whitten now. She took her maiden name back after the divorce. Not that that came as a surprise to anyone." Stella's lips curved upward in a smile. "Once she hears Pete's gone for good, she'll probably dance a jig right around the block."

"Stella sounds like a character," Sam said that night.

The kids were in bed and we were sitting in front of a fire and enjoying a glass of eggnog. The Poodles were spread out on the floor around us like a plush carpet. Bud was upstairs on Kevin's bed.

Some of the Christmas decorations had been put in place while I was away that afternoon. There was a wreath on the front door and an electric candle in each window. A length of pine roping had been wrapped around the banister in the front hall. Now the house was filled with that wonderful evergreen smell.

"But I'm not sure it's a good thing she recommended that you talk to Pete's ex-wife," Sam added. "Ex-wives can be dangerous."

Having met Sam's ex-wife, I was inclined to agree. On the other hand, I was an ex-wife as well. And Bob and I got along splendidly.

Well, most of the time anyway.

"Ex-wives also know where the bodies are buried," I pointed out. "Metaphorically speaking, of course."

"You're still concerned about what John Smith said, aren't you?"

I turned and faced Sam across the couch. "How can I not be? If Smith was right and Pete hadn't had a drink in months, then his death couldn't have been caused by a drunken stupor or intoxicated bumbling in the dark. The smell of gin on Pete's clothing? The empty bottles in his cabin? It looks like someone deliberately set out to mislead the police about what happened. Someone who had a hand in his death."

Neither one of us mentioned the word *murder*, but we were both thinking it.

"I'm not sure what kind of answers I can get from people who hadn't seen Pete in years," I said. "But I know I have to try."

Sam nodded. I wasn't sure whether the gesture was one of acquiescence or resignation. But then he raised his glass and tipped it in my direction, offering a brief salute. "Go get 'em. And let me know what you find out."

I rested my head on Sam's shoulder and wound my arm around his body, pulling us closer together. Perfect.

In my experience there was no point in calling people on the phone to ask them about something they might not want to discuss. Invariably they just hung up on me. When I appeared in person, however, I had much better luck.

Maybe that was because I looked like the elementary school teacher I actually was. Or maybe it was due to my winning personality. *Just kidding.* Most likely it was because I took Faith with me almost everywhere. And who could resist the obvious charms of a big, playful Standard Poodle?

Friday afternoon after school, Faith and I went back to Stonebridge. With the help of some mild internet stalking (thank you Facebook and Instagram) I not only had Penelope Whitten's address, I also knew that she was a stay-at-home mother of two adorable elementary school–age boys, and that she planned to spend the afternoon decorating the outside of her house.

Holy moly. If the average person ran into as many people with bad intentions as I do, they would know better than to put that much information out there for the taking. But considering

Penelope's lack of internet discretion, I could only guess that the worst guy she'd ever run across was her ex-husband, Pete.

Her house was smaller than the Dempsey home and it was located closer to the center of town. The Cape Cod–style home was painted light blue with white trim, and it sat up near the road on a narrow lot. A row of midsize bushes, each one trimmed into a neat square, flanked either side of the front door.

As advertised, Penelope was out in the front yard. At least, I assumed it was she, since the woman I saw was holding a giant ball of Christmas lights that she was attempting—not very successfully—to untangle. As I parked along the curb and got out, the woman lifted her head and glanced my way. Her hair was tucked up into a red knit cap, exposing an unlined forehead, a slender nose, and cheeks that were rosy from the cold. She would have been pretty except for the ferocious scowl on her face.

"Maybe I can help," I offered.

Since I wouldn't be going far, I had rolled down the windows on the passenger side of the car. As I walked across the yard, Faith stuck her head out to watch the proceedings. She was just as eager to see what would happen next as I was.

"Sure, why not? Four hands have to be better than two." The woman shrugged. "I guess you must be Melanie?"

"Um, yes." Sharon had told me this was a town where everybody knew everyone else's business, but even so, that was fast. "And you're Penelope?"

"Penny, please. The only one who called me Penelope was Pete. He was a huge fan of Homer." She yanked on either end of the ball of lights and when they separated slightly, passed one side over to me. "You know, the *Odyssey*?"

"Your husband compared you to Odysseus's faithful, long-suffering wife?" I teased a plug free of the tangle and began to gently work backwards.

"I know. What a joke, right?" Penny smiled grimly. "I didn't have anywhere near twenty years of patience for my errant husband's antics. Half that was more than enough for me."

Since she knew who I was, I assumed that Penny must know the rest of the message I'd come to Stonebridge to deliver. She must have read my mind, because Penny didn't look up from the skein of lights in her hands when she said, "Yes, I heard that Pete died recently. And that he froze to death, which is ironic considering how much he loved cold weather. So you don't have to stand there worrying about breaking it to me. That news was all over town in ten minutes yesterday."

I separated out a single strand of lights, straightened them carefully, then set them down on the dry front steps. "You don't sound terribly broken up about what happened."

"I'm upset for Peter and Christopher's sake. They're my kids, and now they'll never have a chance to get to know their father again. But maybe that never would have worked out anyway."

Now Penny did look up. The expression on her face was fierce. "You want to know how I really feel about my ex-husband's death? I'm glad it happened. That rat bastard had it coming."

Chapter 10

For a few minutes, I applied myself to the task at hand. Thanks to the number of knotted shoelaces I've had to deal with over the years, I'm quite adept at untangling things. Even a mess of lights that looked as though they'd been tossed willy-nilly into a box at the end of the previous holiday season.

"I guess you think that sounds harsh," Penny said eventually.

"I didn't know your ex-husband," I replied. "So it's not up to me to judge."

"Pete was a drunk. That pretty much sums up all you need to know."

I pulled another strand of lights free and set them aside. "He must have had some redeeming qualities. After all, you married him."

"He did," Penny admitted. "Back in the days when he thought alcohol was for social drinking. Before it became a crutch he used to deal with things he didn't want to think about. Before it took over his life and turned him into a man I could barely recognize."

"I'm sorry," I said. "That must have been terrible for you."

"It was." Penny's fingers clenched around the wires in her hands. I hoped the tension in her distracted grasp didn't snap off any lights. "But I'm not the only one whose life was negatively impacted by Pete's behavior. He screwed over his business partners. He shafted his best friend. He even cheated on his mistress."

When I bit back a startled laugh, Penny looked up. "Yes, I knew about her. In case you're wondering, people who drink too much aren't any good at keeping secrets."

"No, I guess not," I said.

Penny wasn't making any headway with her lights at all. I laid my last unknotted strand on the steps with the others and took the remaining lights out of her hands. She seemed relieved to hand them over.

"I didn't deserve to be treated the way Pete treated me," Penny said grimly. "None of us did. Pete had a choice and he chose the booze. Repeatedly. Over his family. Over his career. The drinking was more important to him than anything. He could have stopped, but he didn't."

I thought back to what John Smith had said. I wondered if Pete had been planning to return to his hometown and his family once he was certain he had things under control.

Penny picked up a strand of tangle-free lights. She began to drape it around the bush nearest the front door. There was more vigor than artistry to her application.

"Pete did stop drinking," I said.

She glanced at me over her shoulder. "No. He didn't."

"A friend of his named John Smith told me Pete hadn't had a drink in several months."

Penny just shrugged. "I don't know anyone named John Smith. But Pete called here a couple of weeks ago. He told me some cockamamy story about wanting to make things right. As if I would believe that."

"Maybe he meant it," I said.

"*Meaning it* isn't the problem," Penny growled. "Pete always *meant it* when he said he was going to stop. In that moment, he was sure he was telling the truth. Then he always relapsed anyway. After a while I realized it was safer not to believe anything he told me."

"John said he was going to meetings. That he'd stayed sober—"

"So what?" Penny rounded on me. "So some stranger thinks that Pete was sober? Big deal. I was Pete's *wife*. I was living with the guy and I didn't always know. At least not in the beginning, when Pete was still good at hiding what he didn't want people to see. He was great at sounding sincere and making promises."

She gulped in a deep breath of air. Her face crumpled. For a moment I thought she might cry. Then she gathered herself together and said, "And you know what else he was good at? *Breaking* promises. But you don't have to believe me about that. Talk to his ex-partners, Owen Strunk and Larry Potts at Streamline Search. They'll tell you the same thing."

Faith and I left Penny to finish putting up her lights and drove to Streamline Search in downtown Stonebridge. The company was housed in a two-story brick building with a parking lot out front. Streamline's offices were on the ground floor. I attached a leash to Faith's collar and walked her beside me into the lobby.

A receptionist was sitting behind a low counter that was decorated with festive cardboard candy canes. Christmas music filled the air. The woman looked up and smiled. Then she saw Faith by my side. Her double take was almost comical.

"Is that a service dog?" she asked.

"No. But she's a very obedient pet. I'm here to see either Larry Potts or Owen Strunk. Are they available?"

"Let me check." She reached for her phone. "Do you have an appointment?"

"I'm afraid I don't. I'm only in town briefly this afternoon. Penny Whitten recommended that I come and talk to them."

"Penny sent you. Okay." That seemed to bolster my credibility. "Let me take you into the conference room and I'll go get Larry." Once again, she stared at Faith dubiously. "Is she an emotional support dog?"

"No." I gave her a wide smile. "Just a great companion. Would you like to see her do some tricks?"

Faith tipped her head to one side and stared up at me balefully. Her message was clear: *Tricks are beneath my dignity.*

I sent back a message of my own: *Humor me, this is working. Unless you'd rather go outside and wait in the car?*

Faith just sighed.

"No, I don't need to see any tricks," the woman said brightly. "If the two of you would please follow me?"

She led us down the hallway to a glass-walled conference room. A long rectangular table in the middle of the room was surrounded by chairs. I took a seat at the end near the door. Faith lay down on the floor beside me. We didn't have long to wait.

Larry came striding into the room first. He'd barely finished introducing himself before Owen followed. He paused to close the door behind him.

Both men were in their forties, but that was all they had in common. Larry was tall and slim, dressed in a suit and tie that fit him impeccably. With his carefully styled hair and dark-framed glasses, he projected an image of stability and authority.

Owen, on the other hand, walked toward me bouncing on the balls of his feet. He was already smiling before he reached out to pump my hand heartily. If he'd worn a tie to work that morning, it was gone now. As was his jacket. His shirtsleeves were rolled back, revealing a watch on his wrist that looked complicated enough to launch rockets.

"Nice dog," Owen said, sliding Faith a glance as he grabbed a seat at the table. "That's some hairdo."

Long retired from the show ring, Faith was wearing the easy-to-care-for kennel trim, with a short blanket of dense curls covering her entire body. Only her face, her feet, and the base of her tail were clipped and I'd left a large pompon on the end of her tail. If Owen was impressed by her looks, it was a good thing I hadn't brought along Augie, who was in a show trim.

"Owen . . . let's concentrate, shall we?" Larry ignored Faith and turned to me. "You said that Penny sent you. What is this in reference to?"

"Pete Dempsey."

Larry's lips pursed distastefully. "We heard that he had died. I understand his body was found under a tree in some woods."

"I'm the one who found him," I said.

"Ouch." Owen grimaced. "That can't have been good."

"It wasn't."

Larry declined to offer sympathy. Instead he remained on point. "What do you want from us?"

"I'm trying to understand what happened," I said. "The police think Pete's death was an accident. I'm not sure they're right."

"I see," Larry replied. "Do you suspect that someone from Pete's sordid past might have wanted to harm him? Perhaps someone like his former business partners?"

Owen grinned at that. I merely shrugged.

"What I know so far is that Pete disappeared from Stonebridge approximately five years ago after developing a severe drinking problem," I said. "I gather he'd left a trail of destruction in his wake. Pete ended up in Wilton, where he was homeless and living on handouts. At some point recently, he decided to stop drinking—"

"I sincerely doubt that," said Larry. "Pete's problem with

alcohol wasn't just that he drank. It was that he loved every-thing about drinking. Getting, having, and consuming alcohol became the only thing he cared about. Certainly it was more important to him than the welfare of this company."

Owen bounded up out of his chair. He walked around the room as he spoke. "Pete had a support system of family and friends here in Stonebridge. I can't count the number of times we stepped in—sometimes singly, sometimes together—and tried to get help for him. But Pete didn't want to be helped. Pardon me for being skeptical, but if Pete could have controlled his addic-tion to alcohol, he'd have stopped drinking a long time ago."

"His behavior must have played havoc with your business," I said.

"The three of us started this company together and built it from the ground up," Larry told me. "Pete's drinking cost us clients and it cost us goodwill in the industry. Indeed, his reck-less disregard for industry standards and practices nearly took us under."

"And then there was the money Pete helped himself to on the sly—" Owen muttered. A sharp look from his partner caused him to stop speaking.

"I don't think Melanie needs to hear about that," Larry said smoothly. "Suffice it to say, it was a good thing that Pete parted company with us when he did."

"That happened before he left Stonebridge?"

"Yes. Probably two months earlier. We dissolved our part-nership and Owen and I bought out his share of the business. Much of the money we paid him went to Penny for the chil-dren."

"We hoped that losing his place in the company would serve as a wake-up call," Owen said. "Instead, it only seemed to in-crease his booze budget for a few weeks. And then suddenly he was gone."

"And you didn't know where he went or how he could be reached?" I asked.

Owen and Larry looked at each other. Both men shook their heads.

"It's not as if anyone wanted to go after him," Owen told me. "By that point, Pete had burned every bridge he had in this town."

"And you haven't heard from him since?"

The two men shared another look. Larry sat perfectly still in his chair. Owen was fidgety on his feet. I got the distinct impression that an unspoken message passed between them. Something they didn't want me to know.

"We haven't heard from Pete," Larry said firmly. "And I, for one, haven't given him a second thought. Leaving Stonebridge behind was his choice. If that was what he wanted, I was happy to oblige him."

Owen paused beside my chair. He squatted down and ruffled his hands in Faith's ears. Without looking up, he said, "You might want to talk to Olivia Brent."

Larry frowned. "Owen, don't."

"Don't what?" I asked.

"It's none of our business."

"What isn't?" Now I was really curious.

"At one point, Pete and Olivia were quite friendly with each other," Owen said obliquely.

It only took a moment for understanding to dawn. "Olivia was his mistress," I said. "Penny told me there was someone else."

Larry looked shocked. "Penny told you that?"

Men. They always overestimated themselves and underestimated us.

"Did you think she didn't know?" I asked.

"I *hoped* she didn't know."

"Well, you were wrong." I gathered up my things and stood. "Where would I find Olivia Brent?"

"Probably at the gym," Owen told me. "Or running on the

high school track after hours. That woman really knows how to take care of herself."

Larry still looked annoyed. "She won't be happy to hear from you."

Like that was anything new.

Faith hopped up and we headed for the door together.

"Whatever you do, don't tell her we sent you," Larry called after me.

"I wouldn't dream of it," I said.

Out in the lobby, the same Christmas music was still playing. The receptionist didn't seem to mind. She gave me a cheery wave.

"I hope you got everything you needed," she said.

Not yet, I thought. Not by a long shot. But I would. I'd make sure of that.

Chapter 11

I was blissfully asleep on Saturday morning when the bed gave a sudden lurch and something small and solid bounced onto my stomach. *Bud.* Kevin—the little dog's partner-in-crime—wasn't far behind.

"We're getting a Christmas tree today!" he crowed happily as he climbed up onto the bed. "Get up! Get up!"

Sam rolled over groggily. Lucky man, no errant dogs or children had landed on him. "What time is it?"

"Time to get up," Kev informed him. "Time to go chop down a tree."

"What's all the noise about?" Davey appeared in the bedroom doorway.

Behind him in the hallway were Eve, Tar, and Augie: a Standard Poodle honor guard. Faith and Raven had been asleep on the floor in our room, but now they were up as well.

Everyone looked at Sam and me expectantly. As if they thought we had all the answers. Good luck with that.

"Last night someone told Kevin that we were going tree shopping today." Sam answered Davey's question.

Oh. That might have been me.

Maybe I'd been feeling a little guilty about how much I'd been away this past week. Maybe I'd thought that a fun family outing would be just the thing to restore myself to everyone's good graces. Picking out the right tree, bringing it home and trimming it, had seemed like the perfect activity for us to enjoy together. Too bad I'd overlooked my younger son's rampant enthusiasm for All Things Christmas.

"Good one, Mom," Davey muttered. He didn't even need to be told who was responsible for the early morning wake-up call.

"After we get the Christmas tree, Santa Claus comes," Kev said happily.

"Not right away." I grabbed him, rolled him into my arms, and began to tickle below his ribs. "Once the tree is up, you still have three more weeks to wait."

"Don't want to wait." He tried to push out his lower lip in a pout, but he was laughing too hard to make it work. Instead he squealed and thrust himself away—only to be snatched up by Sam, who smothered him in a big, soft pillow. That led to more squealing.

Bouncing up and down with the movement on the bed, Bud began to bark. After a few seconds Tar and Augie joined in. The two dogs slipped past Davey and leaped up onto the mattress to join the fray.

"You people are all nuts." Davey was still standing in the doorway. He knew better than to come close enough for one of us to grab him.

"*You people*," Sam scoffed. "We're your family. And now that you're a teenager it's our duty to embarrass you. It's in the parents' manual."

"Nuts," Davey repeated. He shook his head and turned away. "I'm going to let the dogs out."

"Good idea," I said.

Everyone in the vicinity understood the word *out*. Even Tar. There was a flurry of scrambling feet and jostling bodies, as an abrupt mass exodus emptied the room. Kevin scooted off the bed and went flying after them. With two boys and six dogs pounding down the stairs, it sounded like someone had turned a herd of buffalo loose in the house.

Sam and I looked at each other. *Alone at last.*

"You don't suppose Davey will let Kev go outside too?" Sam said thoughtfully.

"Of course not. Kev's in his pajamas. There's snow on the ground . . ." I stopped and considered. Then I jumped out of bed and went running after them. "Davey . . . *wait!*"

Mid-morning when we arrived at Haney's Holiday Home, business was hopping. Two cars with trees fastened to their roofs were exiting the property as we approached. Once inside, we saw several more vehicles parked in the small lot.

"Kudos to Frank," Sam said as we headed up the steps to the office. "I was skeptical when I first saw the place, but it looks like he's making a go of this."

I'd have expected my brother to be on hand on this busy Saturday morning—if only so that he could gloat about proving his doubters wrong. But when we entered the building, Frank was nowhere to be seen. Instead, Claire was standing behind the counter and Bob appeared to be taking an order from a customer.

"Merry Christmas!" Claire sang out a cheery greeting.

Tall and slender, she still managed to look svelte dressed in a bulky holiday sweater. An image of Rudolph the Reindeer, complete with 3-D antlers and a blinking red nose, covered her from collarbone to waist. That improbable article of clothing was matched with a green elf cap, perched atop Claire's long, dark hair.

"Doesn't this place look great?" she asked.

"Fabulous," I agreed.

The decorations I'd seen early in the week—garlands of golden tinsel, shiny ornaments, and braided Christmas ribbons—were now hanging on the walls and draped around the counter. The inflatable Santa Claus had been blown up and positioned in the middle of the room. Struck by the chill breeze when we opened the door, he bobbed back and forth in place. The movement made him look as though he was waving hello to incoming customers.

I scooted around behind the counter to give Claire a quick hug. "You've done a fantastic job here."

"Not me," she said. "I wish I could take the credit, but mostly it belongs to Frank."

"Speaking of my little brother, where is he? I thought he'd be here today having a ball."

Bob finished dealing with his customer, then turned to talk to us. "Frank's over at The Bean Counter. Pre-Christmas, we do plenty of extra business there too. It's not like we can slack off at our principle location for the sake of a seasonal fling here. For the next month, he and I will be running ragged trying to keep both places functioning at peak performance."

"Christmas season is a slow time of year for me," Sam said. He worked freelance designing computer software, mostly for long-term clients. "If you want, I'd be happy to pitch in."

"Seriously? That would be great." Bob clapped Sam hard on the shoulder, a gesture of male solidarity that has always looked more painful than gratifying to me. At least they hadn't bumped fists or hips.

"I can help after school and on weekends," said Davey.

"Me too," Kevin offered. He hates to be left out of anything.

"You guys are terrific. Don't be surprised if I take you up on that." Bob's gaze swung my way. "How about you, Mel? You must have a few hours to spare for the family business."

Before I could reply the office door opened, admitting a blast of cold air along with Aunt Peg and Snowball. The Maltese was sporting a new collar and jaunty red leash. When Aunt Peg paused to stamp the snow off her boots on the doormat, Snowball ran ahead into the room. Aunt Peg dropped the lead and the Maltese made a beeline for Kevin who was sitting on the floor.

"Greetings!" Aunt Peg said heartily. "This looks like a lively gathering. What did I miss?"

"Dad said that Sam and I can come and help run this place," Davey announced. "Isn't that cool?"

"Very cool," Aunt Peg agreed. "I've always said you were a useful child." Useful people were her favorite kind. She turned and looked at me. "And you?"

"I have plenty to tell you," I said. "Maybe I can recap while we go pick out our tree?"

After our experience the week before, none of us wanted to venture very far into the woods surrounding the buildings. That hardly limited our choices, however. There were still dozens of pine trees for us to inspect and evaluate.

Sam and the boys went racing ahead through the snow, examining and discarding numerous options in their quest to find the perfect Christmas tree to grace our living room. Aunt Peg and I followed slowly behind as I brought her up to speed on all that had happened since the last time we'd spoken. She had handed Snowball's leash to Kevin and the Maltese was bounding happily through the low drifts. When the boys paused to look at a tree, the little white dog would lower his head and push his nose through the powder until his face was coated with a froth of white crystals. Aunt Peg watched his antics with a bemused smile on her face.

"It does seem like a shame," she said when I'd finished my report.

"What does?"

"That a man is dead and nobody appears to be mourning his loss."

"I gather that was Pete's own fault. By the time he disappeared from Stonebridge, he'd left behind more enemies than friends."

"Hey Mom, hurry up!" Davey called back. "I think we've found it!"

The tree my family had settled upon was a glorious Douglas fir. It stood more than six feet tall, was dark green in color, and had a full, symmetrical silhouette. Best of all, it smelled heavenly. I drew in a deep breath and was flooded with memories of Christmases past.

"Great choice," I said. "It's perfect."

Sam was carrying a chain saw he'd picked up in the office. Davey had dragged along a sled to transport the tree back to the parking area. It wasn't long before the six of us were on our way out of the woods. Snowball had been returned to Aunt Peg's care and Kevin was riding on the sled with the tree.

"Faster!" Kev whooped gleefully. "You guys are too slow!"

"Maybe that's because you're too heavy," Davey told him.

"No." Kev shook his head. "You just need to try harder."

Sam and the boys deposited the sled beside the SUV. As they went into the office to get some rope to tie up the tree, a small pickup truck came bumping up the driveway. Aunt Peg and I had been about to follow the rest of the family inside when the truck pulled into a parking space and John Smith got out.

Abruptly I stopped and turned back. Aunt Peg followed my lead.

"Who's that?" she asked as he came walking toward us.

"John Smith," I told her.

"Excellent," she said under her breath.

His long strides made short work of the distance between us. A knit cap was pulled low over Smith's forehead. His mouth, below the dark moustache, was drawn into a thin line.

"I just came by to tell you I was right," he said.

"About what?"

"Pete wasn't drunk. Not even close. There wasn't any alcohol in his system at all."

"How very interesting," said Aunt Peg.

Smith's gaze swung her way. "And you are?"

"Peg Turnbull. Innocent bystander."

My foot, I thought.

John Smith didn't look terribly impressed either. He looked back at me. "I just thought you should know."

"Thank you," I said. "Are the police aware of that?"

"They're the ones who told me. Guy named Officer Shiner?"

I shrugged. "We barely exchanged names with the officers who were here. Their level of interest didn't seem to require it. Has that changed now?"

"I hope so," Smith replied. "I told them Pete was off the sauce. They didn't believe me any more than you did." He turned and started to walk away.

"His family doesn't believe it either," I said.

Smith spun back around. "You found them?"

"Yes. His name was Peter Charles Dempsey and he came from Stonebridge. He disappeared five years ago and nobody from there has seen him since."

Smith frowned. The downturned moustache gave him a ferocious look. "That can't be right."

"Why not?" asked Aunt Peg.

"Pete's been trying to put his life back together."

"So you said," I agreed.

"Part of the process involved contacting people he'd hurt in the past. Apologizing, trying to make amends. Pete had started doing that over the last month or so."

I shook my head. That didn't jibe with what I'd been told. "Almost everyone I spoke to said they hadn't heard from him in years. His high school sweetheart told me that people had tried to find Pete after he left Stonebridge. But nobody knew where he'd disappeared to."

"They *should* have known," Smith insisted.

"I understand Pete wasn't the most stable character," Aunt Peg said gently. "Maybe he was lying to you about his actions."

"Or maybe the people you talked to were the ones who were lying," Smith replied. "I got the impression Pete had ticked off a lot of folks in his former life."

"He did," I agreed. "People said they were happy to be rid of him when he left."

"That's precisely my point."

Aunt Peg nodded. "I like the way your mind works, Mr. Smith. You're thinking that one of Pete's former associates might have wanted to be rid of him permanently, aren't you?"

Smith eyed us both. "You're darn right I am. Aren't you?"

Chapter 12

Sunday I went back to Stonebridge. How could I resist?

I wondered if Olivia Brent went to the gym on weekends. Pete's business partner, Owen, had implied that she worked out every day. In December, that probably meant somewhere indoors. I figured that checking out the only fitness center in town was worth a try. Because sometimes you just get lucky. And indeed, at the beginning of the day good fortune seemed to be on my side.

I stopped at the gym's front desk and presented myself as an old friend of Olivia's, hoping to surprise her. The attendant smiled cheerfully and directed me around the corner to the weight room. Only one person was currently inside. A petite, elfin woman—blond hair scrunched up in a ponytail on top of her head, corded muscles glistening with sweat—was lifting an implement the size of a small couch.

Seriously, I was impressed.

As I lingered in the doorway, Olivia lowered the bar, then dropped it with a small bounce on the mat at her feet. She reached around behind her and grabbed a water bottle. After taking a long swallow, she screwed the cap back on, then glared across the room at me and said, "What are you looking at?"

That got my feet moving. "Olivia Brent?" I made my way carefully around the various instruments of torture between us.

One brow lifted delicately. "Who wants to know?"

"I'm Melanie Travis. I was told I might find you here."

"So you're Melanie." Olivia didn't look surprised to see me. "Where's the dog? I heard there was going to be one."

Small-town gossip, you had to love it. And I'd thought the dog show grapevine was efficient.

"Just so you know," she added, "I don't like dogs."

"I'm sorry," I said. I meant that sincerely. Anyone who didn't like dogs was missing out on one of the great joys in life. "But Faith stayed home today."

"Dogs should stay home every day. That way they won't bother people." Her emphasis on the last two words made it clear that my presence was every bit as much of an annoyance as Faith's would have been.

"I was hoping we could talk for a few minutes," I said.

"And I was hoping for an uninterrupted workout." Olivia took another drink of water. "Oh what the hell, why not? I know you've seen everyone else. If you'd missed me, I'd have probably felt slighted."

I opened my mouth to speak. She held up a hand to forestall my first question.

"Not here. First I need a shower. You can meet me in the juice bar in fifteen minutes. Grab a table and order me a raspberry banana smoothie. Grande, with extra fruit."

"Got it." If that was the price of Olivia's cooperation, I was probably getting off easy.

The juice bar was on the other side of the building. I ordered two smoothies and sat down to wait. I'd chosen a table from which I could see the gym's front door because I was half-afraid that Olivia might ditch me and use the fifteen minutes to give herself a head start. But twelve minutes later she came glid-ing into the juice bar, tossed a duffel bag on the floor next to the table, and slid into the chair opposite me.

"So Pete's dead," she said. "Tell me about it."

While I did that, Olivia downed half her smoothie in several quick gulps. She struck me as the kind of woman who did everything with gusto. In other circumstances, I would have hoped we'd become friends.

"Well, that's gruesome," she said when I'd finished. "Poor Pete. I wouldn't wish an end like that on anyone."

"I understand that you and he had a relationship," I said obliquely.

Olivia grinned at my choice of words. "Yeah, the kind of re-lationship that broke up my marriage. Pete and I were sleeping together. It lasted two years. Is that what you wanted to hear?"

She'd clearly been hoping to shock me. If so, she'd have to try a little harder than that. "Actually, I was wondering whether you'd seen Pete recently."

"No. Not in years." Olivia seemed to be taken aback by the question. "What do you mean?"

"Pete was trying to get his life back together. He'd entered a program to help him quit drinking. According to his sponsor, he'd been sober for three months. Pete was getting in touch with people whom he felt he'd wronged in the past and asking for their forgiveness."

"Well, that wouldn't have been me." Olivia took another gulp of her drink. "What Pete and I did together might have been wrong by society's standards, but we both went into the affair with our eyes wide open. And for a while, we had a blast together. If Pete had tried to apologize for *that*, I'd have been offended, you know?"

I didn't actually, but I nodded anyway. "Were you sur-prised to hear of his death?"

"Sad to say, not really. The liquor, which I'm sure everyone has talked about endlessly until you're tired of listening to it, wasn't his only problem. Pete always had his demons."

"Like what?" My smoothie was strawberry avocado. The barista had recommended it. I hadn't been sure that the flavors would work together, but the result was delicious.

"Oh you know, just stuff."

"Problems with his marriage?"

Olivia snorted derisively. "Considering who you're talking to, I'd say that's a given, wouldn't you?"

Point taken.

"His job?" I asked.

Olivia waved a hand through the air, dismissing my second guess. "When Pete and I were together, he was living a pretty cushy life. At that point his dark days were few and far between. Whatever was bothering him was something he'd buried pretty deep."

"But he never told you what it was?"

"He never said anything about it at all. Pete hated discussing private stuff. Besides, when he and I had a chance to see each other, we had *much* better things to do than sit around and talk about the past."

"So if Pete didn't talk to you about his problems, who did?"

"Kenny."

That wasn't a name I'd heard before. "Who's Kenny?"

"Pete's best friend from the time they were little kids. The two of them grew up on the same block. They went to the same schools. Those guys did everything together when they were young. Pete was the quarterback on the football team, Kenny was a wide receiver. Pete started Streamline here in Stonebridge, Kenny sells insurance on the other side of town. If you want to know stuff about Pete's early life, you should talk to Kenny. In fact, I'm surprised you haven't already done so."

When she put it like that, I was too. I'd been in Stonebridge for most of the week, so how come this was the first time I was hearing about him?

"Of course, he probably isn't going to want to talk to you," Olivia added.

"Why is that?"

"The two of them didn't part company on the best of terms."

Like I hadn't heard that before. "What went wrong?"

"Same old story, I guess. Kenny wasn't the only one of Pete's buddies who got scammed, but he took it more personally than most. Pete came to him with a surefire business idea. Said the two of them would be partners; he just needed some money for start-up costs. Pete told Kenny they'd be rolling in dough in six months."

"I assume that didn't happen?" I said.

"Not even close. Probably there was never any kind of deal in the works. By that time whatever money Pete managed to score was going straight into the bottle. Kenny certainly should have known better. But Pete could be very convincing when he wanted to be. And Kenny trusted his best friend to do right by him."

"I can understand why he would be bitter. That sounds like a terrible betrayal." I considered for a minute then added, "But what I don't understand is why Kenny would talk about Pete's private problems with you."

Olivia polished off the last of her smoothie and stood up. She crossed the room in three quick strides and flicked the empty plastic cup into a recycling bin. "I thought you knew," she said.

"Knew what?"

"In Stonebridge everyone has the dirt on everyone else's lives. I just assumed someone would have told you."

I hated to ask again but I couldn't help it. "Told me *what*?"

Olivia swept her duffel bag up off the floor and hooked the strap over her shoulder. "Kenny wasn't just Pete's best friend. He's also my ex-husband."

I think my mouth was still hanging open when she disappeared through the doorway.

In a town the size of Stonebridge it wasn't difficult to locate a guy named Kenny who sold insurance. I didn't expect to find him in his office on a Sunday, but like most salesmen he was eager to be accessible to potential clients. Kenny listed alternate phone numbers where he could be reached 24/7. So I gave him a call on his cell phone.

Kenny picked up after just two rings. His ex-wife had spent the morning at the gym. Kenny was at a dog park. That was a lucky break. Maybe he and I could bond over our mutual love of dogs.

Kenny told me he had a Great Dane named Rufus. I told him I had five Standard Poodles. He asked me if I was interested in discussing liability insurance. He informed me that someone with multiple large dogs ought to have an umbrella policy in place. I said I was interested in discussing his former good buddy, Pete Dempsey.

That was when Kenny hung up.

A brief internet search supplied directions to Stonebridge's only dog park. When I arrived, there were six dogs racing around the large enclosure. A harlequin Great Dane was playing tag with a Border Collie that looked agile enough to run rings around him. A brindle Boxer appeared ready to join their game. I was betting that the Dane's name was Rufus.

Five minutes of watching from my car allowed me to match most of the dogs with their owners. Kenny was tall and skinny with watery blue eyes and a prominent nose. Dressed in a woolen peacoat, standing with his shoulders hunched forward and his hands shoved deep in the pockets of his jeans, he looked like he was freezing. I got out of my car and ambled over.

"Go away," he said as I approached.

The hostility in his tone caused several nearby dog owners to turn and have a look at us. As if by consensus, they followed his dictate and removed themselves from the vicinity. I didn't think that was what Kenny had in mind.

"You don't even know what I'm going to say yet," I told him.

"I can guess," he mumbled.

"Go ahead."

"Go ahead and what?"

"Guess," I said. I was standing right in front of him now.

Kenny scowled. "I'm not playing your game."

"No games. I'm just trying to figure out who disliked your old friend Pete enough to want to kill him."

Kenny lifted his fingers to his lips and gave a loud whistle. Rufus, still busy playing with his friends, ignored him. "It wasn't me."

"I didn't think it was," I said.

That got his attention. "Why not?"

I opted for honesty. "If you didn't murder him five years ago when he swindled you out of money and slept with your wife, you probably weren't going to do it now."

"Then why are you here?"

"Maybe I'm hoping you have some ideas. You're the man who knew Pete better than anyone. Did he have any enemies?"

Kenny barked out a laugh. "That's rich. Would you like a list?"

"Sure. Or you can start by telling me what you told Olivia. She said Pete had his demons. I'm wondering what they were."

"That stuff's old news." When he blew out a breath, condensation swirled in the air between us. "I'm not going to rehash what went on in high school. Certainly not with *you*."

"I thought you might be interested in seeing justice served."

"I can't imagine why. Will justice return my money? Will it bring back my marriage?"

When I didn't reply right away, Kenny shook his head. "Yeah, I didn't think so."

Rufus came wandering by. Kenny reached out and snagged the Great Dane's collar. He pulled a leather lead out of his pocket and snapped it on. The pair started to walk away, then Kenny stopped and looked back. "If you figure out who did it, let me know. I'd like to buy the guy a beer."

Chapter 13

At least my trip to the dog park hadn't been a total loss.

Though Kenny had been determined not to talk to me, an interesting tidbit had still slipped out. *I'm not going to rehash what went on in high school*, he'd said. Pete's past life encompassed a lot of years. Now I was pretty sure my search had just been narrowed down considerably.

I had to wait until Tuesday to get back to Stonebridge again. In the intervening day-and-a-half, we brought our new Christmas tree into the house and decorated it, I managed to sneak out for some surreptitious Christmas shopping, and the Poodle pack did their best to make me feel guilty that none of the running around I was doing included them. That led to numerous long walks around the neighborhood and the distribution of more peanut butter biscuits than were strictly necessary. Aunt Peg wasn't the only one who knew how to play me like a harp.

Monday at school my ability to concentrate was sadly lacking. In my defense, I wasn't the only one. Now that Christmas was almost upon us, half the students I tutored had already left for holiday vacations in far-flung locales. The other half were dreaming of the parties they planned to attend or the presents Santa would be leaving beneath their Christmas trees. If any serious schoolwork was being performed during this lead-up to the holiday, I certainly wasn't aware of it.

By the time I left Howard Academy on Tuesday afternoon, I felt nothing but a sense of relief that I was finally on my way back to Pete's hometown. I had a hunch that I was closing in on something important and I was hoping that Pete's high school girlfriend, Sharon LaRue, might be able to help me figure out what it was.

Planning ahead that morning, I'd left Faith at home with Sam and the other Poodles for company. That seemed like a better alternative than making her sit in the high school parking lot again.

This time when I walked in the school's front door, I knew where I was going. I didn't pass a single person on my way to the assistant principal's office. Nor was anyone sitting at the outer desk. Apparently Howard Academy wasn't the only school dealing with the effects of the upcoming holiday.

Sharon LaRue's office door was slightly ajar. I knocked lightly and waited until she looked up from a paper she'd been studying and acknowledged my presence. Today her tawny hair was loose around her shoulders. The style made her look both younger and prettier. A wool sweater dress hugged her generous curves.

Sharon had a pair of reading glasses perched on her nose. She removed them and set them carefully to one side of her desk before greeting me with a half-smile.

"Melanie Travis," she said. An ability to remember names was probably helpful in her position. "I didn't expect to see you again."

"Do you mind if I come in?"

"No, but I'm a little pressed for time." She glanced at a

clock on the wall. "I can spare ten minutes though. What's this about?"

"As you may know, I've been speaking with some of Pete Dempsey's former friends and family."

Sharon nodded. "Pretty much everyone in town is aware of that. I have to admit I'm not sure what you hope to achieve. Pete left Stonebridge a long time ago. Nobody here has any desire to dredge those memories back up."

"It appears that Pete's death may not have been an accident," I said.

It took Sharon a moment to absorb what I'd said. Then her body went utterly still. "What are you talking about?"

"When Pete died, there was no alcohol in his system. And according to a current friend of his, Pete hadn't had a drink in months. As part of the program he'd joined to get sober, Pete had been making contact with people from his past."

Sharon shook her head. "I can hardly believe that. This is the first I've heard of it."

"So he didn't attempt to get in touch with you?"

"Heavens no. Why would he? Our relationship ended years before his problems began. Pete and I had both long since moved on."

A picture was sitting on the corner of Sharon's desk. She reached over and turned the frame around so I could see photograph within. An attractive man with grizzled gray hair and a wide smile was standing with his arm around a younger woman who was mugging for the camera.

"That's my husband, Steve, with our daughter Amy," Sharon told me. "Steve and I got married our freshman year in college. Our parents thought we were too young to know what we wanted, but it will be twenty-three happy years next June. So you see, I was lucky. When Pete broke up with me, I met the love of my life. If he'd attempted to get in touch with me after all this time, the only thing I would have had to say to him is *thank you.*"

"Most people in Stonebridge don't share your equanimity," I said. "A couple of them have alluded to something that might have happened to Pete a long time ago. Maybe while he was here in school?"

"Something like what?"

"I don't know. That's why I came to see you. Last time we spoke you implied that Pete had led a charmed life when he was young. But nobody's life is perfect, especially not in high school. I'm wondering if something could have happened that you didn't mention. Some kind of unresolved issue that might have plagued him later."

Sharon thought for a minute before answering. "There was one thing. Not an issue, exactly. More like a rivalry. You met Pete's brother, Tyler."

"Just briefly," I said. "He wasn't eager to talk to me."

"That's not surprising. Tyler was never eager to get involved with anything that had to do with Pete. Those brothers were always competitive and unfortunately for Tyler, he was usually on the losing end of things. I remember when he was a sophomore, he went out for the football team. As you can see, this isn't a big school. It's not like our sports teams can afford to turn away anyone who wants to play, you know?"

I nodded.

"Pete was a senior by then and he was the quarterback. He made it clear to the coach that he wasn't going to play on any team that included his little brother. He didn't even want Tyler sitting on the bench. He insisted his brother be relegated to the stands with the parents, the nerds, and the rest of the kids who couldn't hack it."

"That terrible," I said.

"I totally agree with you. But that's how those two were with one another. They fought over everything, no matter how trivial." Sharon pushed back her chair and stood. "Pete's disappearance was the best thing that ever happened to Tyler. Even if it's by default, he's the favorite son now."

Sharon walked past me and headed for the door. I turned and followed.

"I guess you heard that their mother isn't doing well?"

"Yes, you mentioned that before."

"I don't think poor Betty has long to live. And, of course, the news of Pete's death must have come as a huge blow to her."

"If Pete had tried to contact his mother," I asked, "would Tyler have given him access?"

Sharon frowned. "Truthfully, I don't know the answer to that. You'll have to ask him yourself."

"If you had to guess?" I pressed.

Sharon leaned toward me. Her voice dropped to a whisper. "Pete and Tyler were Betty's only children and their father has been dead for years. So now there's an inheritance to consider too. Under those circumstances, do I think Tyler would have allowed Pete back in their mother's life? No way in hell do I see that happening."

I left the high school and drove to the Dempseys' house, planning to have a conversation with whomever answered the door—Tyler or Betty, either one was fine with me.

Since the last time I'd been to Meadow Lane, Christmas decorations had gone up around the neighborhood. The houses on either side of the Dempsey home had fairy lights on their eaves, ornate wreaths on their front doors, and pine roping wrapped around their mailbox posts. Compared to the holiday festivity that surrounded it, the house I parked in front of looked plain. Almost somber.

A gauzy curtain in a front window flicked open as I got out of my car. It fell back into place when I was on the brick walkway. Once again, Tyler Dempsey didn't wait for me to reach the door before he opened it and stepped outside.

"You shouldn't have come back here," he said.

I gazed up at him. Sunlight glanced off the snow around me and I had to lift my hand to shade my eyes. "I've been talking to people about your brother."

Tyler grimaced slightly. "I suppose you think I should care about that."

"In your place, I would."

"That's hardly relevant, is it? You and I know nothing about one another. I doubt we have anything in common."

"I was hoping we could talk." I started up the steps.

Tyler folded his arms across his chest. "I will not have you in this house."

"Fine," I snapped. "Then out here. Maybe you'd like to get a coat?"

He reached inside around the doorframe. There must have been a coat rack there because a leather jacket appeared in his hand. Tyler shrugged it on, then pulled the door closed behind him. He walked down the two front steps, passed me, and kept going.

"We'll talk in your car," he told me. "I won't have the entire neighborhood listening to my business."

The interior of the Volvo was only slightly warmer than the crisp air outside. As Tyler made himself comfortable in the passenger seat, I turned on the engine and blasted the heat.

"There's no need to warm the car on my account," he said. "I won't be here long. You need to understand that my mother is very ill. She doesn't have long to live."

"I'm sorry," I said.

"I don't want your condolences. What I want is for you to go away and leave us alone. Pete's descent into alcoholism was very distressing for my mother. His subsequent departure even more so."

"I understand that she and your brother were very close."

He closed his eyes briefly before speaking again. "Yes, they were. Which is why she felt Pete's failures as a son, and a husband, and a father, all the more keenly. Though his disappearance came as a terrible shock, over time it also served to ease some of her turmoil. At least in his absence, Mother wasn't served a daily reminder of her son's deficiencies."

I stared at him across the seat. "Is that your mother's opinion or yours?"

"Let me tell you something, Ms. Travis. The only reason you and I are having this conversation is so I can make it clear that my brother's untimely demise is a topic Mother must be shielded from at all costs. Knowing what happened could only cause undue stress at a time when her life must remain as peaceful as possible."

"You didn't seem particularly upset by the news of your brother's death."

Tyler frowned. "That's an unnecessarily personal observation. Not all families are happy ones, Ms. Travis."

He reached for the door handle. I was running out of time.

"Pete had started contacting people from his past, people he'd known in Stonebridge. I'm sure his family must have been at the top of that list." I finished what I wanted to say in a rush: "Pete got in touch with you, didn't he?"

Tyler's hand stilled. The car door remained closed.

"Not that it's any of your business," he said after a minute. "But yes, he and I spoke several weeks before he died. Pete tried to convince me that he'd stopped drinking. He told me he was putting his life in order."

"It was true," I said softly.

Tyler turned and looked at me. "Was it? If you truly believe that, you are a more gullible person than I. In the course of our conversation, Pete and I agreed on just one thing—that our mother's health and happiness was paramount. To let her hope that her older son had finally been restored to her, only to lose him once again to a relapse would have been tragic. A shock like that could have killed her."

I shook my head. "Maybe that should have been your mother's choice to make."

"No," Tyler said stubbornly. "Pete and I agreed. We made a deal. For once in his incurably selfish life, my brother put someone else's needs ahead of his own."

"What kind of deal?"

"If Pete stayed sober until the new year—if he managed to go a full four months without a drink—I would tell Mother that we had been in contact. Together she and I would welcome him home."

"But you never expected that to happen," I said.

"No, of course not. I was quite certain Pete wouldn't be able to uphold his end of the bargain." Tyler reached for the handle again. This time he pushed the door open before turning back to me. A draft of cold air came streaming into the warm car. "And as it turned out, I was right."

"Not entirely," I told him. "Pete's accident wasn't caused by alcohol. He wasn't drunk when he died."

Tyler's reaction wasn't what I'd expected. He merely shrugged.

"And yet the end result is still the same, isn't it? One way or another, Pete's reappearance in our lives would have had a devastating impact. You've only confirmed what I said from the beginning. I was right to remain silent. Good day, Ms. Travis. I hope we won't have occasion to meet again."

I'd have been tempted to slam the car door, but Tyler closed it softly behind him. Then he turned away from me and walked to his house. I watched until he went inside. Tyler never looked back.

Chapter 14

Wednesday afternoon after school, Sam was busy working and Davey, Kevin, and I were gathered around the kitchen table.

Davey, having summoned me to this get-together, had also supplied the refreshments. In front of each place setting was a mug of hot chocolate with pieces of candy cane floating on top. A plate of my favorite cinnamon Christmas cookies sat in the middle of the table. Next to my seat was a thick pad of lined paper accompanied by two pens.

Color me intrigued.

The Poodle pack, including honorary member Bud, had followed us out to the kitchen. As Davey, Kev, and I found our seats around the table the Poodles jostled for position on the floor.

Predictably, Tar flopped down beneath Kev's chair. He was ever hopeful that food would drop into his mouth and Kevin was the most likely benefactor. Augie went straight to Davey. Faith and Eve lay down beside me. Raven and Bud curled up next to each other on the big dog bed tucked against the wall. Christmas music wafted through the room.

The stage was set. But for what?

"It's time to make Christmas lists," Davey announced.

Kev nodded his head in agreement. "It was my idea."

"Your idea?" Somehow that didn't come as a surprise. At almost-four, my younger son loved *everything* about Christmas. But still. "More lists? New lists? Additions to your previous lists?"

Kevin had begun to giggle. Davey was grinning too.

"I could have sworn you both gave me your Christmas lists before Thanksgiving." Seriously. They'd have handed them over before Halloween if I'd been receptive to the idea.

"They're not for *us*, silly," Kev informed me.

Davey waved a hand around the room. "They're for the Poodles."

"And Bud!" Kev added.

You know, in case there was any doubt. Which there hadn't been.

I gazed around at the canine corps. Now that we'd settled into our seats, most of the Poodles were snoozing contentedly. There was a basket of dog toys in the corner, but no one had opted to pull something out and start a game. Well-muscled, well-fed, with bright eyes and dense shiny coats, none of our dogs looked as though they lacked for anything.

Except perhaps for Tar, who was sadly lacking in brainpower. He'd flipped over on his back and was now lying with his tongue hanging out of his half-open mouth and all four feet pointing up in the air. Somehow I didn't think a Christmas list would help that.

"The Poodles have a stocking that we hang with all the others," I pointed out. "This year, Bud will be included. Do they *need* a list?"

I took a sip of my hot chocolate. It was rich and delicious. I had to hand it to Davey. The addition of crushed candy cane was pure genius.

"Everybody needs a Christmas list," he informed me. "Otherwise how will you know what to put in their stocking?"

"*Santa Claus* knows." I leveled Davey a warning look. "Santa Claus knows everything."

Kev frowned as he puzzled something through. Thankfully it wasn't Davey's gaffe. "If Santa knows everything, how come *we* made lists?"

"You guys were being helpful. Santa Claus is very busy this time of year."

"I know." Kevin nodded solemnly. "He was in the mall yesterday. Santa is everywhere."

"Kev was excited about making lists for the dogs," Davey said. "Wouldn't it be a good idea to be helpful on their behalf too?"

Put like that, what mother could possibly refuse?

I pulled over the pad of paper and uncapped one of the pens. "Okay. Who wants to start?"

"Me, me!" Kevin's hand shot up in the air. "The Poodles need biscuits and bones, and a new sock with a tennis ball in the toe because Augie threw the last one over the fence."

I looked up. "He did?"

"It was an accident," Davey said. "Tar was chasing him."

Oh. "What else?"

"Bud needs a winter coat," Kev told me. "Otherwise he's going to be cold in the snow."

"Bud has plenty of hair." I never dressed the Poodles up in clothing or costumes. Dogs in fashionable outfits just weren't my thing. "Plus, he lives in the house. He never has to stay outside if he doesn't want to."

"A coat," Kev repeated firmly. "Santa will understand. He lives in the North Pole. I bet his reindeer wear coats too."

"Bud is more likely to chew up a coat than wear it," I mentioned.

Kevin ignored me. "It should be plaid." He thought for a moment, then added, "Red and white with silver stars on it."

"Stars?" I repeated faintly. *Where was I going to find a plaid dog coat with stars on it?*

Davey was grinning again. He glanced at the paper in front of me. "Are you writing all that down?"

Kevin hopped up from his seat and came to have a look. He couldn't read yet, but he stared at the writing on the pad anyway. "Does that say *plaid*?" he asked. "It needs to say *plaid*."

PLAID, I wrote down in big block letters. WITH SILVER STARS.

I was pretty sure I was going to regret this.

Later that night, my cell phone rang. I didn't recognize the number. Everyone was gathered in the living room, watching Charlie Brown and Snoopy celebrate Christmas on TV. I carried the phone around the corner into the hall so I could hear.

"Is this Melanie?" a woman's voice asked. She sounded older and not entirely sure of herself. I wished she would speak up.

"Yes, it is. Who is this?"

"Stella Braverman. Do you remember me?"

I pressed the device closer to my ear. "Of course, Stella. How are you?"

"I'm well. Thank you for asking. But I need you to do something for me."

"Oh?"

"Well, not exactly for me. It's for my neighbor, Betty Dempsey. You've met her son, Tyler."

For a second, my breath caught. "Yes, I know who Betty Dempsey is. What does she need from me?"

"Betty wants to talk to you," Stella told me. "She wants to know what happened to Pete. She wants to hear it from you. In your own words."

"I'm not sure that's possible," I said. "Tyler has been very clear about the fact that he doesn't want me to see his mother. To be honest, I'm not even sure he's broken the news to her about Pete's death."

"No, he didn't. That coward." Stella's voice rose. "But I did. Betty deserved to know."

Good for her, I thought. Unfortunately that still didn't mean that I could do as she'd requested.

"I'm not sure how you expect me to get past Tyler," I said.

"Same way I do," Stella replied with a snort. "You wait until he's left the house, then you take my key and let yourself in."

"Stella, I live in Stamford. Even if you called me as soon as Tyler went out, by the time I got to Stonebridge, he could be back."

"That's why I set something up for tomorrow afternoon. Tyler's going to be called away between two and three o'clock. Can you make that?"

As plans went, it sounded far from perfect. There were a dozen questions I wanted to ask. And probably several good objections I should have made. But I realized immediately that this was likely to be my only chance to hear what Pete and Tyler's mother had to say about the rivalry between her two sons. And maybe to discover how far one of them might have gone to retain his place in the spotlight.

In reality, there was never any doubt about my reply.

"Yes," I said. "I can make that."

"Again?" Sam lifted a brow later the next morning when I informed him of my plans for the day.

"I suspect this will be my last visit to Stonebridge. I've already spoken to Pete's ex-wife, his business partners, his former best friend, his mistress, his brother, his neighbor, and even his high school girlfriend." I stopped and sighed. "You'd think I'd have an idea what caused Pete's death by now."

"Yes," Sam agreed drily. "You're usually quicker on the uptake. While you take another drive up the coast, the boys and I will be doing our bit and covering the office at the Christmas tree farm this afternoon. With Howard Academy having early dismissal on Fridays, I volunteered you to do the same tomorrow. I believe Aunt Peg intends to join you."

"Oh joy," I said. "She probably wants to spend the afternoon pumping me for information I don't possess."

Sam leaned down and brushed a kiss across the top of my head. "Maybe you'll learn something interesting today."

One could only hope, I thought.

Promptly at two o'clock, I pulled into Stella Braverman's driveway and coasted to a stop. Luckily the short strip of macadam was located on the opposite side of the house from the Dempsey home. Due to the clandestine nature of our business, I thought it wiser not to park on the street where the Volvo would be highly visible to passersby.

As I exited the car, Stella was already coming out her back door. She was dressed in furry boots and a hooded parka and had a determined look on her face. She was holding a key in her hand.

"Good, you're punctual," she said. "Let's go. I don't know how long Tyler's going to be gone. Trust me, it'll be better if he doesn't see us. Last time he caught me he tried to take my key away. Thank God Betty didn't let him, or we'd be out of luck today."

There was a well-worn path in the snow between the back of the two neighboring houses. Stella was spry for a woman her age and she obviously knew where she was going. I was happy to let her take the lead.

She elbowed aside a glass storm door, inserted her key in the lock, then shoved the inner door open. I followed her into a dark kitchen. As we paused to open our coats and wipe our boots on a thick fiber doormat, Stella reached over and turned on the lights.

"Betty?" she called out. "It's me and Melanie coming in the back door. We'll be right in to see you."

"Take your time, dear," a thin, reedy, voice called back. "I'm not going anywhere."

The living room opened directly off the kitchen. It too was only dimly lit. As we entered the room, a burst of light to one side drew my gaze. A television with its volume muted was showing what appeared to be an infomercial for cooking utensils.

"Turn that thing off, would you? The TV is nothing but an annoyance. I don't know why Tyler thinks it keeps me company." Betty Dempsey spoke up from the opposite side of the room.

A frail woman with gaunt features and wispy gray hair, she lay half-reclining on a low couch. The lower part of her body was covered by a light blanket and her head and shoulders were resting on a plump bank of pillows. She was staring at me with interest.

"You must be Melanie," Betty said. "Pleased to meet you. I hope you don't mind if I don't get up."

"Of course not. It's a pleasure to meet you too, Mrs. Dempsey." There was an upholstered chair beside the couch. I walked over and took a seat. When I leaned forward, the two of us were on the same level.

"I'll just give you ladies some time to get acquainted," Stella said. "If anybody needs me I'll be in the kitchen brewing some tea."

"I'm terribly sorry for your loss," I said.

Betty nodded somberly. "Thank you. My son's absence has been a hole in my life for these last years. In my condition, the only bright spot I have to look forward to is that I'll be seeing him again soon. I know you were there when he was found. Would you tell me what happened?"

I took my time relating the story, pausing for Betty to ask

questions or add comments. I told her that Pete wouldn't have suffered. I mentioned that his best friend, Snowball, had been by his side at the end.

That part made Betty smile. She sat up and folded her hands together on the blanket. "That boy always did love animals. Back when he was young, Pete was always bringing home strays and nursing them back to health."

"What about Tyler?" I asked casually. "Did he like animals too?"

Betty's gaze narrowed. Her body might have been weak, but her perception hadn't dulled. "Stella has kept me apprised of your escapades around town. I'm sure you've already heard an earful about those two boys and how they treated one another. Now that I have nothing else to do but sit and think, I look back on it and I think maybe that was partly my fault."

She paused and drew in a deep breath. One hand fluttered upward. She placed it over her heart. "Pete's birth was the answer to many prayers. I'd had two miscarriages before he arrived. The doctors weren't sure I'd ever be able to carry a baby to term. My husband and I called him our little miracle."

It was easy to imagine that Tyler would have found that a hard act to follow.

"When Pete's drinking spiraled out of control it ruined my life too." Betty's voice was growing fainter. I hoped my visit wasn't tiring her out. "That boy had every opportunity handed to him and he threw it all away. When I was diagnosed, I asked Tyler to try and find his brother. Did he tell you that?"

I nodded in silence. Unexpected tears pricked the corners of my eyes. I had no desire to cover up Tyler's misdeeds but I couldn't break this woman's heart by telling her that shortly before his death, Pete had wanted to come home. And her younger son had prevented him from doing so.

"Tyler thinks he needs to protect me," Betty said softly. "He's wrong about that, but he never listens. His father was the same way. He tried to shield me from things he thought I was better off not knowing. But of course I knew anyway. I've always known. I could see what was right in front of me."

She leaned back and rested her head on the pillows. Her gaze grew misty. I had no idea what Betty was talking about. Or if indeed, she was still talking to me at all. She seemed to be lost in a reminiscence of times past.

"What was right in front of you?" I asked.

"Life," Betty whispered. "Beautiful, miraculous life. A little girl with hazel eyes just like Pete's, who I never had a chance to know. I should have spoken up, but instead I let time pass. Then it was too late and I had to watch her grow up from afar. Pete should have made things right. That I allowed him not to will always be my biggest regret."

As she was speaking, Betty's lips curved in a small smile. I wondered if she was picturing a little girl with hazel eyes.

"I wasn't aware the Pete and Penny had a daughter," I said.

"They don't," Stella said from behind me. She walked into the room carrying a tea tray. "Betty, how about a nice, warm cup of tea?"

Betty blinked several times before focusing her gaze on her friend. "That would be lovely. Will you pour?"

I turned to Stella. "Betty was just talking about—"

"It's time for tea," Stella said. "Then we'll have to go. We wouldn't want anything about our visit to upset Betty."

"No, of course not," I agreed.

The tea was quickly poured and drunk. Fifteen minutes later, we'd said our good-byes and Stella had locked the door to the Dempsey home behind us.

"You'd better be on your way," she told me when we reached her driveway. "We don't want Tyler to come home and find you here."

Stella kept walking toward her house. I stopped beside my car.

"Betty was telling me about a little girl," I said.

Stella paused and looked back. "Betty's on a lot of medication these days. Sometimes her thoughts wander. I'm sure it wasn't anything important."

I didn't believe that for a minute. In fact, I was pretty sure that the opposite was true. It seemed to me that Betty's memories might be more significant than anything else I'd learned thus far. Now I had to figure out how to make that nugget of information fit with everything else I knew.

On the drive home, I realized the answer was easy. I'd dump everything in Aunt Peg's lap and let her make sense of it. Friday afternoon at Haney's Holiday Home was going to be interesting indeed.

Chapter 15

When Aunt Peg blew into the office at the Christmas tree farm the following afternoon, Faith and I were waiting for her.

She was carrying Snowball under her arm and moving with the determined stride of a woman on a mission. It was no wonder Aunt Peg wasn't walking the silky-haired Maltese on a leash. He probably wouldn't have been able to keep up.

"*Well!*" She stopped in front of me and propped her free hand on her hip. "It's about time."

It was a good thing there weren't any customers in the office right then. Anyone with an ounce of sense would have taken one look at the expression on Aunt Peg's face and run for the hills.

Which said nothing for the quality of my brain cells, because instead I stood my ground, grinned in the face of her obvious wrath, and said, "Time for what?"

Aunt Peg snorted indelicately. She set Snowball down on the plank floor, then unzipped her parka, pulled it off, and tossed it behind the counter. Her scarf and hat followed. Then she turned back to me.

"Is your phone working?"

"I believe so."

"Can you make calls with it? Send an e-mail? Maybe a text?"

"All possibilities," I confirmed.

Aunt Peg gazed at Faith who was lying beside the woodstove, and shook her head sadly. Faith flapped her tail up and down in support. "Then for heaven's sake, what is *wrong* with you? It's been how long since we spoke . . . a month?"

"Actually less than a week—"

"Indeed the silence on your end had become *so* deafening I'd begun to look for smoke signals."

"Now that's just silly," I said.

"You wouldn't think so if you were in my shoes. Thank goodness for Snowball. Otherwise I'd have been entirely lacking in suitable companionship."

"I'm going to tell your Poodles you said that," I mentioned.

Snowball came bounding out from behind the counter. He had his teeth fastened on the end of Aunt Peg's wool scarf and was dragging it along the floor behind him. As the Maltese went racing by, I leaned down and scooped him up. The scarf came with him.

It took a minute to pry the two apart. By the time I'd succeeded in doing so, Aunt Peg seemed to have settled. She sat down in the rocking chair. I walked over and deposited Snowball in her lap. I'd just reached down to give Faith a pat when the door opened again and a family of four—two smiling adults and two exuberant children—came inside.

Most of the customers I'd dealt with so far were old hands at locating and chopping down their own trees. Many had brought the tools they'd need to do the job with them. This family was similarly prepared. All I had to do was hand out candy canes, show them where the sleds were waiting by the side of the building, and point them in the direction of the Christmas tree forest.

In the brief lull that followed, I quickly told Aunt Peg about my visit with Betty Dempsey the previous afternoon. She sat and mulled that over while I dealt with two more sets of customers, one who needed help getting their tree tied to the roof of their car, and a second who wanted to negotiate a price for the inflatable Santa Claus—a decoration that wasn't for sale.

"Are you thinking what I'm thinking?" she asked when we again had the cozy office to ourselves.

I lifted a brow and waited. Before voicing my suspicions, I wanted to hear what Aunt Peg had to say. As usual, she didn't disappoint.

"It sounds to me as though the little girl whom she watched from afar might be Betty's grandchild."

"I agree," I said. "And there's more."

This time I backtracked to my conversation with Pete's ex-mistress, Olivia, about her former lover's demons. After that, we got sidetracked when I mentioned Rufus the Great Dane. Somewhat predictably that led to a discussion of Aunt Peg's aversion to dog parks.

Customers came inside to pay for a tree they'd picked out and when they left, I once again picked up the thread of my story. I'd now worked my way around to Pete's high school sweetheart, Sharon LaRue. By this time, Aunt Peg was sitting up straighter in her seat. Considering the state of the rocking chair, that wasn't an easy feat.

"There was a photograph on Sharon's desk," I said.

"Let me guess." She placed Snowball on the floor and stood up. "Was it a little girl with hazel eyes?"

"Not quite," I admitted. "It showed her husband and a grown-up daughter whose eye color I didn't bother to notice at the time. Sharon told me that she and her husband had married when they were very young. During their freshman year of college, in fact."

"I'd say that's rather interesting timing." Aunt Peg walked over to the window in the back wall. She stared at the forest thoughtfully. Though it was only mid-afternoon, we were close to the shortest day of the year. The sun was already dropping in the sky. "What did she have to say about Pete's high school peccadilloes?"

"She told me that Pete's only problem back then was his rivalry with his brother. That if there were unresolved issues in his life, they'd have had to do with his family."

Aunt Peg glanced at me over her shoulder. "And you believed her?"

"At the time I had no reason not to. But now . . ."

"You're wondering," Aunt Peg said. "As am I."

At that moment, the happy family of four returned to pay for their tree and to browse through our selection of Christmas ornaments. Twenty minutes passed before I was able to get back to Aunt Peg. In the meantime, she'd wandered outside and helped another family wrangle their tree from sled to vehicle. As I stepped out onto the porch to check on their progress, I realized how dark it had grown and turned on all the outdoor lights.

The area surrounding the office and its outbuilding was well-lit but the dense woods were not. Frank had asked me to stay open until five o'clock, but I doubted we'd see any additional shoppers that afternoon.

Aunt Peg and I made short work of checking out the last tree buyers. As their vehicles' taillights disappeared down the driveway, all appeared quiet. I closed the office door firmly to keep the warmth inside.

"It looks as though we're done for the day," Aunt Peg said with satisfaction. "Let's get back to what really matters. What else do you have to tell me?"

"One last thing. John Smith said that Pete had been contacting people he'd wronged in the past."

"I know that. I was there." She flicked a hand impatiently, waving me on.

"Several people I spoke with in Stonebridge told me that they'd heard from him. But not Sharon. She was adamant about the fact that they hadn't been in touch in years."

"Maybe he hadn't worked his way around to her yet," Aunt Peg said dubiously.

I didn't believe that. I was pretty sure Aunt Peg didn't either.

"Or maybe she was one of the first people he contacted," I said. "And she was lying to cover up the fact that she knew exactly what Pete was doing and where to find him."

Aunt Peg was nodding as I spoke. Now she said, "That information needs to go to the police. Those new details added to the autopsy result ought to be enough to convince them that their initial conclusion about Pete's death was incorrect."

If not, her tone implied, she would browbeat the officers in charge until they changed their minds.

"You and I can go together tomorrow morning," I said.

"Excellent." Aunt Peg picked up her scarf and wrapped it around her neck. "Now that we have that settled, Snowball and I are going to take a walk. I've discovered that caretakers of small dogs must adapt to the needs of their tiny bladders. Are the lights on out back?"

"Yes, I turned everything on a few minutes ago. While you do that, I'll close the cash register. Then we can all leave together."

Faith elected to stay inside the warm office with me. She watched as I counted the day's receipts, and then I tucked them into a bank pouch that went in a small safe beneath the counter. I was leaning down and fiddling with the combination when a blast of cold air signaled that the door had opened once again. Aunt Peg and Snowball were back sooner than I'd expected.

Then I heard the rumble of a low growl from Faith and quickly readjusted my thinking. The big Poodle had been greeting incoming strangers with warmth and equanimity all afternoon. But whoever had entered the office now clearly did not meet with her approval.

Slowly I rose to my feet. Sharon LaRue was standing in the doorway.

"Oh," I said, surprised. "What are you doing here?"

Sharon nudged the door shut with her foot. "We need to talk. What's the matter with your dog?"

I glanced at Faith. "Nothing. She's fine."

"She's not fine. She's growling." Sharon still hadn't advanced into the small room. "I can hear it. Does she bite?"

"Only people she doesn't like."

Faith probably rolled her eyes at that, but I didn't look over to check. The Poodle's instincts were always spot-on. If there was something about our unexpected visitor she didn't like, I was willing to trust her response. I remained behind the counter and I kept my gaze firmly fixed on Sharon.

"How did you find me here?" I asked. I wasn't aware that she and I had ever discussed my connection to the Christmas tree farm.

"I had dinner last night with my Aunt Stella. She had several interesting things to tell me."

Aunt Stella. My breath jammed in my throat.

What an idiot I was. I'd overlooked one of the chief characteristics of small, insular towns. One way or another, almost everybody had a connection to everyone else.

"She told me you went to see Betty Dempsey yesterday."

"That's right. Betty asked to see me. She wanted to talk to me about Pete's death."

"I heard that's not all you and she discussed."

Hand held low, I gave my fingers a soft snap. Faith padded quietly around the counter to my side. Once there, she pressed her body against my leg. Clearly, she was still uneasy. And because of that, so was I.

Sharon could no longer see Faith, but she still didn't step

away from the door. That was just as well. The office was a small space. Even standing on the other side of the room, the other woman still felt uncomfortably close.

Sharon wasn't looking at me, however. Instead her gaze was sliding dismissively over the colorful jumble of holiday decorations that Claire had hung on the walls. "Geez, what were you thinking when you put up all this crap? It looked like the North Pole exploded in here."

Affronted on Claire's behalf, I said, "Did you come here to discuss the décor?"

"No, I came to tell to you to stop sticking your nose into everybody's business." Her eyes returned to me. "Betty's an old lady. She's sick. Sometimes she doesn't know what she's saying."

"Betty seemed perfectly lucid to me." That might have been a stretch, but I went with it anyway.

"That's not for you to judge. You don't even know the Dempseys."

"You're right," I agreed mildly. "I couldn't possibly know them as well as someone like you who's been friends with them for years." I paused a beat, then added, "Or possibly more than friends."

Sharon still hadn't unbuttoned her coat. Or taken off her hat. She wasn't wearing gloves and now she shoved her hands deep into her pockets. She glared at me angrily.

"You want to talk about Pete?" she snapped. "Fine, let's do that. Pete Dempsey was a spoiled, selfish, rotten excuse for a human being and I'm glad he's dead."

"Did you kill him?" I asked.

"Not me. The booze did that."

"Pete hadn't been drinking when he died," I told her. "He didn't freeze to death because he collapsed in a drunken stupor. He died because someone hit him over the head with a tree branch and left him lying in the snow."

Sharon scowled. "Don't look at me like you think I ought to be sorry about that. Nobody in Stonebridge is sorry. Pete's death wasn't a loss to any of us. When he left town, we were all happy to see him go."

"But that was the problem, wasn't it?" I prodded gently. "Pete was coming back. He'd gotten sober and he'd been contacting people from his past. You told me you hadn't heard from him in years, but I think you lied about that. I'm guessing you were one of the first people he called."

"No, that's not true." Sharon's deep chuckle had an ugly edge. "I *should* have been the first person Pete apologized to. But I wasn't. He took his own sweet time getting around to me."

She shook her head as if she could hardly believe it. "And even then—when he was trying to make me believe he wanted to be a better man—Pete still couldn't admit that what he'd done to me was wrong. He had the nerve to say that my life turned out fine in the end, so what right did I have to be upset with him?"

"Wow." I winced. "That would have pissed me off too."

"I know. *Right?*"

For a brief moment Sharon and I were in perfect agreement. Then I spoiled our accord by saying, "You were pregnant at the end of your senior year of high school, weren't you? Is Pete Amy's father?"

Sharon didn't reply to my question directly. Instead she said, "I was only eighteen years old. I had no idea which way to turn. When I told Pete, he said, 'That's your problem. You find a way to deal with it.' Then he left for college."

I didn't want to feel sympathy for her, but hearing her story I almost couldn't help it. "In your place, I'd have been furious," I said.

"Fury was a luxury I didn't have time for," Sharon snapped. "Steve and I were married six weeks later."

"Did he know?"

"Not right away. But later on, yes. He and I have a great relationship. We had our issues in the beginning, but we worked through them."

Issues indeed, I thought. How great could a relationship be when it was founded upon a lie?

Sharon thrust out her chin. "Steve loves Amy. In every way that matters, he *is* her father."

Something—a spark of apprehension—flashed in her eyes. Right then I knew: Steve wasn't the one who was the problem.

"Amy doesn't know who her real father is, does she?"

"No, of course not. Why would I have told her something like that? My daughter doesn't need to know that her father is a lying, cheating, bastard who abandoned me as soon as he found out she existed."

"Pete wanted to tell her the truth, didn't he?" I was guessing, but the anguished expression on Sharon's face confirmed that I was right.

"There was no way I could let him do that," she said. "I wasn't about to let Pete ruin Amy's life the way he ruined mine. He refused to claim her back then. It was too late for him to want to be her father now."

"I agree," I said.

Casually I stepped out from behind the counter, like we were just two women having a perfectly normal conversation. Earlier I'd left my phone near the woodstove. As Sharon continued to speak, I slid my gaze that way.

"I had no choice but to protect Amy." Her voice rose with the conviction that she'd been right. "Amy was *mine*. Not his. But Pete refused to accept that he'd lost any right to his daughter twenty-three years ago when he walked out on me. I wasn't about to let that scumbag come back and dismantle the life I'd built for myself."

"What did you do?" I asked, inching toward the back of the room.

"I told Pete he could take his stupid atonement ritual and

shove it. His reappearance would have destroyed Amy and *for what*? To make himself feel better? That was never going to happen. Not while there was a single breath left in my body."

It was a chilling statement of intent. I heard Faith whimper softly under her breath. It was almost as if she knew what was coming.

"So now you know why I've come." Sharon's lips flattened into a hard line. "I have to protect my family. The story I told you ends here, today, with you and me."

She withdrew her hand from her pocket. It was holding a gun. Sharon lifted it and pointed it at me. "Stop right there, Melanie. Don't move."

Chapter 16

I froze in place and held up a hand. *As if that would help.* "Wait. Let's talk about this."

"I have nothing more to say. Except maybe that I'm sorry it's come to this." Sharon looked at me across the short expanse. "Although it's your own fault."

"It hasn't come to anything yet," I said quickly.

There was no way I could get to my phone. I cast my gaze around the room, searching for a weapon. The only thing I saw was a thick piece of firewood. That would be ironic.

"How did you do it?" I asked, stalling for time. With the barrel of a gun pointed at my midsection, what choice did I have?

"It wasn't hard," Sharon said dismissively. "After I got over the shock of hearing from Pete, I told him that I wanted to meet with him in person. But not in Stonebridge. I insisted on coming to him."

"And he was all right with that?" I asked, surprised. I wouldn't have thought Pete would want his old friends to see how he was living.

"It wasn't as if I gave him a choice. Pete knew the only way he could get to Amy was by going through me. I told him if I was satisfied with our conversation, I would let him talk to her."

"But you never had any intention of doing so," I said.

"Of course not." Sharon looked at me like I was daft. "We met outside this building. This place was deserted then. Pete was all alone out here in the middle of nowhere."

She must have initially gotten together with Pete after Mr. Haney died and before Frank purchased the property. The Christmas tree farm would have been closed then. And empty.

"I asked Pete to show me where he lived and he did." Sharon shuddered. "It was disgusting. I couldn't believe he'd sunk that low. After I saw that, all I had to do was go home and come up with a plan."

"It was a good plan," I told her. "Pete's death appeared to be an accident."

"That was the idea." Sharon sounded smug. "I decided to show up with a couple bottles of gin and get Pete so drunk that he passed out. After that, it would be easy enough to turn off the dinky little stove and leave him there in the cold." She stopped and frowned. "But Pete refused to cooperate. Considering our past history, maybe I should have expected that."

Yeah maybe, I thought. "Then what did you do?"

"I told Pete I wanted to go for a moonlight walk in the snow with him. And he fell for it. Can you believe it?"

I shook my head. Honestly, I couldn't. The male ego was a wondrous thing.

"I took one of the liquor bottles with me. I was sure that when he got chilly enough, I could convince him to warm up with a drink. But then I saw that branch just lying on the ground. It was perfect, like fate had placed it there for me. Once I hit him over the head, Mother Nature did the rest."

"Presumably except for dumping the gin on him and leaving the empty bottles in his cabin," I said drily.

"Yes, except for that." My sarcasm had gone right over her head.

"You fooled the police last time," I said. "But they'll be suspicious about a second death here. If you shoot me with your gun, you're not going to be able to explain that away."

"That won't be a problem." Sharon sounded remarkably sure of herself. "The police will think this was a robbery gone bad. Probably kids looking for drug money. A remote location and a woman alone with a cash register? It's the perfect setup."

Damn, I thought. *She was right.* Except for one thing. I wasn't alone. Apparently Sharon didn't realize that.

"Plus," she added, "you don't strike me as the kind of person who would meekly hand over the cash to stay safe. Probably everybody knows what a pain in the butt you can be."

Well, okay. She might be right. But that meant I wasn't about to let her meekly shoot me either. Not if I could figure out a way to stop her.

Faith was still making low noises. Her whimper had turned into an angry whine. She didn't know a thing about guns but she must have felt the palpable edge of menace in the air. The Poodle came out from behind the counter on her toes with her shoulders arched. The hair on her neck and shoulders was standing straight up.

"Don't even think of siccing that dog on me." Sharon cut Faith a glance. "If you do, I'll shoot her first."

I cupped my hand around Faith's muzzle and quickly maneuvered her around behind me. "Nobody's going to be shooting anybody."

"I wouldn't bet on that if I were you."

From somewhere outside, there came a blood-curdling scream. At the same moment the door to the office came flying inward.

The solid wooden panel hit Sharon hard from behind, catching her squarely across the shoulders. She stumbled and went staggering forward. Her arms flailed in the air as she tried to regain her balance. It didn't happen.

I briefly registered the panicked look on Sharon's face before whirling around to grab Faith. As Sharon fell, her finger tightened on the trigger. With a roar that sounded impossibly loud in the small space, the gun discharged.

Faith and I hit the floor together. I was on top, and the big dog cushioned my frantic dive without complaint. I heard the sound of a loud pop. To my surprise, it was followed by the whoosh of escaping air.

I'd started to raise my head, but immediately ducked down again as something red and white went flying past us. I was still trying to process that when the unidentified missile suddenly shot upward. Several large splinters of wood came raining down from the cabin ceiling. A loud plop followed.

Quickly I disengaged myself from Faith and scrambled to my feet. Right now, there wasn't time to think about anything but getting to the gun.

Sharon had dropped the weapon when she'd used her hands to break her fall, but she was already looking around for it. From my vantage point I could see that the gun had skidded across the floor and come to rest beside the counter. I went racing after it, but I didn't get there first.

Aunt Peg beat me to it.

She crossed the room in four quick strides and scooped up the gun, handling the piece with the calm assurance of someone who was accustomed to riding to the rescue. Then she spun around and trained the weapon on Sharon, who'd risen slowly to her knees.

"I don't think so," Aunt Peg said.

"Who the hell are you?" Sharon spat out. She dusted off her hands and started to get up.

"You may think of me as the cavalry," Aunt Peg said with a wolfish smile. "The police are on their way. I'd rather you remain on the floor until they arrive. I'd hate to have to use this, but I will if I need to."

Sharon grimaced as though her knees were hurting, but she lowered herself back down on the wooden planking. A small, mean part of me was gratified to see that she appeared to be in pain. Having threatened to shoot us, Sharon was getting off easy, in my book.

On the other side of the room, Faith was up and moving well. She'd trotted over to the far corner and was busy examining something crumpled on the floor. Satisfied that she was in good shape, I turned to Aunt Peg.

"That was a rash move," I said.

"But effective. At least you might credit me that."

"The shot went wild," I pointed out. "You could have gotten me killed."

Aunt Peg just shrugged. *All's well that ends well.*

It was easy for her to be so blithe about it. There hadn't been a gun pointed in her direction. Meanwhile the aftershock of my near miss had left me feeling unaccountably grumpy.

"It took you long enough to make your move," I said.

"I was listening to what Sharon had to say." Aunt Peg flicked a quick glance my way. "After all, it's not as though you've gone out of your way to keep me apprised."

"You could hear us from outside?"

"Of course. I was on the porch. This old building is hardly soundproof. Those wooden walls have gaps wider than my little finger."

I took a sudden look around. "Wait a minute. Where's Snowball?"

"Don't worry about him, he's safe in my van. I stashed him there when I rounded the building and saw Sharon's car. I thought perhaps I might need to have my wits about me. It's a good thing I'd done so, because when I heard her threaten Faith, I knew I had to intervene."

"When you heard her threaten *Faith*?" As I recalled, that had happened a good minute after Sharon had threatened to shoot *me*.

"Precisely." Aunt Peg nodded. "That's when I knew things were about to get serious."

I opened my mouth. Then shut it again. Upon reflection, there was absolutely nothing I could say to that. Instead I went to check on Faith.

She was still in the corner, sniffing at something. From afar, it looked like a discarded bundle of clothing. But when I nudged the Poodle aside and took a closer look, the object of her curiosity turned out to be the remains of our inflatable Santa Claus. The bullet Sharon fired had missed both Faith and me, but it had struck Santa directly in the middle of his red vinyl chest.

The cheery, life-size, holiday figure was a goner. Under the circumstances, it seemed like a small price to pay.

Chapter 17

"Do you hear something?" Aunt Peg asked. She lifted a hand to her ear.

Sirens. A minute later, the still-open doorway revealed several sets of flashing lights coming closer through the trees.

Hopefully it was just my imagination that Aunt Peg appeared to surrender the gun with reluctance when the first police officers came through the door. She was enough of a menace when she wasn't holding a weapon. I hated to think that she might be developing a fondness for firearms.

Aunt Peg and I took turns explaining the situation to the responding officers while Sharon listened in stony silence. Her gun and the demolished Santa Claus were enough to get her taken into custody. In addition, the officers promised to pass along what we told them about Pete Dempsey's death to their superiors.

Sharon immediately hired a lawyer. Thanks to his quick work, she was out of jail the next day. I couldn't help but wonder what kind of reception she would receive from the good folks of Stonebridge upon her return to town.

Later I heard from Aunt Peg—who followed each new development avidly—that Sharon's attorney was discussing such things as mitigating circumstances and a conspicuous lack of hard evidence with the DA. Apparently, the blameless life the assistant principal had led thus far would also work in her favor.

Now that the police and the courts were handling things, I put that adventure behind me and threw myself into preparations for Christmas. *Better late than never.* Once the upcoming holiday finally had my full attention, it all came together beautifully.

On Christmas morning, everything was perfect. Or as near to perfect as things could ever be in a family with one child starry-eyed over Santa's visit, a teenager and five Standard Poodles who were all too clever for their own good, a semi-trained mutt, and two adults who had resigned themselves to living in a constant state of near-lunacy.

Of course we were awake early on Christmas morning. That was a given. Several inches of new snow had turned the outdoors fresh and white overnight. When we lit a fire in the fireplace and turned on the Christmas tree lights, the entire living room glowed.

The boys tore into their presents, greeting each new gift with appreciation, even the clothing and books. When Kevin reached for a small box that was tucked way back beneath the tree, Sam and I shared a private smile.

"What do you suppose that is?" Sam asked.

Kev held up the box and shook it, like he'd seen his brother do.

"That sounds like more clothes," Davey predicted. He was busy examining a new wireless controller with thumb sticks.

"I hope it's not socks," Kevin said seriously. "I have lots of those."

"I don't think Santa brought you socks," I told him. "Open it and see."

Kevin yanked off the bow and opened the box. A peanut butter dog biscuit was sitting on top of a bed of tissue paper. He frowned, perplexed. "Why did Santa bring me a dog biscuit?"

"Maybe it goes with what's underneath," Sam said. "Keep looking."

Davey stopped what he was doing to watch too. So we were all paying attention when Kevin pushed aside the tissue wrapping and began to shriek. Jumping to his feet, he held up a red plaid dog coat decorated across the back with a spray of silver stars.

"Santa brought it!" Kevin exclaimed. "I knew he would."

Sam had gone from store to store until he'd found the perfect chew-resistant jacket. Meanwhile I'd bought a length of silver fabric and made stars. I'd spent the last several nights, after the boys were in bed, sewing them on. The look on Kevin's face when he'd opened the present made the extra effort well worth it.

Bud was immediately brought forward and buckled into his new coat. The little dog stood in place for a few seconds, whipping his head from side to side to examine his new outfit. Then he leapt away and began to race around the room.

As Kevin cheered and the Poodles watched in bemused wonderment, Bud shot across the living room floor and gave a sudden flying leap that landed him on the couch. From there, he hopped to a nearby chair, then skimmed across a tabletop before landing on the floor again.

He was about to repeat the circuit of the room when Sam stepped in and scooped him up. "I think we'd better let them take this game outside before the Poodles decide to join in the festivities and they wreck the place."

Great idea.

Aunt Peg showed up when we were seated at the kitchen table, eating a Christmas breakfast of French toast and slab-cut bacon. Having gone directly from presents to food, we were all still in our jammies. I was surprised Aunt Peg was out and about so early on Christmas.

"I needed to make an early holiday delivery," she explained as she joined us and helped herself to a plate of food. "Snowball has gone off to his new home."

"*On Christmas morning?*"

We were all aware of Aunt Peg's firm objection to puppies being given as presents on the busy holiday. That she would even consider participating in such a scheme herself came as a shock. Aunt Peg, however, remained unruffled.

She slid another slice of bacon onto her plate and said, "It took this long to get things settled, since nobody seemed to know precisely who Snowball belonged to. Not surprisingly, Pete didn't leave a will. So I took myself over to Stonebridge and talked to his family. They didn't want anything to do with the poor little dog."

I lifted my head in surprise. "You spoke with *Tyler?*"

"Of course. You're not the only one around here who gets to ask questions. I talked to Betty too. She asked me if I might be able to find Snowball a good home. So that's precisely what I did."

"But still," said Sam. "Christmas morning?"

"This was a special case. The Butlers are a retired couple. Their children are grown and have families of their own. This year no one was making the trip home for the holiday. So Ned and Sally would be spending a quiet day by themselves."

I gazed around our lively table crowded with loved ones. I couldn't help but feel sorry for anyone who had to spend the holidays alone.

"I'd extended some feelers in the Maltese community," Aunt Peg continued. "Their local rescue put me in touch with Ned. Apparently he'd proposed to Sally forty years ago on Christmas Day, and sealed the deal with a Maltese puppy. They'd been dog owners ever since, until they lost their last pet three months ago."

"That's sad," said Kevin. The rest of us nodded.

"Recently Sally had indicated to Ned that she might be ready to open her heart to a new dog. At their age, she thought an adult dog might suit better than a puppy. So Ned contacted the local Maltese club. He and I spoke on the phone, then he came and met Snowball. The two of them hit it off beautifully. Ned wanted to surprise his wife on Christmas morning and, under the circumstances, I was happy to oblige."

"That was a very nice thing you did," Sam said softly.

I couldn't seem to talk past the lump in my throat, so I just nodded again. Even Davey looked subdued. Not Kevin. He was shaking his head.

"Ned should have asked Santa Claus for a dog," he said with impeccable three-year-old logic. "Santa would have brought him one."

I reached over and ruffled my son's hair. "But this way Snowball got a great home. And with Aunt Peg helping out, Santa had more time to spend making children happy."

"Oh." Kev considered that. The thought of Santa Claus working hard on his behalf made him smile. "Well done, Aunt Peg."

Well done, indeed.

Melanie's Favorite Cinnamon Cookies

These cookies are great for busy moms. They're delicious and easy to make, and most people already have the ingredients in the pantry. Enjoy!

Ingredients
1¼ cups of butter
⅔ cup of sugar
⅓ cup brown sugar
1 egg yolk
1¼ cups of flour
1¼ teaspoons cinnamon
¼ teaspoon salt

Preheat your oven to 300 degrees.
Mix the butter, the sugar, and the brown sugar.
Add the egg yolk and blend well.
Stir together the flour, cinnamon, and salt. Add the dry ingredients to the creamed mixture and blend well.
Place the dough by rounded teaspoons on an ungreased cookie sheet. Bake for 20–25 minutes. Cool on the cookie sheet for a few minutes, then transfer to wax paper or a wire rack to finish cooling.

Yield: about 3 dozen cookies (unless you make each cookie twice as big as it should be like I do, in which case you will have half that many.)

Here Comes Santa Paws

Chapter 1

"Guess what I found in my Christmas stocking this morning?" Aunt Peg said.

I paused, holding the phone to my ear. Where Aunt Peg was concerned, a guess was a risky venture. Seventy years old and sharp as a bee sting, she made it her mission to keep me on my toes.

Her interests were wide ranging, encompassing everything from her beloved Standard Poodles, to global politics, to the psychology behind reality TV. But most of all, she enjoyed stirring up trouble.

And since I was the one who was usually left holding the bag when her escapades backfired, you can probably understand why I stopped and thought before I answered. And then attempted to dodge the question entirely.

"Christmas is still two and a half weeks away," I replied. "Why would anyone be leaving presents in your stocking now?"

"That's what I'd like to know," she huffed. "And this most certainly wasn't a present. At least not a welcome one."

"Oh?"

"Oh?" she mimicked. "Is that all you have to say?"

"I'm waiting for more information."

"So am I."

I sighed under my breath. As usual, I didn't have time to waste. I'm a wife, a mother to two growing boys, and a special needs tutor at a private school. I also have five Standard Poodles of my own, plus a small spotted mutt, who thinks he's another Poodle.

And Christmas was coming.

So I needed to move this conversation along. "I'm a little busy here," I said. "Give me a hint. Animal, mineral, or vegetable?"

"Animal."

Hmm.

I'd fully expected her to say *mineral*. If Santa had left a lump of coal in Aunt Peg's stocking, I wouldn't have been surprised. She and I both would have had a good laugh about that.

Well, I would have anyway. But no such luck.

"Puppies!" Aunt Peg announced. She'd obviously grown tired of waiting for me to come up with an answer on my own. "Some depraved person tucked a litter of three into my Christmas stocking. The poor things look like they're no more than five weeks old."

"What?" I yelped.

Faith, the big black Poodle who was lying draped across my lap, lifted her head and tipped it to one side. My shriek had probably hurt her ears. Faith and I have been together for nearly nine years. She knew what I was thinking almost before I did. Now she had to be wondering what was the matter. I patted her reassuringly.

When she settled back down, I returned to the conversation. "You can't be serious. Are you saying that somebody snuck into your house last night with an armful of puppies?"

The thought defied belief, but I still had to ask.

"Good Lord, Melanie, do try to keep up. Of course nobody came inside the house. Otherwise the dogs would have raised the alarm, and I would have confronted the intruder with a shotgun."

Aunt Peg doesn't actually have a shotgun. Just so you know. She does, however, stand six feet tall and have a grip that can make a grown man wince. Even her glare is fearsome. Given a choice, most people would probably rather face down the weapon.

"I'm talking about the stocking that's hanging from the mailbox post at the end of my driveway," she said. "I put it up last week and it looks quite festive, if I do say so myself. It's *supposed* to be a holiday decoration. Nobody was meant to put it to use."

"Christmas puppies," I said with a slow, happy, smile. "Cool."

"Cut that out," Aunt Peg snapped. "This isn't a holiday fairy tale. Those puppies were abandoned. They're homeless."

"Not anymore," I pointed out. I was glad she couldn't see that I was still smiling. Even Faith looked happy now. Talking about puppies has that effect on both of us. "Now they have you."

"I suppose they could have done worse," Aunt Peg grumbled.

You think?

Margaret Turnbull was an acknowledged authority on all things canine. A longtime Standard Poodle breeder and an experienced dog show judge, she adored dogs of all shapes and sizes. She understood their moods and their personalities. She could shape their characters and predict their actions. And every dog Aunt Peg had ever met adored her right back.

Those three puppies had no idea how lucky they were.

"What breed are they?" I asked.

I knew she'd have an answer ready. A normal person might have labeled the puppies cuddly or cute. Not Aunt Peg. I was sure she'd already been busy assessing the tiny canines' features and cataloging their good qualities. It was no surprise that she came up with a quick reply.

"Australian Shepherds, unless I miss my guess. Two blacks and a blue merle. Maybe not entirely purebred, but close enough to have the look. They seem healthy enough, even after having spent part of the night outside. But I still don't understand what they're doing here. Why would someone have left them at the end of my driveway?"

"Probably because your reputation precedes you," I said. "Maybe someone had an accidental litter and was too lazy to do right by them. They figured you'd give the puppies a good home."

"Find them one is more like it," she replied. "I'll fatten them up, worm them, get them their shots, then locate some lovely people for them in January. They're young and appealing. That will help."

"I love puppies," I said dreamily. It had been years since I'd had a litter of my own. "Can I come and see them?"

"I thought you were busy." Aunt Peg's tone was arch.

"That was before you told me you had puppies. See you soon!"

I disconnected before she had time to argue. I was sliding Faith off my lap when my husband, Sam, walked around the corner into the living room. Tall and fit, he carried himself with an easy grace. When he smiled—which he did often—his gray eyes crinkled at the corners. Right now, however, Sam was looking uncharacteristically disgruntled.

His blond hair was mussed, as though he'd been raking his fingers through it, and his denim shirt was partially untucked. I knew Sam had been working in his home office. It didn't look as though things had been going well. No doubt he'd been eager for a distraction.

"Was that Peg?" he asked. "Did I hear you say that she has puppies?"

"Yes, and yes," I replied. "I'm going to go play with them. Want to come along?"

"I wish." He sounded envious. "But *some* of us aren't already on Christmas break."

That was meant to be a jab at my employer, Howard Academy, and their famously liberal policy toward school vacations. The purpose of the extended recess was to allow students' families ample time for their trips to the beach or ski slopes. Fortunately, it also gave teachers and administrators the same three weeks off. None of us complained about that.

I hopped up from the couch, braced my hands on Sam's shoulders, and planted a quick kiss on his lips. "You work for yourself. Doesn't that mean that you get to set your own hours?"

"Sure," he said. "But it also means that if I don't sit down and actually do the work, no one else will either."

The rest of our canine crew must have been keeping Sam company in his office. Now they came trailing into the room behind him. Poodles come in many colors, but all of ours are black—not surprising since most of them are interrelated. All our Standard Poodles were also former show dogs. Each had titles and a long, impressive name that nobody ever bothered to use now that they were retired from the show ring.

Leading the way were the two males, Tar and Augie. Tar wasn't the brightest Poodle we owned, but with numerous Bests in Show on his résumé, he was the most accomplished. Augie belonged to our older son, Davey, who had handled him to his championship. Both dogs were cocky and bold, and they thought they ruled the house. I was pretty sure that one day the three female Poodles would set them straight about that.

Aside from Faith, we also had Sam's older bitch, Raven, and Faith's daughter, Eve. Those girls were funny and sweet, and

smarter than the average child. The bitches were less rambunc-
tious than the boys, but they definitely knew how to get their
point across when they needed to.

Completing the pack was our newest addition, Bud. A small
black-and-white dog of indeterminate heritage, he had been
rescued from the side of the road the previous year and had
quickly become every bit as much a member of the family as
the Poodles were.

Laces clenched between his teeth, Bud was dragging a shoe
behind him. It appeared to be one of Davey's sneakers. There
were several dozen dog toys scattered throughout the house,
but without fail, the little mutt tended to help himself to something that was supposed to be off-limits.

I rescued the shoe and set it on a nearby table. Bud wagged
his stubby tail and gave me his doggy grin. Heights didn't deter
him for long. We both knew he was just waiting for me to turn
my back so he could recapture his prize.

"So what's the story with the puppies?" Sam asked. "I know
Peg wasn't expecting a litter. How did she end up with one?"

"She says they're Christmas orphans. Aussie look-alikes,
apparently. Dumped at the end of her driveway and in need of
good homes."

He gazed at me askance. "Not here. Don't get any ideas
about that. We already have a houseful."

"Does that mean there's no room at the inn?" I lifted a
brow.

Sam got the none-too-subtle Christmas reference. He grinned
reluctantly. "Not unless one of them is pregnant and riding a
donkey. In which case, I may be forced to reconsider."

I walked out to the front hallway and grabbed a coat and
scarf from the closet. "I won't be gone long. Try not to work
too hard while I'm away."

"You'll pick up Kevin on your way home?"

Four-year-old Kevin was our younger son. Mornings, he attended Graceland Nursery School. Like Davey, who was in his first year of high school, Kev still had another week before his Christmas vacation began. I'd be gone from Aunt Peg's in plenty of time to swing by and get him. Or so I thought.

"Sure," I said. "I can handle that. No problem."

I've never seen a puppy that wasn't adorable, and the three in Aunt Peg's kitchen were no exception. The two males were black with tan markings. A ruff of white hair formed a wide ring around their shoulders and chests. The lone female was a blue merle with bright blue eyes. All three stared at me inquisitively when I sat down on the floor beside the low, newspaper-lined pen Aunt Peg had erected for them.

She and I lived in neighboring towns in lower Fairfield County, Connecticut, so it hadn't taken me very long to find my way to her kitchen. From my home in North Stamford, it was just a short trip down the Merritt Parkway to her house in back country Greenwich.

At ten o'clock in the morning, the scenic highway had been nearly empty. Though the Stamford mall and trendy Greenwich Avenue were bound to be thronged with holiday shoppers, I'd gone well north of either destination. Christmas carols blasting from my radio, I'd spent the trip singing along. Thankfully, I'd been alone, so no one else had had to suffer through it.

Aunt Peg had met me at the front door, with her pack of Standard Poodles eddying around her legs. The dogs and I were old friends, and I'd greeted each one by name. They'd then formed an honor guard around us as I followed Aunt Peg through the house.

Her kitchen was cozy. It smelled like warm scones. And best of all, there were puppies. It was like the trifecta of all good things.

Except that now Aunt Peg was hovering above me as I sat on her floor. Her hands were propped on her hips, and she was frowning downward at the three Aussie puppies, who were frolicking happily in their pen.

"They're just *babies*," I said, delighted. I reached out and picked up the blue girl. Her hair was silky soft, and when I lifted her to my face, she nuzzled my chin with her nose. I inhaled the delicious scent of puppy breath. "They're not even steady on their feet yet."

"I told you they were young." Aunt Peg sighed. "Those puppies should never have been separated from their dam this early. It's criminal what some people will do."

I glanced up over my shoulder. "You have no idea who left them here?"

"None, even though I've given it plenty of thought. I know every dog in the neighborhood—or at least I thought I did. And I can't think of a single one who could have produced puppies that look like these."

Aunt Peg's neighborhood had formerly been farm country. The barns and meadows were now long gone, however, and the narrow lanes had been widened and paved. Her road held half a dozen single-family homes, each on a generous five acre lot. Roaming dogs were a rarity there. Nevertheless, I was sure Aunt Peg would have been well acquainted with the local canine population.

"Have you given them names yet?"

Aunt Peg growled under her breath. Naming implied ownership, and we both knew it. Still, she had to call them something, didn't she?

She motioned toward the puppy I had snuggled in my arms. "I call her Blue."

"I would never have guessed," I said with a straight face.

"That one's Black." Aunt Peg pointed at the male puppy who was trying to climb out over the low wooden rail.

Now I was biting back a grin. "I foresee a problem with your naming strategy."

"Not at all." Her chin lifted. She indicated the second boy. "His name is Ditto."

"Oh, that's excellent!" I sputtered out a surprised laugh. "Well done."

"Bear in mind those are only temporary names," Aunt Peg said firmly. "The puppies' new owners will naturally want to change them."

"Naturally," I agreed. "When the time comes."

"Let's hope it's sooner rather than later."

"But not until after the holidays," I pointed out.

Aunt Peg nodded in agreement.

I put the blue girl back in the pen and rescued the boy puppy who was still trying to scramble over the side. He jumped into my hands and immediately began to wriggle around, asking to be lowered to the kitchen floor. I was about to oblige him when my cell phone sounded. Currently, I had it set to squawk like an angry bird.

Aunt Peg spun around and stared at my coat. I'd left it slung over a nearby chair. My phone was in the pocket. "What is that unearthly noise?"

"Cell phone." Still holding the puppy with one hand, I beckoned with the other.

"It sounds ridiculous," Aunt Peg sniffed. She reached over and fished through my pockets.

"Yes, but it's loud so I can always hear it," I told her. She handed me the device, and I held it to my ear. "Hello?"

"Melanie!"

The caller was female. That much I knew immediately. But she was whispering, so I didn't recognize her voice right away. There was no mistaking the urgency in her tone, however.

I lifted the phone away and looked at the caller ID. "Claire? Is that you? Why are you whispering?"

"Melanie, you have to come right away. It's horrible. She's dead!"

A sudden chill washed over me. Claire was family. Married to my ex-husband, Bob, she was stepmother to my older son, Davey. She was also a dear friend. Whatever she needed, I would be there for her.

Quickly I lowered the black puppy to the floor, then gripped the phone with both hands. Aunt Peg was staring at me in concern. I shook my head. I still had no idea what was going on.

"Slow down," I said to Claire. "Take a deep breath. Then tell me what's wrong. Who's dead?"

"Lila Moran. She's a new client of mine. I was just dropping off a few things at her house. She wasn't even supposed to be here. But she is. She's lying on the floor and there's blood everywhere."

Chapter 2

"What's the matter?" Aunt Peg hissed.

I ignored her. She leaned down and poked my shoulder. Hard. I quickly angled away so she couldn't grab the phone out of my hands.

"It's Claire," I said. "Something's happened. Give me a minute."

"Oh God." Claire moaned. "Is that Peg? Don't tell her it's me. I can't deal with her right now. Melanie, you have to come and help me. I don't know what to do."

There was no use in pointing out that Aunt Peg already knew whom I was talking to. Claire clearly wasn't thinking straight. I hoped that meant she was wrong about the dead body too.

"Claire," I said slowly. Calmly. "Breathe." I waited a moment while she did so. "Now tell me what happened."

"I just did!" she wailed, her voice still edging toward panic. "Lila is *dead*!"

Out of the corner of my eye, I saw Aunt Peg flinch. She'd heard that.

"Are you sure?" I asked Claire.

"Of course I'm sure. She's lying right here in front of me."

That wasn't what I'd wanted to know. Not at all.

"Where are you now?" I asked.

"I'm standing in her living room."

"You're alone?" I confirmed. "You're sure you're not in any danger?"

"No," she replied firmly. Then her voice quavered. "At least I don't think so. Oh God, what made you ask *that*? Do you think the person who did this to her is still *here*?"

"I don't know," I said. "I don't know anything yet. Listen to me, Claire. I want you to turn around and walk outside. When you get there, lock yourself in your car. As soon as you've done that, hang up with me and dial nine-one-one. Okay? Can you do that?"

"I'm leaving," Claire told me. "I'm getting out right now. And I've already called nine-one-one. I did that right away. The moment I saw her. In case I was wrong and somebody could still help her. But they can't. It's just that I was just hoping . . ."

There was a moment of silence. I was afraid I'd lost her. Then her voice returned, and I exhaled sharply.

"Okay, I'm outside now. I'm walking toward my car."

"That's good," I said. "Wait in your car until help arrives. The dispatcher said they're sending someone, right?"

"Yes . . . yes, she did," Claire stuttered. "She said help would be here in less than ten minutes. But you have to come too. Melanie, you can't leave me here to face this by myself. I need you!"

"I'm on my way," I said. I was already pushing myself to my feet. "I'll be there as soon as I can. Where are you?"

"Oh. Right. I forgot that part." Claire giggled. I hoped she wasn't becoming hysterical. "I'm in New Canaan. On Forest

Glen Lane. It's off Weed Street. I'm at the gatehouse for the Mannerly estate. Do you know where that is?"

"No, but I can find it. I'll be there soon. Are you in your car yet?"

"Yes," she said, and I heard a door thunk shut. "I'm locked in."

"Good. Just stay there," I told her. "Don't move."

"Hurry, okay?" Claire's voice was shaking again. *"Please?"*

I shoved my phone in my pocket and grabbed my coat off the back of the chair. Aunt Peg cleared the Poodles out of our way as we hurried toward the front door, then down the outside steps to the driveway. She fired questions at me as we ran.

"Who's dead?" she immediately wanted to know.

"A woman named Lila Moran."

Aunt Peg frowned. "Who's she?"

"Claire said she was a client."

"Claire's arranging an event for her?"

"I don't know," I said. "Maybe."

Claire had her own event planning business. Her specialty was over-the-top children's birthday parties, but she also worked with a number of corporate clients. Earlier in the fall, Claire had come up with a brilliant idea to expand the services her company offered. She'd announced her availability to act as a personal Christmas shopper for busy Fairfield County residents. She'd quickly found herself with as many customers as she could handle. Perhaps she'd met Lila Moran that way.

"How did the woman die?" Aunt Peg demanded.

"I don't know that either. Claire didn't say."

"Who killed her?"

I stopped and stared. "How would I know that?"

"You were the one on the phone with her," Aunt Peg snapped in frustration. "I thought surely Claire must have told you *something.*"

"She told me she needed help," I said simply. "So I'm going to help her."

"I'm coming with you," Aunt Peg decided suddenly as I reached my car.

We'd dashed out of the house together. Aunt Peg hadn't even stopped to grab a jacket. We hadn't had any snow yet this winter, but the morning temperature was barely above freezing. Aunt Peg was dressed in a cotton turtleneck, jeans, and sneakers. We'd been outside for only thirty seconds, and already she looked cold.

"No, you're not," I told her. I was holding the car key, but my hand stilled above the door handle. This was non-negotiable.

"I can help too," Aunt Peg said firmly.

"You'll freeze," I pointed out.

"No, I won't. Your car has a heater."

So much for the easy excuse.

"Claire doesn't want you there," I said.

Aunt Peg had started to climb into the Volvo. Now she paused. "Did she say that?"

"Yes."

Aunt Peg's eyes narrowed. I knew she was getting ready to argue again.

"Look," I said. "All I know is that something horrible has happened and that Claire stumbled on the scene. She's understandably upset and she needs our support. What she doesn't need is for you to show up and tell everyone what to do. The police are already on their way. The situation is being handled. Just let me go and get her through this, okay?"

"I guess so," Aunt Peg muttered. She stepped away from the car. "If you insist."

"I'll call later and tell you everything," I said as I slid into my seat.

"You'd better," Aunt Peg replied darkly.

I probably violated a few traffic laws between Greenwich and New Canaan. But I got there quickly and that was all that mattered. Nevertheless, it looked as though half the local police force had already beaten me to the scene.

New Canaan was a quiet, affluent, mostly residential town. There were no shopping malls or fast food restaurants. The town boasted more parks than gas stations. Residents valued their privacy and sent their children to the town's excellent public schools.

Crime was unusual in New Canaan. Violent crime was almost unheard of. So I wasn't surprised that whatever had taken place inside the gatehouse at the Mannerly estate had resulted in a sizable police presence.

Forest Glen was a narrow, winding lane, so I'd already slowed my car to well below the speed limit before the estate came into view. A forbidding-looking wall—its stone base topped by black, wrought-iron spikes—was the first indication that I was nearing my destination. The property itself was densely wooded. I drove for another quarter mile, without seeing a single break in the trees, before I finally arrived at a wide double gate. It, too, was made of iron and stood at least eight feet tall.

Both sides of the gate were open, but a police cruiser was parked across the driveway, blocking access. As the Volvo coasted closer to the entrance, I sat up in my seat and attempted to peer down the driveway. It was deeply shadowed by a solid thicket of tree trunks and encroaching underbrush. A canopy of tangled branches arched in the air above it.

About thirty feet inside the property, and barely visible in the gloom, was a small vine-covered building. Presumably, that was the gatehouse where I would find Claire. I turned on my signal and started to pull over. Immediately, a police officer stepped out into the road to wave me past.

I stopped and rolled down my passenger side window. The officer leaned down and looked inside.

"Ma'am, I'm going to need you to move along," he said.

"I'm here for Claire Travis," I told him. "She's the woman who called and reported what had happened. She's waiting for me at the gatehouse."

At least I hoped she was. I couldn't see her car. But nor could I imagine that the authorities would have let her leave so quickly—certainly not before they'd questioned her and begun to try to figure out what was going on.

"Claire Travis," he repeated slowly. "And you are?"

"Melanie Travis." For once, the fact that I still used my first husband's name actually came in handy.

"You're a relative?" he asked.

"We're sisters," I lied. "Claire called me right after she dialed the emergency number. I was in Greenwich, and I came straight here. Whatever's going on in there, Claire needs my support."

He considered for a few seconds, then nodded. He gestured toward the other side of the road. "Park over there out of the way, and I'll walk you in."

I parked the Volvo and got out. The officer watched with approval as I locked it behind me.

"Stick close to me," he said when I'd joined him in the driveway. "And don't touch anything. Your sister's sitting on a bench behind the gatehouse. As soon as the detectives are finished inside, they're going to want to interview her. I'm not sure if they'll let you stay for that part, but you can wait with her until they're ready."

They would let me stay, all right, I thought. Otherwise Claire and I would both be leaving. But I knew better than to voice the sentiment aloud.

The driveway in front of me was long and barely lit by the weak winter sun. By the time we reached the gatehouse, I still hadn't been able to catch even a glimpse of the main house anywhere ahead of us. The bulk of the estate appeared to be entirely shielded from the road by the overgrown forest.

Idly, I wondered if it belonged to a Hollywood icon or some dot-com billionaire. Clearly, the owner possessed a fanatic need for seclusion. I could well imagine he or she wasn't going to appreciate the authorities mounting an investigation on the property. Even here on the outer edge.

The closer we came to the gatehouse, the more dilapidated it appeared. The compact, one-story building had small windows and faded clapboard siding. Its roof sagged in one corner. There was no Christmas wreath on the front door, nor any holiday lights. Nothing brightened the dwelling's drab exterior.

The officer bypassed the front entrance without pausing. He walked me around the gatehouse to the other side.

I saw Claire's car first. Her red Civic was parked in a small cleared area beside the driveway. Then I finally saw Claire. She was seated on an ancient wooden bench placed just outside the building's back door. Her head was lowered; her shoulders slumped. *Forlorn.* That was the first word that came to mind.

The low branches clustered over the spot must have provided shade in the summer. But the limbs were bare now. Slapping and rattling in the light breeze, they looked threatening, almost malevolent, as they hung down over the small clearing.

I was already hurrying toward her when Claire looked up and saw us. Quickly, she jumped to her feet. A look of relief lit up her face.

Claire was statuesque and slender, with long, dark hair that was now mostly hidden beneath a knitted cap. Her bulky down parka was zipped all the way up to her chin, and she had fuzzy mittens on her hands. Her face was alarmingly pale. The only spot of color was her nose, which was red from the cold.

"Your sister's here, Ms. Travis," the officer said. "She said you called her and told her to come."

Claire's startled gaze found mine. "Sister?" she murmured.

Quickly I closed the gap between us. I gathered her in my arms for a strong hug. "Just go with it," I said under my breath. "I had to talk my way in. So now we're sisters."

Claire stepped back out of my embrace. The smile she aimed at the policeman made his cheeks flush. "Thank you, Officer Jenkins. I feel so much better now."

"Good." He ducked his head. "I'm sure Detective Hronis will be out to speak with you shortly. I'd better get back to my post." He turned and retreated down the driveway.

"Look at you. You're freezing!" I grasped Claire's hands in mine and rubbed briskly back and forth. "How long have you been sitting out here?"

"I don't know. Maybe fifteen minutes?"

"Why?"

She shrugged. "They told me to sit down and not move. Something about messing up evidence. I didn't really think about it. I just did what they said."

That didn't sound at all like the Claire I knew and loved—a woman who ran her own company and was happy to be in charge. I wondered if she was in shock.

"Your car isn't evidence," I said firmly. "Let's go sit inside there. It's got to be warmer, and at least we'll be out of the wind."

I waited until we were sitting in the Civic's bucket seats and Claire had removed her mittens and scrubbed her hands over her face before saying, "Now—before the police come to ask you questions—tell me what happened."

She sucked in a breath. "I don't know where to begin."

"Start at the beginning. Tell me why you came here this morning."

"Lila is . . . she was . . . a client," Claire said slowly. "You know I started the personal shopper thing, right?"

"Of course." I'd been half-tempted to sign up for her services myself.

"I figured that with Christmas coming, it might prove to be a popular sideline to the event planning. But let me tell you, I had *no* idea. I've been swamped."

"That's because you're good at what you do," I said. Claire was still jittery. She needed to relax. So I started with the easy stuff. "Walk me through how it works."

"Generally, someone hears about my services, they get in touch, and we agree to meet. Mostly, it's guys because . . ." Her lips quirked in a half-smile. "You know."

"They're lazy, and they hate to shop?"

She nodded. "Either that or they're just unimaginative. And some have jobs that take up so much of their lives, they don't have time to think about anything else."

"So you meet up with a client," I prompted.

"That's right. We talk about their Christmas lists and the people they need to buy gifts for. They tell me about their preferences and the kinds of things they like to give, like maybe books or wine. I take some notes about the people I'll be shopping for and make suggestions about things that might work. After that, we discuss how much they want to spend, and then I'm pretty much good to go."

"So you did all those things with Lila Moran?"

"Yes. About three weeks ago. In fact, we met right here at her home."

"So why did you come back this morning? Were the two of you supposed to meet again?"

"No." Claire frowned. "That's what's so strange. Lila wasn't supposed to be here at all. After I've bought a few presents for a client, I usually go ahead and gift wrap everything. Then, if they don't want to be bothered picking stuff up, I can deliver. That was what Lila had asked me to do."

"Tell me what you saw when you arrived."

"Nothing." She stopped and shook her head. "I mean, everything *seemed* normal. I had no reason to think it wouldn't be."

"Had you made a delivery for Lila previously?"

"Yes, last week. I went in the back door, piled the packages on her kitchen table, and left. I thought today would be the same. So I drove back here and parked. I unloaded her things from my trunk and let myself in."

"How did you do that?" I asked. "Do you have a key?"

"No, but Lila keeps one under the flowerpot on the stoop."

Both our gazes swiveled that way. The empty clay pot was now sitting on its side. "Not exactly high-tech security," I said drily.

"Believe me, nothing about this place is high-tech," Claire told me. "Lila grumbled about that a lot. The estate was built in the early twentieth century. It seems like the gatehouse has hardly been touched since."

"So you walked into the kitchen . . ."

"Yes. I was juggling several parcels and trying not to drop the key while I closed the door behind me, so I didn't notice anything right away. Except there was an odd smell . . ." Her voice trailed away.

I knew it was better not to let her dwell on that. "Go on," I said sharply.

"I put the packages down on the table, and that's when I saw her." Claire closed her eyes briefly.

"Where was she?"

"Lying on the floor in the living room. At first, all I could see was Lila's lower legs and feet. The rest of her body was curled around the other side of this big upholstered chair. I thought maybe she'd tripped and fallen. I hoped she hadn't been seriously hurt." Claire looked stricken. "Can you imagine?"

"I know," I said quietly. "I know."

She braced herself and continued. "So I went to try and help her. I thought I could do that. How stupid of me. Because then I walked around the chair, and that's when I understood. Lila's eyes were open. There was a bullet hole in her chest. She was beyond anyone's help."

Chapter 3

We sat in silence for a minute.

Then I asked, "What did you do next?"

"I screamed bloody murder," Claire retorted. "Then I backed up as fast as I could. I yanked out my phone and started calling for help."

A sudden knock on the side window of the compact car startled both of us. Claire and I jumped in our seats. I spun around and saw an unfamiliar face staring in at us.

The man was probably in his forties. He had bushy brown hair and what looked like a wiry build, now covered by several layers of clothing. His nose was broad, his cheeks were fleshy, and his lips were pursed. Judging by his expression, he was not happy.

Now that he had our attention, the man straightened and stepped away from the car. He beckoned impatiently with two fingers. He wanted us to get out. And to hurry up about it.

Detective Hronis, I assumed. It was a good thing I'd heard his name earlier, because he didn't bother to introduce himself.

"I thought I told you to wait over there," he said to Claire.

"Yes, but—"

"She was cold," I told him. "It's freezing out here. Didn't that occur to you before you went inside?"

His gaze swung my way. "Who are you?"

"Melanie Travis. Claire's sister," I added for good measure. I'd already told the lie once, so I figured I might as well run with it.

"What are you doing here?"

"Apparently, I'm looking out for my sister's welfare. Which is more than can be said for you. If Claire hadn't called emergency services, you wouldn't even be here. She was trying to be a good citizen and do the right thing—and look how she got treated in return. I understand that you need to talk to her, but you have no right to mistreat her while she waits for you to get around to doing it."

Hronis looked taken aback. He glanced over at the wooden bench, then back to the car. "Could be, you're right," he admitted, then turned to Claire. "Ms. Travis, you have my apologies. I should have thought that through before I left you sitting out here."

"Thank you," Claire replied. She sounded surprised.

That made two of us.

"Now if you don't mind, I'd like you to step inside so we can talk," he said. I saw Claire go still. Hronis must have noticed, too, because he added, "We'll go in through the front door. There's a small office on the other side of the cottage. My men are still working, but you won't able to see a thing from there. I promise."

Claire looked shaky, but she nodded.

"I'm coming too," I said.

Hronis held up a hand. He looked ready to argue. Then he glanced at Claire and changed his mind. "You can come," he told me. "But only if you stay out of the way and keep your mouth shut. This is her story, and I want to hear it in her own words. You got that?"

"I've got it," I confirmed. I was happy to remain quiet—just as long as Claire didn't say anything that might get her in trouble.

Normally, I wouldn't have been worried about that. Claire was smart and had plenty of common sense. I'd never seen a sticky situation she couldn't talk her way out of. But today's circumstances were far from normal. And ever since I'd arrived, everything about Claire had radiated uncertainty.

So although I'd told Detective Hronis that I would stay out of the way, I grasped her hand and gave it a firm squeeze. I made sure that my shoulder was level with hers as we walked around to the front of the gatehouse. And when she strode through the front door, I was mere inches behind her.

The detective preceded us through the doorway and immediately took a hard right. Eyes cast downward, Claire quickly followed.

I had only a few seconds to gaze around the interior of the cottage before doing the same. The dwelling appeared to consist of just a few rooms. I glimpsed a stone fireplace in the hallway and an artfully decorated Christmas tree in the living room. Other than that, there wasn't much to see.

The furniture inside the home was shabby, and the floorboards were warped beneath my feet. The wallpaper in the hall looked as though it might have dated from the middle of the previous century. There was an old water stain on the ceiling.

It occurred to me that someone who could afford to hire Claire to do her Christmas shopping should also have been able to afford to upgrade her furnishings. The gatehouse was part of the larger estate, however. I supposed that meant it was a rental. Probably everything inside had come with it.

Once we'd entered the small office, Detective Hronis closed the door behind us. He stepped over to the window and pushed aside a pair of heavy damask drapes. The weak winter light that filtered down through the trees around the gatehouse didn't help much.

Someone had placed two ladder-back chairs so that they were facing each other in the center of the room. A third was pushed against a wall. I thought about moving it to join the others, then decided against it. I'd be able to see and hear everything from where it was.

I unbuttoned my coat and pulled it off. I unwound my scarf, then tossed both items on a narrow bench nearby. Claire did the same. Her hat followed. She shook out her long hair. It rippled down to the middle of her back.

The detective watched us get comfortable. He unfastened his overcoat but left it on. When we were ready, he waved us both to our seats. As Claire sat down, she shivered slightly and crossed her arms over her chest.

"Are you warm enough now?" Hronis asked her.

"Yes, thank you. I'm fine," she replied. The answer was automatic. Seconds later she amended it. "Well, not fine. But I'm okay."

"Good. Then let's begin. What was your connection to the deceased woman, Lila Moran?"

"She was a client of mine," Claire said. "I like to think we were becoming friends."

"Ms. Moran hired you to do something for her?"

"That's correct." She briefly outlined the scope of her services. I was happy to see that Claire was keeping her answers short and to the point. That would give the detective less opportunity to trip her up.

"It sounds to me as if you hadn't known her very long," he said.

"No, we first met about a month ago. Some people wait until the last minute to think about Christmas shopping. But Lila was super organized. She wanted to have everything finished in plenty of time, so she could enjoy the holiday without having to worry about it."

"And that's why she employed you?"

"Yes." Claire nodded. "That's why all my customers employ me. I do the worrying for them."

Hronis shifted in his chair. I didn't blame him. The hard wooden seats could have used a cushion.

"How did Ms. Moran find out about your services?" he asked. "Would that have been in response to an advertisement you ran?"

"Some people do come to me that way," Claire agreed. "Others find me on Facebook or Instagram. In Lila's case, a friend of hers for whom I'd planned a children's party recommended me to her."

"I see," he replied. "Is that unusual?"

"Not at all. Anyone who works for himself will tell you that good word of mouth is the best recommendation you can get. I love when former customers bring me repeat business or send me new clients."

Claire glanced over at me and smiled. Due to my connections at Howard Academy, I'd sent several customers to her myself. Hronis observed the exchange with interest. Evidently he didn't miss much.

"Let's move on to today's events," he said. "What brought you to Ms. Moran's house this morning?"

"I had a delivery to make." Claire had already indicated that was one of the services she offered. "Lila told me she expected to be working late tonight and she wouldn't have time to pick up the presents I'd bought for her. One was for a Christmas party she planned to attend this weekend. I offered to drop everything off to make sure she got it in time."

"Those were the wrapped packages that are sitting on the kitchen table?" the detective asked.

"That's right."

"So if I'm understanding this correctly, when you arrive you expected the house to be empty?"

"Yes."

"You intended to come inside, drop off your parcels, and leave. Is that right?"

Claire nodded. And frowned. I could understand why. It sounded to me as though she was being made to answer every question twice.

"But you didn't do that," the detective said.

"No. I did not."

"Why not?"

"Because as soon as I put the packages down on the table, I could see . . ." Claire stopped speaking. She waved a hand in the air ineffectually. "I could see . . ."

"What did you see?" Hronis prompted.

Claire had been sitting up straight, but now her body slumped. She blinked rapidly several times. Suddenly she looked as though she might cry.

I started to rise. But then a slight shake of Claire's head made me settle back in my seat—not happily. "Is this really necessary?" I asked the detective.

He nailed me with a hard look. "If it wasn't, we wouldn't be here." His voice gentled as he turned back to Claire. "Think back, Ms. Travis. What exactly did you see?"

"I saw Lila's feet," she said slowly. "And her lower legs. I thought maybe she had tripped. Or fallen."

"Did you notice anything else?"

"No. Not until . . ." She sighed. "Not until I stepped around the chair. I thought I might be able to help her."

"What did you do then?"

"I backed away very quickly and called for help."

Hronis leaned forward in his seat. "Did you touch Ms. Moran?"

"No." Claire shook her head vehemently. "I did not."

"And yet you knew she was dead."

"There was . . ." Her hand came up and flapped in the air again. "There was a lot of blood."

"I see." The detective paused, as if he was gathering his thoughts. I suspected he already knew exactly what he was going to say next. "You told the dispatcher that there had been an accident at this address."

"Did I?" Claire asked. "I don't remember."

"You did," he said. "What was it about the scene you saw that made you believe it was an accident?"

"I don't think I really did believe that. I was upset, and probably babbling. It was the first thing I thought to say. Because the alternative was just too horrible to contemplate. All I wanted was for someone—anyone—to come and help."

Detective Hronis nodded, as if acknowledging that her reply made sense. "Just a few more questions," he said.

I glanced at my watch. I was surprised to see that the two of them had been talking for nearly half an hour.

"How familiar are you with Ms. Moran's home?" he asked.

"Excuse me?" said Claire.

"How many times had you been here previously?"

"Twice," Claire answered without hesitation. "Once when Lila and I initially met and she agreed to hire me, and then a second time when I had other presents to drop off."

"Nothing other than that? Maybe when the two of you got together socially?"

"No," Claire replied.

"Even though Ms. Moran was someone you felt you were beginning to think of as a friend?"

"Detective," I broke in before Claire could speak. There was a warning note in my tone. "What is this about?"

He held up his hands in front of him, a protest of innocence. I wasn't fooled for a minute. I doubted Claire was either. Detective Hronis was fishing for something. Perhaps trying to get

Claire to admit to a deeper relationship than she and Lila had actually possessed.

"I'm just wondering whether or not Ms. Travis might have noticed anything that was different about the house on this visit," he said. "Maybe something that had been moved or was out of place. That's all."

All, my foot.

"I wouldn't know about that," Claire replied frostily. She stood up. "I've already told you everything I know. Are we finished?"

"Almost," the detective said. He remained seated as she walked over to the bench where her outerwear lay. "Just one last thing."

Claire picked up her hat and jammed it on her head. "What's that?"

"When you arrived here this morning, you entered through the back door."

"That's correct."

"Was the door open or closed when you got here?"

"Closed. I had to juggle the packages into one arm so I could turn the knob."

The detective tipped his head to one side, considering. "It wasn't locked, then?"

"Yes, the door was locked when I arrived. I knew where to find the key."

"You knew where to find the key," he repeated slowly. Meaningfully. "Even though you'd only been here twice before?"

"Look," Claire said firmly. "Lila knew I was coming this morning. And she certainly didn't want—or expect—me to leave her nice presents sitting outside on the stoop. She told me to let myself in and put them on the kitchen table."

"Inside the house," Hronis said. "With the key."

"No," I snapped. "With a sledgehammer."

I got up and grabbed my coat too. I was *so* ready to be done with this.

"You're not helping," he growled at me.

I gave him a look that said the feeling was mutual. Just so we understood each other.

Detective Hronis finally rose to his feet. He was taller than both of us, and he seemed to enjoy having that height advantage. He gazed down at Claire and said, "Something terrible happened here. Since you knew Ms. Moran, I would think you'd want to help us get to the bottom of things. Anything you might know, or suspect, or that you're even wondering about—no matter how small or insignificant—now would be the time to speak up."

Claire did him the courtesy of thinking about it before she replied. "No," she said finally. "I'm sorry I can't be more helpful, but I've said everything I have to say."

"You're sure about that?"

I rolled my eyes, but Claire managed a second civil answer. "Yes, I'm sure."

"All right." The detective sounded resigned. "We're going to need you to stop by the police station to get fingerprinted. If you could take care of it this morning, that would be best."

Claire's body stilled. She looked shocked. Clearly she hadn't expected that. "Am I a suspect, Detective Hronis?"

"Right now, all I can tell you is that we'll be investigating every possible connection we see." He walked over to the door and opened it. "I trust the fingerprinting won't be a problem?"

Claire tossed her head. Then she preceded him through the doorway. "No, it won't be a problem."

She left the house without looking back. I paused before following her.

"I hope you find whoever did this," I said to the detective.

"Don't worry," he told me. "We will." He slipped a hand in his pocket and pulled out a business card. "If your sister thinks of anything else she wants to talk about, tell her to call me at this number."

That didn't seem likely, but I took the card anyway.

I'd intended to catch up with Claire but by the time I walked out the front door of the gatehouse, her Civic was already heading down the driveway toward the road. When Claire reached Forest Glen, she turned the car in the direction of town and sped away.

I stood and stared after her. That was odd. She was the one who'd asked me to come. So why hadn't she waited so we could leave together?

I hoped it wasn't a bad sign that Claire had been in such a hurry to escape.

Chapter 4

Unbelievably, after all that, I was still on schedule to swing by Graceland Nursery School and pick up Kevin before heading home. With everything that had transpired since I'd left earlier that morning, it felt like it ought to be at least dinner time.

I spent the trip back to Stamford brooding about Claire's precipitous departure from the Mannerly estate. And wondering if there was more to the situation, and perhaps to her relationship with Lila Moran, than she had wanted to let on.

But those thoughts vanished as soon as Kev saw my car and quickly separated himself from the rest of the children who were waiting in front of the school. I immediately switched gears and turned into Mom again. It was a relief to be able to let everything else go—at least for the time being.

My younger son was four and a half, going on twelve. He had floppy blond hair, two skinned knees, and boundless energy. His body seemed to be made of equal parts rubber and lightning. Kevin asked more questions than I knew how to answer, and gave the best hugs of anyone I knew.

As he came racing toward the car, I got out and I waved to

the two teachers who were supervising school dismissal. Kevin threw open the Volvo's back door and hopped into his car seat. He buckled himself in while I got his backpack settled on the floor at his feet. I checked the belts he'd fastened, then hurried around to the driver's seat. Preschool pick up was busy. There was already a line of cars forming behind us.

"How was school?" I asked once we were underway.

"Great!" Kevin crowed. Pretty much everything makes him happy.

Before we'd even left the school property, he was already gazing out the side window. Red cars are his favorite. He likes to count how many we pass on the road.

"What did you do today?"

"We're working on Christmas presents. One!" Kev pointed as a red Mazda went speeding by.

"That's nice. What are you making?"

"It's a secret." He laughed. "I can't tell."

"Who are you making them for?"

"Mo-om." He groaned. "That's a secret too."

"Okay." I glanced back over my shoulder. "I thought you and I could work on putting together another frame for Davey this afternoon. You know, since Bud ate the first one."

Kevin had come up with the idea to make his brother a customized picture frame for Christmas. He'd envisioned one that was the right size to hold the win picture commemorating Davey's last dog show with Augie—the one where the Standard Poodle had finished his championship. The plan was to take a plain wooden frame and glue dog biscuits all around the outer edge for decoration.

I'd thought that was a wonderful idea—until Bud had sniffed out our half-finished project and helped himself to all the edible parts, destroying the remainder of the frame in the process. Now we needed to buy new supplies and start over. And find a better hiding place.

"Two!" Kevin crowed. This time it was a pickup truck.

"What do you think?" I asked. "Should we stop at the crafts store?"

"Sure. Look, three!"

Four and a half is a great age. Everything is just that easy.

Life stopped being easy as soon as we got home an hour later. That was when I found out that Aunt Peg was coming to dinner.

"Did we invite her?" I asked Sam.

"We didn't have to," he informed me. "She invited herself."

It figured.

"Peg said she'd wasted half the morning waiting for you to call her," Sam mentioned. He was holding our packages from the craft store as Kevin and I stood in the front hall, shedding our outerwear.

I hung up my winter coat in the closet. Sam deftly nabbed Kev's mittens before they hit the floor. The Poodles were waiting for us to finish. Those dogs were all opportunists. They knew I felt guilty for leaving them, and that meant everyone would get a biscuit.

"As you might imagine, that came as a surprise to me." Sam slanted a look in my direction. "Since I thought the two of you were together. When you didn't get back to her, Peg decided to take matters into her own hands. She's coming over to find out for herself what's going on."

"Oh," I said. I had forgotten to call Aunt Peg. Possibly on purpose.

Sam followed me to the kitchen. "That 'oh' sounds like the beginning of a story."

My husband knows me well. In my life, there's almost always a story. And this one was a doozy.

"Claire called while I was at Aunt Peg's house," I said as I handed out the dog biscuits, one to a customer, with an extra scratch under the chin for Faith.

"Mom was playing with puppies," Kevin told him. I'd filled him in on that part on the way home. "They have silly names."

"Larry, Moe, and Curly?" asked Sam.

I was pretty sure Kev didn't know who the Three Stooges were. He giggled anyway. "No! They're Black, Blue, and Ditto."

Sam grinned. "With names like that, it sounds like she doesn't intend for them to be around for long." When it mattered, Aunt Peg was all about finding the perfect name for a new puppy. "How's Claire doing?"

"She's had better days," I replied, frowning. "So have I."

I looked at Kev meaningfully. Sam got the hint.

"Hey squirt, why don't you run up to your bedroom and find a book for us to read?" he said. "Take your time. Pick out something really good."

"Okay." Kevin's eyes lit up. He loves to pretend he knows how to read. "Come on, Bud. You can help." The two of them went flying out of the room.

Sam waited until Kev was out of earshot, then said, "I'd give him two minutes. Three, if we're lucky. Talk fast."

So I did. I summarized what had happened first. Then I summarized what I knew about the morning's events. That part didn't take very long, because I didn't know much. I was already running out of useful things to say when Kevin and Bud returned.

Kev was holding out a battered copy of *Go, Dog. Go!* Really, I should have seen that coming.

"I'm ready," he said, thrusting the book at Sam. "I'll read the first page. Then it's your turn."

So we tabled the rest of our discussion for later.

Davey's school bus dropped him off at the end of the driveway at four o'clock. When he walked in the back door, he was looking down at his phone. Davey had turned fourteen in September and had shot up in height around the same time. He had my first husband's lean build, and also his dark brown eyes. He glanced up at me as he kicked out a foot to shut the door behind him.

"Did you know Aunt Peg is coming for dinner?" he asked. "She says she's bringing barbecue from that new place that just opened up in Cos Cob."

"You're texting with Aunt Peg?"

I was standing in the middle of the kitchen. Kevin and I had just finished working on Davey's present. Kev had run upstairs to hide the frame in the back of his closet. I was cleaning up the supplies we'd used. Quickly I shoved the glue out of sight in a nearby drawer.

"Sure." Davey held up the screen. "See?"

"I didn't know Aunt Peg knew how to text."

"Everybody knows how to text." He dropped his backpack on a chair and headed straight for the refrigerator. "Except you."

"I know how," I informed him loftily. "I just choose not to. I would rather talk to someone. Conversation is a dying art."

"Yeah." Davey smirked. "Hold that thought." He grabbed a banana and disappeared.

Aunt Peg showed up at six o'clock. "I was going to wait until a more fashionable hour. But this barbecue smelled too good not to eat right away. I hope everybody's hungry."

She shoved two large parcels into my arms, then stooped down to say hello to the Poodles, who were swarming around her legs eagerly. As usual, they greeted her like a long-lost savior. From what, I wasn't entirely sure. Most days, I'm pretty sure those dogs have a better life than I do.

Bud refused to join the fray. Instead, he stood off to one side, keeping a beady eye on the food. The little dog had been half starved when he came home with us. Now he never missed a meal.

Davey's head popped over the railing on the second floor landing. "Do I smell brisket?" he asked.

"You most certainly do." Aunt Peg looked up at him, and Eve took the opportunity to lick her neck. "Along with pulled pork, baked beans, coleslaw, and corn bread. Enough for everyone to have an enormous helping."

Davey came bounding down the steps. "You ought to come to dinner more often."

"Someone ought to invite me more often," Aunt Peg said crisply. She braced a hand on her knee and rose to her feet as Sam and Kev came around the corner from the living room.

"I'm pretty sure you have a standing invitation," Sam said. He sniffed the air, then grabbed the bags out of my arms. "But we don't need to haggle about that now. Let's eat."

The table was already set, and drinks were already poured. All we had to do was find our seats, open the containers, and dig in. By unspoken agreement, none of the adults brought up the topic that had brought Aunt Peg to our house until dinner was finished and the two boys had left the room.

Davey had homework to do. Before going upstairs, he set up a movie for his younger brother in the living room. I cleared the table while Sam brewed coffee for the two of us and heated water for Aunt Peg's Earl Grey tea. The Poodles were lying on the floor around us. They knew they didn't get leftovers from the table, but they remained ever hopeful that one night we'd relax the rules. I gave Faith a pat instead, and retook my seat.

"This is the point in the evening where you're supposed to offer me dessert," Aunt Peg said. "A piece of cake would do nicely."

"We don't have cake," Sam said. "How about an Oreo?"

She did not look amused.

"How about a recap of the day's events?" I offered.

Aunt Peg nodded. "That will suffice."

I told her everything that had happened after I'd left her house and gone rushing to New Canaan. Sam had already heard an abbreviated version of the story and I meant to give

Aunt Peg the same. But since she stopped me every few seconds to ask questions, the retelling expanded greatly in length.

"So who is this woman, Lila Moran?" she asked at the end. "What do we know about her?"

"Not very much," I replied. "Mostly just that she's a new client of Claire's."

"Age? Occupation? Marital status? Reason she doesn't do her own Christmas shopping?" Aunt Peg lobbed questions at me faster than I could shake my head.

"If you want all those answers, you should be talking to Claire," I said, exasperated.

"I would be—if I hadn't assumed that you'd already done so. From the sound of it, the two of you were together for more than an hour. It didn't occur to you to request some pertinent facts?"

"We were busy," I hedged. "And then the moment we weren't, Claire was gone."

"Gone where?" asked Sam.

"I wish I knew. One minute we were talking to Detective Hronis, and the next Claire had disappeared. I'd thought we'd walk out together, maybe compare notes about the interview. But the detective stopped me to give me his card, and before I could get away, Claire had left. It was almost as though she couldn't wait to escape."

"How very unexpected." Aunt Peg frowned.

"I thought so too. Claire merely had a business relationship with the woman. It was just bad luck that she was the one to discover the body." I looked back and forth between Sam and Aunt Peg. "It's not as though she could have anything to hide. *Is there?*"

"It seems to me that ought to be the first thing you find out," Aunt Peg said.

"Tell us more about the place where Lila Moran lived," said Sam. "You called it a gatehouse?"

"Yes. It's a cottage situated just inside the entrance to a very large estate. I can't imagine who would own a place that looks like that. The property is really overgrown, and the gatehouse is decrepit. It's kind of creepy."

"Creepy?" Aunt Peg perked up. She loved anything that sounded mysterious.

"Everything looked neglected. The outer edge of the estate is like a wild forest. Nobody's pruned back those trees in years. Even in winter, the branches are thick enough to block the light from getting through. The whole place gave me an eerie feeling."

"Or maybe it was the dead body that did that," Sam murmured.

"Even a small home in New Canaan costs a bundle," Aunt Peg mused. "It seems odd that someone would let a property that size fall to ruin. Did the place have a name?"

"Claire referred to it as the Mannerly estate."

"Mannerly?" Aunt Peg's eyes widened. She sat up suddenly. "As in Josephine Mannerly?"

"Could be." I shared a glance with Sam. Neither one of us knew who she was talking about. "The name fits."

"Well then, I suppose *that* would explain a few things."

"Who's Josephine Mannerly?" Sam asked.

"Really?" She stared at the two of us. "You've never heard of her?"

We figured that was a hypothetical question. We both declined to answer.

Aunt Peg's gaze moved past us to Faith and Eve, who were sleeping side by side on the floor. Their bodies were aligned from the tops of their heads to the bases of their tails. "One might think the Poodles have a better grasp of local history than my own relatives do."

"And one might be right," I conceded.

I stood up and went to pour myself a second cup of coffee.

It wasn't decaf. That probably meant that I'd be up all night. But caffeine made my brain work better. And when Aunt Peg was conducting an interrogation, I needed to keep my wits about me.

I lifted the pot and tilted it in Sam's direction. He shook his head. Smart man.

I'd barely sat back down at the table before Aunt Peg said, "Josephine Mannerly was the most stunning debutante ever to make her debut at the Grosvenor Ball."

I swiveled in my seat in surprise. "You *knew* her?"

"Many, many, years ago our families socialized in the same circles, so we were slightly acquainted with one another. I was several years younger than Josie, but that didn't matter. Everyone in my set knew who she was."

Reminiscing made Aunt Peg smile. "It wasn't as if we had a choice. Our mothers pointed Josie out to us. They extolled her grace and feminine virtues. For those of us who might have been inclined toward hoydenish behavior, Josie was held up as a model of ladylike comportment."

I bit back a smile. It didn't surprise me in the slightest that Aunt Peg had been known as a young hoyden. Apparently little had changed in the intervening decades.

"Josie's father had scads of money," she continued. "I believe most of it came from copper mines and railroads. When the Second World War broke out, he was too old to serve but like many men of his generation, he signed up anyway. Tragically, he was killed in France when Josie was barely a toddler."

Aunt Peg sighed. "I don't think Josie's mother ever recovered from the loss. The family was living in the city at the time—eighteen rooms on Park Avenue, if I remember correctly. Back then, the estate in New Canaan was merely a weekend retreat. Over the next two decades, Ada Mannerly immersed herself in the New York social whirl, and that meant Josie did too. Josie was an only child, and Ada's life revolved around her."

"That doesn't sound like a good thing," I said.

"I'd imagine it wasn't," Aunt Peg agreed. "Especially since the society pages chronicled their every move. I doubt that Josie enjoyed even a modicum of privacy during her teenage years. And of course, the reporters called her a poor little rich girl. Then, to everyone's dismay, that proved to be oddly prescient."

"What happened?" asked Sam. He was listening to the story just as avidly as I was.

"It was only a year or so after Josie made her debut that tragedy struck again. Her mother drowned in a boating accident off Nantucket. Josie had barely turned twenty at the time. The relationship she had with her mother had been her whole world, and then suddenly her mother was gone too. Josie disappeared after that."

"Disappeared?" I gulped. "What do you mean?"

"Josie withdrew from society," Aunt Peg replied. "She stopped going out. She refused to take her friends' calls. She abandoned the New York apartment and moved to Connecticut. Aside from the servants, she lived all alone in that big house and saw no one. It was as though she'd fled from everyday life."

"That must have been fifty years ago," Sam said wonderingly.

"Nearly half a century," Aunt Peg agreed. "Once upon a time, Josephine Mannerly was dubbed the Deb of the Decade. But to the best of my knowledge, nobody has seen or heard from her in years."

Chapter 5

"Do you think she's still alive?" I asked.

"I don't see why not," Aunt Peg replied. "Surely the press would have reported on her death if she wasn't."

"Is she still living in that house?"

Aunt Peg stared at me across the table. "How would I know that?"

The question made me laugh. "You seem to know just about everything else about her."

"Oh pish," she said. "I was an impressionable young girl and Josie was being held up to me as a paragon, a living example of everything I was meant to strive for. So of course I studied her closely. But that was decades ago. All the information I have about her is sadly out of date now. Not only that, but I hadn't given her a thought in years until *you* brought her up."

"Strictly speaking, I only mentioned her estate," I pointed out.

"*And* jogged my memory," Aunt Peg shot back.

"Stop squabbling you two." Sam held up a hand for silence. "You're both overlooking the most important question. Considering who Josephine Mannerly is, what was Lila Moran doing in her gatehouse?"

"Presumably, living there," I said. "Possibly renting it."

"Yes, but why?" Sam persisted. "Why would a very wealthy woman, one who's lived as a recluse for years, allow that? Why would she want anyone in there?"

"You're right, that is puzzling," Aunt Peg agreed. "We need to find out more about Lila Moran. Who she was, and where she came from."

"Or we need to let the police hunt down that information," I said.

"Don't be ridiculous. It's not as though they're going to tell us what they find out. We should do a little snooping around on our own."

Of course she would say that.

"And I know just the place for you to start," Aunt Peg added with satisfaction. "Isn't it handy that we have someone right in our own family who can answer our questions? You need to talk to Claire and find out what she knows."

For once, Aunt Peg and I were in full agreement. I did need to talk to Claire. And Aunt Peg's questions weren't the only ones I had.

I understood why Claire had called me when she'd discovered Lila Moran's body in the gatehouse. I have an uncanny tendency to stumble upon unfortunate situations myself. So I can see why someone might think I possess useful experience in that regard.

So I'd been happy to drop what I was doing—playing with puppies, let's not forget!—and dash to Claire's side. I'd been ready to offer whatever kind of help or support was needed. I'd even been prepared to run interference between Claire and the authorities.

What I hadn't expected was to find myself standing alone on that cold driveway, watching Claire flee—as though now that I'd served my purpose, she couldn't get away from me fast enough.

That demanded an explanation. And it had better be good.

The next morning I called Claire and told her we had to talk. She told me to meet her at the Stamford Town Center. Considering the conversation I wanted to have, that location wouldn't have been my first choice.

Stamford Town Center was a large shopping mall downtown. It had seven levels and more than a hundred stores, which were wrapped around a central atrium. The place was bright, and noisy, and fun. On a normal day, it attracted shoppers from all over Fairfield County.

So I could picture what the mall would look like now, in mid-December. With just three weeks until Christmas, the place would be a veritable madhouse—which Claire must have known. If she hoped that threatening to drag me to that holiday shopping mecca would permit her to avoid me again, she'd need to rethink her plan. I was made of sterner stuff than that.

We'd arranged to meet at Barnes & Noble, on the fourth level. The exterior of the store was draped in pine roping and twinkled with fairy lights. Christmas music played quietly in the background. When I stepped inside the wide entrance, Claire was already there.

Browsing through a selection of bestsellers on a front table, she looked up and smiled as I approached. Claire was wearing a white merino wool tunic, paired with burgundy leggings. There were suede booties on her feet, and some professional had done amazing things to her eyebrows.

I had on jeans and sneakers. The puffy down jacket I'd worn outside was now slung over my arm. I'd brushed my hair that morning before running out to drop Kevin off at preschool, and I'd meant to put on lipstick.

It was kind of funny to realize that the same man had managed to marry both of us.

"Books," I said, nodding toward the table. "Someone has good taste. Are you shopping for yourself or a client?"

"Oh, please. Do you even have to ask?" she said with a grin. "I'm like the cobbler whose children have no shoes. I'll be lucky if I have time to fit in my own shopping on Christmas Eve. I need a present for a quiet ten-year-old boy. His mother wanted a Nerf gun. I suggested a book on astronomy."

"Looks like you won," I said.

"We're compromising. He's getting both. Come on, the children's section is in the back. I'm sure I'll be able to find something there."

The Claire who'd just greeted me was aeons away from the shell-shocked woman I'd spent time with the previous morning. Perhaps her hasty departure had had nothing to do with me. Maybe she'd simply been eager to put the whole distressing episode behind her. Even so, it seemed surprising that less than twenty-four hours later, Claire appeared to have nothing more weighty on her mind than the need to search for perfect gifts.

It took us less than ten minutes to locate just the right book. Claire declined an offer of gift wrapping and placed the purchase in her roomy tote. Over the next hour, I followed her from one store to the next. I watched as she examined goods ranging from alpaca scarves to cell phone chargers and Swiss Army knives.

"Sorry I'm so busy," Claire said as she hopped on an escalator to travel to an upper level. "I guess this isn't what you hoped to be doing when you said we should get together."

I stepped on after her. "The point wasn't to get together. I want us to talk about yesterday."

Claire sighed. "There isn't much to say. You were there. You know what happened."

"Not everything. I still have questions."

She spun around to look at me. "You *always* have questions." Her tone sounded almost accusing.

Claire wasn't paying attention, and she stumbled slightly when we reached the next level and the stairs flattened beneath us. Quickly she caught herself and found her footing. She strode away.

"If that annoys you, you shouldn't have asked me to help," I said to her retreating back.

Claire's steps slowed. Then stopped. We were standing in the line of traffic beside a display of giant candy canes. Harried shoppers dodged around us. Half of them were on their phones. All were intent on their own problems. No one paid attention to us.

A loudspeaker somewhere was piping out "Joy to the World." Not so much where I was standing.

Claire's shoulders stiffened. She turned to face me. "You're saying this is *my* fault?"

"No," I replied calmly. "I'm saying that we need to talk."

"Does it have to be now?"

I shrugged. "That's the only reason I'm here."

An elf popped his head out of the candy cane display. He said to Claire, "For Pete's sake, lady, just talk to her, wouldja? Maybe then she'll leave you alone." The elf looked at me. "Right?"

"Right," I agreed. At this point I'd take help anywhere I could get it—even from a guy with pointy shoes and bells on his cap.

Claire lifted a finger and pointed. "Upstairs."

"We just came up," I said.

"There's a food court up there," the elf told me helpfully. "Maybe she's cranky because she's hungry."

"Maybe she's cranky because she wants both of you to butt out," Claire snapped back.

"See?" He waggled a finger. "Cranky. Feed her. It'll help. Trust me, I know these things."

Neither one of us said a word until we were on the next escalator heading upward. Then, to my surprise, Claire suddenly dissolved in a fit of giggles. "Trust me," she mimicked, "I know these things. Poor guy. I guess Mrs. Elf must be hard to live with."

"Hey, don't knock it," I said. "We're taking his advice, aren't we?"

"I guess." Her good humor vanished as quickly as it had come. "Are you really going to make me relive what happened yesterday?"

"Not all of it," I told her. "I just want to go over a few things."

The frozen yogurt stand was selling cups of raspberry whipped yogurt topped with chocolate chips. Claire and I each bought a double. It was still early, so the food court wasn't mobbed. We were able to find a small table overlooking the atrium.

Down below in the center of the mall, children were running and playing in a life-size gingerbread house. Despite the distance, we could hear their delighted shrieks of laughter. Giant holiday ornaments hung from shiny ribbons attached to the ceiling above us. Everywhere I looked, people were feeling festive.

Christmas was in the air. Except perhaps at our small table.

I dipped my spoon into my frozen yogurt and savored the first bite. "This is good."

"Of course it's good," Claire replied. "It's probably made of sugar." She peered down at the cup as if she was hoping to see a list of ingredients. "And possibly artificial flavor and food coloring."

"It's yogurt," I grumbled. She was raining on my parade. "That means it's practically health food."

"Uh-huh. And Santa Claus is alive and well and living at the North Pole." Nevertheless, Claire ate another spoonful. "You're the one who wanted to talk. I'm here. I'm listening. Have at it."

So much for chitchat. And on to the main event.

"Tell me about Lila Moran," I said.

"What about her?"

"Start with anything you happen to know. Where did she come from?"

Claire stopped and thought. "I don't believe Lila was a Connecticut native. At any rate, she was living in Massachusetts before she came here. She'd been in New Canaan for about a year."

"Why did she move here?"

"She took a job in Stamford. Officer manager for an advertising agency. James and Brant?"

I shook my head. I hadn't heard of them, but that didn't mean much. "And you met through a mutual friend?"

"That's right. Karen Clauson. Her husband works at James and Brant too. They have three kids. I planned four parties for them this year."

"Four?" I looked up.

"Three birthdays, plus an office function. Melanie, what's this about?"

"I was talking to Aunt Peg last night—"

Claire groaned.

"Yeah, I know. But she was curious about Lila Moran and so am I. It turns out that many years ago Aunt Peg knew the woman who owns the estate where Lila was living."

"I don't know anything about that." Claire crunched a chocolate chip with her teeth. "I never went any farther inside than the gatehouse."

"Did you ever ask Lila how she came to be living there?"

"No. Why would I?"

"Maybe because you were curious?" One could only hope.

Claire shook her head. "Lila wasn't very chatty about personal stuff. Although she did complain about the place a couple of times. The furnace was iffy. A downstairs window was warped. I asked her why she didn't get those things fixed, but she said it wasn't up to her. There was a caretaker who was supposed to be looking after the gatehouse, but he never got around to doing anything. That ticked her off pretty royally. She said once that she probably wouldn't be staying around much longer."

"And now she's dead," I said quietly.

When Claire grimaced, I regretted my blunt statement. It turned out that wasn't the problem.

"And I'm apparently a suspect," she retorted. "Which is utterly ridiculous. You heard what that detective said. They're investigating every connection. Even mine."

"Is that what you're so upset about?" I asked.

"I'm not upset," she shot back.

I helped myself to some more raspberry yogurt and waited her out.

"All right," Claire said after a minute. "I'm upset."

"I can tell," I said. "So talk to me. Do you have any thoughts about who might have wanted to harm Lila?"

"Of course not." She shoved another spoonful in her mouth. "Why would you even ask that?"

"Because you knew Lila and I didn't. And because you explained to me how your business worked. You would have talked with Lila about her friends and family. She'd have described the people she wanted you to buy presents for. Information that might be useful for Detective Hronis to have."

"*Useful.*" Claire snorted. "You know that's Peg's favorite word."

I nodded. I did know that. Sometimes she referred to me as a useful person. It was supposed to be a compliment.

"Do you know something?" I prodded.

"Not about that," Claire said firmly. "Not even close. Think about it, Melanie. Who in their right mind would buy a Christmas present for someone who wanted to kill them?"

The question probably shouldn't have made me laugh, but it did. Even Claire managed a small smile.

"Then what?" I asked. "I know something's bothering you. And I don't have all day to hang around this mall, waiting for you to speak up. Come on, Claire, let's hear it."

"Has anyone ever told you that you're a giant pain in the posterior?"

"Sure. It happens all the time. Now spill."

Claire finished her last spoonful of yogurt. She pushed the cup to the side. "There is one thing."

Finally, we were getting somewhere. "What's that?"

"The woman who died yesterday in the gatehouse? I don't know who she was, but Lila Moran wasn't her real name."

Chapter 6

"Shut the front door," I said.

Claire laughed at the expression on my face. "It's not often I manage to surprise you."

"Well, you've certainly done it now. What makes you think that?"

"A month ago, before the first time Lila and I got together, I did a background check on her."

She certainly had my attention. I leaned forward in my seat. "Why?"

"Because I'm a woman who runs my own business. And sometimes due to the nature of that business, I meet with clients alone in their homes. So mostly I do it for my own safety. You know, to make sure the people who want to hire me don't have any prior arrests or a history of past craziness. And of course, it also helps to know that when they contract my services, they actually have the money to pay me."

"I had no idea," I said admiringly. "I guess I should have. It only makes sense."

"Of course it does," she agreed.

"And what did Lila's background check reveal?"

"Not nearly enough." Claire frowned. "That was the problem."

"What do you mean?"

"With most people, in addition to that other stuff, you can also find out things like when and where they were born, their parents' names, and where they went to high school or college. You know, basic facts. But in Lila's case, none of that information existed."

I didn't get it. But then again, I'd never done a check on anyone. "How is that possible?"

"Good question. As far as I could tell, Lila Moran—the woman who was living in that gatehouse—came into existence about five years ago."

My eyes narrowed. "She made up a new identity."

"Something like that. Obviously I don't know for sure, but I'd never seen anything like it before."

"Did you ask her about it?" I demanded.

"No." Claire looked pained. "It didn't seem like it was any of my business."

"Not your business?" I repeated incredulously. "That's crazy. You ran a background check on a prospective client—and she flunked your query Big Time. Under those circumstances, why would you go to work for her?"

She winced at my tone but answered my query in a calm voice. "For starters, because Lila was recommended to me by someone I know and trust."

"The woman you mentioned earlier?"

"Yes, Karen Clauson. Not only is she a reputable person, but she and her husband are good clients too. So if I had turned Lila away without even meeting her, how would that have looked?"

"Gee, I don't know," I snapped. "Maybe like you were using your brain?"

Claire pushed back her chair and stood up. "You see? That's why I didn't want to tell you. I knew you'd think I'd done something stupid."

"Claire, I'm sorry." I blew out a breath. And felt like an utter ass. At least now I knew why she'd been avoiding me. "I shouldn't have said that. Please sit back down."

Reluctantly she did so. She folded her hands on the table and stared at me without saying anything. It was left to me to make amends.

"Okay," I said. "That was the first reason. Was there another?"

Claire nodded.

"Are you going to make me beg?"

"I'm thinking about it."

"How about if I go and get you another helping of frozen yogurt? Will that help?"

"My mood, yes." She smiled grudgingly. "My waistline, not in the slightest. The second reason was because once I'd met Lila, I found that I actually liked her. I mean, I knew there was something hinky about her background. But in person, she didn't seem like she was a deranged psychopath. Or indeed anything out of the ordinary at all. After I got to know her a bit, I even found myself trying to come up with reasons why she might have needed to become somebody else."

"Such as?"

"Maybe Lila was trying to escape from an abusive husband," Claire told me seriously. "Or she could have been part of the witness protection program."

Both options sounded pretty far-fetched to me. But for Claire's sake, I was willing to play along. "I suppose those could be possibilities."

"You don't have to sound so skeptical. I would have asked her eventually, you know." Claire frowned. "I just thought I should wait until we had more of a relationship."

Now that would never happen. The depressing thought hung in the air between us. Claire hadn't just suffered the shock that came with finding a dead body. She'd also lost a friend.

"You should have told Detective Hronis about this," I said.

"No way," Claire replied. "He thinks of me as a suspect. I've watched enough episodes of *Law & Order* to know that unless you have a lawyer with you when you talk to the police, you should say as little as possible. And you especially shouldn't bring up something they might somehow find incriminating. Besides, the authorities have plenty of resources. By now, I'm sure they already know."

She was probably right about that.

Claire reached across the table, picked up my empty yogurt cup and spoon, and added them to her own. There was a trash container just behind us. She turned around and dumped everything in. People were standing around the edges of the food court waiting for tables. It was time for us to move on.

We both stood up. Claire gathered up her purse and the big tote. She checked something on her phone. "I still have two more stops to make. Are we good now?"

"We're good." I reached over and gave her a firm hug. "We're always good, even when we don't entirely see eye to eye."

"So what happens next?"

"What do you mean?"

"You're going to keep asking questions, aren't you?"

I wondered if it was my imagination that she sounded almost hopeful. "Do you want me to?"

Claire hesitated only briefly before nodding. "I hate this. It reminds me of last time." Her beloved brother had been murdered several years earlier. That tragic event had been the beginning of our relationship.

I was tempted to give her another hug, but Claire wasn't crumbling. Instead, her chin lifted defiantly.

"Plus," she said, "this kind of attention isn't good for my business."

"We can't have that," I agreed.

She pulled out her phone again and went to work. A minute later, she looked up. "I sent you Karen's contact info. She knew Lila better than I did. You should start with her."

When I got home, Sam was closeted in his office, working. So I grabbed the Poodles, plus Bud, and took the crew for a mile walk around the neighborhood. Our backyard was big and totally fenced in, and the dogs loved to hang out there. But aside from the occasional game of tag or tug-of-war, they rarely used it to exercise.

That was left to me. But what the heck. The walks were good for me too. And they gave me a chance to admire my neighbors' Christmas decorations.

The Standard Poodles knew how to listen, so they were loose. Bud listened too—but then he was apt to make a unilateral decision to explore other options. So he was on a leash. When Raven and Eve saw something interesting a few houses away and dashed on ahead of us, the little dog looked up at me and whined.

"No," I said.

Bud wagged his tail hopefully.

"You know why."

He cocked his head to one side and gave me a doggy grin.

Dammit, he was adorable. I hardened my heart anyway. "Don't try to tell me you won't steal the baby Jesus from Mrs. DeLeo's crèche, because I know better. Last time, you dragged it all over her yard before I caught you, and I had to have his little gown dry cleaned."

Faith woofed under her breath. She'd enjoyed that.

Augie and Tar, busy peeing on every tree we passed, had lagged behind. Now the two male Poodles caught up with us. Surrounded once again by his buddies, Bud relaxed and we continued our walk.

Despite the lack of snow on the ground, the street looked

ready for the holidays. Nearly all the houses had Christmas wreaths on their doors. Many had festive lights twined around their trees and bushes. One enterprising person had positioned a sleigh, with a blow-up Santa Claus and eight plastic reindeer, in the middle of his front yard. The neighborhood dogs had been barking at that for a week.

Sam and the boys had put up our outdoor lights a few days earlier, but we had yet to buy a wreath or a tree. That event was scheduled for the upcoming weekend when we planned to visit Haney's Holiday Home, a Christmas tree farm in Wilton owned by Bob and my brother, Frank. Now in its second year of operation with them at the helm, the business was turning out to be an unexpected success.

When I returned from my walk, Sam and I had lunch together. Then I dashed out and picked up Kevin at preschool. When I called Karen Clauson after that, I found out that Claire had already smoothed the way for me. Not only did Karen know who I was, but she also said she'd be happy to speak with me.

"With three kids, I'm running around like crazy this time of year," she told me. "But I've got half an hour free this afternoon. Why don't you stop by?"

Karen also lived in Stamford so I told her I'd be there shortly. Leaving Sam in charge of the child and the dogs, I jumped back in the Volvo and quickly headed out.

Shippan Point was a small peninsula that jutted out into Long Island Sound in the southernmost part of the city. It was a neighborhood of large homes, yacht clubs, and private beaches. Karen and her husband, George, lived in a gracious three-story house with a large yard and views of the water.

A brisk breeze was blowing in off the Sound when I got out of my car in front of their home. I arranged my scarf more tightly around my neck and walked across the lawn. The cold air was bracing, but I still had to stop for a minute to appreciate the view. Even in winter, it was amazing.

I heard the front door open and looked up as a woman stepped out onto the wide porch. She was thin as a twig and had on leather boots and a cashmere turtleneck dress. A wide belt accentuated her enviably small waist. The woman's blond hair was gathered into a high ponytail that swung gently when the wind hit it.

She stood with her arms crossed over her chest, probably for warmth. Her hands pegged her as middle aged, but her face had the taut look of a much younger woman. As I went to join her, her smile was immediate and friendly. I could already understand why Claire liked her.

"I'm Karen," she said, extending a hand. "And you must be Melanie." She nodded toward the expanse of water, winter gray and rolling with whitecap-tipped waves. "It's beautiful, isn't it?"

"It certainly is," I agreed.

"Most people move here because they want to be near the shore in the summer. But I prefer this time of year, when everything looks so wild and untamed. It makes me feel small, like Mother Nature's making sure we understand who's actually in charge."

"I never thought about it that way before."

Karen laughed. "George says the same thing. He thinks I'm crazy. But as long as he can spend six months a year on his sailboat, he's willing to put up with frigid winters beside the Sound."

She had left the door open behind her and turned back to it now. "Let's go inside and warm up. I've got a fire burning in the living room. And there's a pot of coffee in the kitchen, if you'd like some."

"That sounds wonderful." I pulled off my coat and scarf and hung them on a coatrack near the door. "Thank you for agreeing to see me."

"As I'm sure you can imagine, Lila's death came as a huge shock to all of us. To tell you the truth, I'm happy to be able to talk about it with someone. The whole thing has left me feeling anxious, and even a bit jumpy. I just never expected to know someone who . . ." She stopped and cleared her throat softly. "This isn't the kind of place where you think something like that will happen."

I nodded. "I understand how you feel."

"Maybe this will sound morbid, but I keep thinking that if I can learn more about what took place, maybe that will help me to understand. I spoke with Claire briefly, but she sounded so fragile that I didn't want to press her for details. So when she told me that you were there with her yesterday . . ."

"You figured you'd get your questions answered while you were answering mine?" I asked.

"Yes, something like that. Let's get our coffee and sit down. We've got half an hour until my two youngest get home from school. We should put it to good use."

Karen's coffee was strong and hot, and the fire crackling in the fireplace gave the spacious living room a cozy feel. We found seats on two matching love seats that faced each other across a low butler's table.

"I understand you were the person who referred Lila Moran to Claire," I began.

"Yes, I was. Claire's done several events for us. Well, for me, really—George doesn't care a fig about the kids' birthday parties—and she's always done a phenomenal job. Whenever anyone asks for a recommendation, I'm always happy to send business her way."

"I'm sure Claire appreciates that."

"I'd imagine she did." Karen frowned. "Until this time."

"That was hardly your fault. I know Claire enjoyed working with Lila and getting to know her."

"Yes, she would have. Lila was like that. She made friends easily. She'd only been at James and Brant about a year, but she very quickly found her stride. It wasn't long before she fit right in."

"She was the officer manager there?" I asked.

"That's right."

"So you must have met Lila through your husband."

Karen blinked. She looked surprised by the question. "I guess I did, although not directly. James and Brant is an advertising firm. The principals like their people to be seen out and around, so George and I attend a number of functions each year. As soon as Lila joined the company, it was inevitable that our paths would begin to cross."

"How well did you know her?"

"I would say we were friends—which doesn't mean that we were particularly close. Lila and I led very different lives. I'm a stay-at-home mom and happy in that role. Lila was a career woman. She was ambitious, always keeping her eye out for the next opportunity. She never said as much to me, but I think she viewed the job at James and Brant as a stepping stone rather than an end destination."

My coffee had begun to cool. I picked it up and took a sip. "Claire didn't know much about Lila's background. Things like where she grew up or went to college. I was wondering if you know more?"

"Not really." Karen paused to consider. "I guess we never got around to talking about those things. George probably has that information. He's one of the partners in the firm. I'd be surprised if he didn't see her résumé before she was hired. I could ask him about it if you want."

"That would be great. Thank you." I appreciated that Karen was trying to be helpful, but it sounded as though she didn't know any more about Lila than Claire had.

In the fireplace a log snapped and fell, sending a spray of sparks shooting into the air. Karen stood and picked up a pair of tongs. She rearranged the remaining wood to her satisfaction, then reached into a nearby bin and placed a new log on top of the pile. The flames quickly licked upward, seeking the fresh fuel.

"You look like an old hand at that," I said as she retook her seat.

"It's hard not to be when you live on the water in Connecticut. A toasty fire goes a long way toward taking the chill out of the air."

I nodded. She was right about that. "I know this is a difficult question. But do you have any thoughts about why someone might have wanted to harm Lila?"

"You mean kill her," Karen replied flatly.

"Yes."

"I heard she was shot."

"She was," I affirmed. "Do you know of any enemies she might have had?"

"None." Karen sighed. "That's what makes this whole situation so incomprehensible. I watch the news. I know that bad things happen. But I just never expected my family to be impacted by a violent crime like this. Please . . . tell me what happened. I heard Lila was found in her living room. Do you think she came home and interrupted a burglar?"

"I suppose that could have been the case." I considered that idea. "Although there didn't seem to be much in her home that anyone might have wanted to steal. And nothing else in the room looked as though it had been disturbed."

"Was the door locked when Claire got there? Do you think Lila admitted her killer to the house? Could it have been someone she knew?"

"Claire went in through the back door. She used a hidden key to let herself inside," I said. "I don't know whether or not the front door was locked—and maybe it wouldn't have mattered."

Karen looked up. "Why is that?"

"The gatehouse where Lila was living is pretty old. And it's seriously in need of upkeep. It didn't appear to be very secure."

"Oh," Karen said abruptly. "Oh my."

"What's the matter?" I asked.

"What you said just reminded me of something. It was a couple of months ago. With winter coming, Lila mentioned that her furnace needed to be repaired. I told her I could recommend someone. But she said there was a caretaker on the property who was supposed to do stuff like that. I said, 'Good, then you're all set,' but she shook her head and gave me the oddest look."

I sat up straight. "Did you ask why?"

"I did." Karen frowned, thinking back. "At first she didn't want to talk about it. But then she finally admitted that she was afraid of the guy. She didn't like him coming inside her house. Lila said he was convinced that she had something of his, something he wanted back. I didn't think any more about it at the time, but now I wonder. Do you think she was right to be worried?"

Chapter 7

"Yes," I said. Lila was dead. *Did she even have to ask?* "Have you talked to the police about that?"

"No." Karen appeared shocked by the suggestion.

"Because that sounds like useful information they should have."

She still didn't look convinced. "A detective showed up at James and Brant yesterday afternoon. George told me all about it. The detective talked to everyone. People who knew Lila much better than I did."

"But maybe they didn't know about this," I pointed out. "Was anyone else there when you and Lila had that conversation?"

"Let me think." Karen paused. "Yes, Chris was there. Chris Sanchez. She's one of the account reps. And she would have been at work yesterday. I'm sure she must have told the detective what Lila said."

I wasn't nearly as sure of that as she was. But Karen sounded so relieved to be off the hook that I decided not to press the issue.

"In fact," she said, standing up, "if you want to find out more about Lila, Chris is the person you should talk to. She and Lila have worked side by side for the past year. She would have known her better than I did."

Karen crossed the room to the desk in the corner. She opened a drawer and took out a pen and a sheet of paper. Then she got out her phone and wrote something down. "Here's her number. Call Chris. Tell her I sent you. I'm sure she'll be able to help you."

At least Chris would be able to tell me whether she'd passed along Lila's fear of the caretaker to the police. "Thanks," I said. "I appreciate it."

"Do you know what I think?" Karen asked as she accompanied me to the door. "That this was a totally random event. Like maybe Lila was just in the wrong place at the wrong time. And the police will catch the guy quickly so we can all put this behind us." She nodded firmly. "That's what's going to happen."

"I hope you're right," I said.

Shippan was in South Stamford. My house was in North Stamford. The offices for James and Brant were downtown, which meant I'd be driving virtually right past on my way home. So when I got out to my car, I took a shot and called Chris Sanchez.

It was mid-afternoon so I figured she'd be at work. If I was lucky, maybe she'd be able to spare a few minutes to talk to me.

Chris sounded wary when she answered her phone. Since she hadn't recognized my number, she probably thought I wanted to sell her something. She thawed slightly when I introduced myself, and by the time I told her that Karen had put me in touch, Chris had become positively chatty. When I asked if I could stop by the office, she had another idea ready.

"Don't come here," she said. "There's a Starbucks on the

corner. I can meet you there in fifteen minutes. Would that work?"

"That's perfect," I told her. "But I don't want to drag you away from things you're supposed to be doing."

"Don't worry about that. I'm happy to take a break. This place is a madhouse today. Of course, Lila's murder came as a huge shock to everyone. But her loss impacts us on a practical level, too, because suddenly we're without an office manager. Nobody will even notice if I duck out for a few minutes."

I beat her to the coffee shop, picked up a caffè mocha, and grabbed a table. Chris came flying in two minutes later. She looked to be in her early thirties. Her skin was lightly freckled, and her dark hair was gathered into a messy bun on the top of her head. She'd run out of the office without bothering to put on a coat, which probably accounted for her speed.

Chris paused just inside the door and took a look around. I was the only single woman sitting alone, so she gave me a small wave. I waved back and smiled. She stopped at the counter to buy an espresso and a slice of lemon pound cake.

As she slipped into a chair opposite me, Chris set the cake plate and two forks on the table between us. "This is big enough to share. And that way I only have to worry about half the calories. I hope you're Melanie, otherwise I am offering sweets to a total stranger. And that could probably get me in trouble."

"Yes, I'm Melanie," I said with a laugh. "And I never mind when someone offers me cake. Thank you for agreeing to talk to me."

"Hey, like I said, it was a good excuse to escape the mayhem." She was already digging into the pound cake. "How do you know Karen?"

"Actually, we just met earlier. She and I were talking about what happened to Lila Moran."

Chris looked up. "Why?"

"Because I was at Lila's house yesterday morning, after her body was discovered."

"Oh." Chris took a swallow of her espresso. "So are you some kind of plainclothes cop or something? Because we talked to those guys yesterday."

"No. Claire Travis, the woman who found Lila, is a good friend of mine. She was in a panic, and she called and asked me to come and help."

"Claire Travis." Chris stared at me. "And you're Melanie Travis?"

I nodded.

"Friends, not relatives?"

"Claire is married to my ex-husband," I said.

She barked out a laugh. "How's that working out?"

"Surprisingly well."

"I guess so." Chris shook her head. She looked bemused. "Considering that you were the one she called, and now you're here talking to me. Is Claire the personal shopper?"

"That's right."

Chris helped herself to another piece of cake. At this rate, I wouldn't get a single bite. "Lila mentioned her the other day. The rest of us were complaining about all the Christmas shopping we still had to do, and Lila started bragging that she was already finished. So of course we wanted to know how she'd managed that. Made me think I should consider trying it next year."

"Claire does a great job." I was always happy to give her a plug.

"Except that her client is dead," Chris mentioned.

"That's not Claire's fault."

"You sure about that?"

"Of course I'm sure." I huffed out a breath.

She lifted her head and studied me. "Even though she stole your husband?"

The accusation was so absurd that it made me laugh. "Claire didn't steal my husband. Bob and I had been divorced for years before the two of them even met."

"Maybe that's just what they want you to think," Chris said.

"You have a suspicious mind. I like that in a woman." I sipped my drink. My third coffee of the day. No wonder I was getting a buzz. "Do you mind if I ask a few questions?"

"Have at it," she invited. "I'll answer the ones I like and ignore the ones I don't."

That sounded fair enough. Especially considering that I'd lost control of this interview a long time ago.

"How well did you know Lila Moran?"

Chris shrugged. "Not as well as you might think, since we'd worked in the same office for a year. We got along well enough in our professional setting."

"But apparently you weren't friends," I said.

"No, not really."

"Are you friends with the other people you work with?"

Chris nodded. "Most of them, yeah. But Lila was different."

"How?"

"She always seemed to hold herself apart. Lila didn't talk about her family, or her hobbies, or her plans for the weekend. She listened when the rest of us were sharing stuff, but she almost never joined in."

Interesting. That wasn't at all the impression I'd gotten from Karen.

"How did the other people in your office feel about her?" I asked.

"Like maybe you're thinking it was just me she didn't get along with?" Chris grinned. "Nope, that wasn't it. If you asked around, I'd imagine you'd hear that none of us liked her much." She paused, then added, "Except maybe the partners."

"Oh?"

"Well, you know, they're important."

"And you aren't?"

"Not in Lila's eyes, we weren't. The partners were the big shots. She was always going out of her way to try and impress them." Chris pulled a face. "Or if we had a client stop by, Lila would suddenly turn into the sweetest woman you ever met. The rest of us weren't fooled by that act."

She picked up the last piece of lemon cake with her fingers, tossed it in her mouth, and chewed happily. There went that chance. I hoped it had been good.

"I'll tell you what," Chris said after she'd washed the cake down with a swallow of espresso. "The woman was a hypocrite. The office may be in an uproar now, but after things get back to normal, I won't be the only one who's happy not to have to deal with her crap anymore."

"Karen mentioned a conversation she and Lila had concerning the caretaker on the estate where Lila was living," I said. "She told me you were there too."

"Was I? I don't remember that. All I knew was that she lived in some fancy place in New Canaan."

"Lila needed to have her furnace fixed," I prompted. "And she was afraid of the man who was supposed to come and do it."

"Really? That's odd." Chris looked down at the empty plate and frowned. She seemed more upset that there was no more pound cake than she was about Lila's murder. "Why didn't she just hire another guy?"

"Because the caretaker is responsible for the property," I told her. "It was his job. None of this sounds familiar to you?"

"Nope." She shrugged. "Not one bit. But Lila could be a pretty tough cookie when she didn't get her own way. I can't imagine her being afraid of some repairman."

"That's what Karen told me," I said again.

"Then she must have spent more time chatting with Lila than I did." There was plenty of snark in Chris's tone. "Which is not surprising, considering that her husband, George, is a partner."

It felt like our conversation had come full circle. I started to gather up my things.

When I stood up, Chris remained seated. She didn't appear to be in any hurry to return to her office. "I do know one thing about Lila you didn't ask about," she said as I was putting on my coat. "She had a boyfriend."

I sank back down in my chair.

"At least she mentioned a guy once. We were talking about how hard it is to meet single men in Fairfield County, and she said she had someone. Mostly, I think, so she could lord it over us that she had a man when the rest of us were still looking. The guy had a really snooty-sounding name. That's why it stuck in my mind. Lincoln Landry."

"You're right." I smiled. "He sounds like a trust fund baby."

"Which probably means he works in a gas station." Chris laughed. "That would serve her right."

"I don't suppose you know how I can get in touch with him?"

"Seriously? Google is your friend. With a name like that, how hard can he be to find?"

"How come we don't have a Christmas tree yet?" Kevin asked that night. "Everyone else has one. How will Santa Claus find us if we don't have a tree?"

It was Kev's bedtime. He'd had a bath and a story, and now he was tucked beneath the covers. Bud was snuggled on the quilt at the foot of his bed. I'd been just about to turn off his light.

And now Kevin wanted to talk. Of course.

"What's that?" Sam came walking around the corner. Faith was lying down in the doorway. She'd been waiting to accompany me back downstairs. Sam stepped over her and entered the room. "You don't think Santa will be able to find you?"

"Not without a tree, and lights, and ornaments," Kevin said plaintively.

"You wrote him a letter, didn't you?" I asked.

Kev nodded.

"And you put your address on it, right?" said Sam.

"I did," Kevin confirmed. "Davey helped. Do you think Santa will read it?"

"I know he will," I told him. "One of the elves will give it to him. Santa Claus reads all the letters children send him."

"He'll see the return address," Sam added. "That's how he'll know where you are."

"Plus, we'll be getting our Christmas tree on Saturday," I said.

Kev brightened briefly. Then he frowned. "That's still two whole days away."

"What's going on? Where is everybody? Is someone having a party in here?" Davey stuck his head in the room. Augie was with him. That big Poodle hopped over Faith too. Then he saw Bud on the bed and jumped up to join him.

At this rate, I was never going to get that child to sleep.

"Kevin thinks we need a Christmas tree," I said.

"Smart kid." Davey and Kevin high-fived. "Of course we need a tree. We're going this weekend."

"We should have one already." Kev pouted. He's single-minded. And stubborn. I have no idea where he gets that from.

"Well, sure," said Davey. "But remember last year, when we went to the Christmas tree farm in Wilton and cut down our own tree? Don't you want to do that again?"

Kevin nodded.

"We can't do it during the week because it takes too long, and by the time I get home from school, it's already starting to get dark. That's why we're going Saturday morning."

Kev considered that for a few seconds. "First thing, right?"

"First thing," the three of us repeated solemnly.

"Promise?"

"We promise," we said.

"Pinky swear?"

"Enough!" I laughed. I got up off the bed and shooed Augie down too. Bud could stay. He always did. "If you don't go to sleep, it will never be Saturday."

"Okay." Kevin closed his eyes. "Turn off the light."

We all snuck out. I closed the door most of the way behind us.

"That kid's crazy for Christmas," Davey said as we all went trooping down the stairs. "Was I that bad at his age?"

"You were worse," I told him.

Claire called later that night. She was whispering into the phone. "Melanie, you have to help me!"

Oh no, I thought. Not again.

I'd been sitting on the couch, reading a book. Faith was lying on the cushion next to me. When I snapped upright, she jumped up too.

"Claire," I said urgently, "where are you?"

"I'm at home. Where do you think? It's almost ten o'clock."

My shoulders relaxed. Okay, so there wasn't any immediate danger. I gave Faith a reassuring pat. She turned a small circle and lay back down.

"What's the matter?" I said.

"I've lost my gold bracelet. The one Bob gave me when we got married. I've looked all over the house and it isn't here. So I thought back to the last time I saw it, and I realized there's only one place it could be."

I squeezed my eyes shut. *Don't say it*, I prayed. *Please don't say it.*

Claire said it. "It's in Lila's cottage."

"No, it's not," I told her firmly. "Think again. I'm sure there are plenty of other places you might have lost it. Besides, weren't you wearing mittens that day?"

"Not when I first went into the gatehouse. I took the mittens off because I knew I'd have to use the key. The bracelet must have slipped off my wrist when I put all those packages down on the table. I remember feeling something tug and I was going to check on it, but then I saw Lila and everything else flew straight out of my mind."

I sighed. Unfortunately that sounded plausible. "If your bracelet was in the gatehouse, the police will have found it by now."

"Maybe," she allowed. "But it could have rolled under a piece of furniture and nobody noticed it. So I have to retrieve it before that detective gets his hands on it and decides it somehow makes me look guilty."

"Claire, that's not going to happen."

"You don't know that," she wailed. Then her voice dropped to a whisper again. "This is important, Melanie. I need that bracelet back before Bob realizes it's gone."

"I wouldn't worry about that," I said, biting back a smile. After all, the guy was my ex. "Bob isn't that observant."

"He notices more than you think. And I always wear the bracelet, so he's bound to notice that it's not on my wrist. Will you help me?"

"Claire, think for a minute. Even if the police haven't found your bracelet, I know they will have removed the spare key. So how are we going to get inside the gatehouse?"

"Remember that warped window I told you about? It doesn't close all the way, so it can't be locked. I'm sure I can get us in."

I swallowed heavily. This was *so* not a good idea. "Just to clarify, you're proposing that we break into a crime scene?"

"When you put it like that, you make it sound crazy," Claire grumbled.

Frankly, I couldn't think of any other way to put it. Faith was listening to our conversation. Even she looked concerned.

"Yes," she confirmed. "That's what I want to do. And there's nobody else I can ask to come with me. *Please?*"

"When?" I said. I still wasn't making any promises.

"Tomorrow morning. I'll pick you up at seven-thirty, and we can go together. Trust me, we'll be in and out of there in five minutes. Ten, tops."

I did trust Claire. But I still had a sneaking suspicion that things weren't going to go as smoothly as she thought they would.

"We're out in ten minutes," I said. "Whether we've found the bracelet or not."

"I swear," she replied.

I ended the connection and gazed down at Faith. The big Poodle still looked worried. In dog years she was old enough to be my mother. Maybe that was why she'd always felt compelled to watch out for me. Even when I did things she didn't approve of. Perhaps especially then.

"It'll be a quick trip," I told her. "Nobody will even know we were there."

Faith lowered her head and rested her muzzle between her paws. She wasn't convinced of the wisdom of this plan. Sadly, I couldn't blame her.

Chapter 8

As it happened, I never got around to mentioning the plan to Sam. I did tell him that he was in charge of getting both boys off to school the next morning. That was cause for a raised eyebrow.

"Claire's picking me up early," I said. "There's something we need to do."

"Do I want to know?"

"Probably not." I smiled to soften the sentiment. I knew it hadn't worked when I heard Sam's next question.

"Do I need to start raising bail money?"

"I hope not," I told him cheerfully.

Sam didn't think that was funny. That put him and Faith on the same team, which wasn't reassuring.

"I hope you know what you're doing," I said to Claire the next morning when I climbed into her car.

We were close to the shortest day of the year and the sun was barely up. The temperature outside was frigid, and there was frost on the grass in my yard. The air smelled like snow. I wondered if that meant some was on the way. I hadn't had time to look at a forecast.

"Of course I don't know what I'm doing," Claire replied. She put the Honda in reverse and backed down the driveway. "That's why I asked you to come along."

That was just peachy.

"Faith thinks we're nuts," I mentioned.

"Faith's a dog. We don't have to take her opinion into account unless we want to." Her gaze swiveled my way. "Which we don't. I'm guessing you didn't tell Sam where you were going?"

"Not exactly," I admitted.

"Good."

Claire turned her eyes back to the road and drove. It wasn't long before we were on Forest Glen Lane. The Mannerly estate loomed into view.

"Oh, look," I said when we reached the entrance. "There's a gate across the driveway."

"There was a gate there two days ago," Claire replied drily. "Didn't you notice?"

"Two days ago it was open," I pointed out. "Now it's closed. Uh-oh."

"No problem." Claire pulled the car over beside an entry box, discreetly painted black, that I hadn't noticed on my previous visit. "How do you think I got in the other day? Lila gave me the code."

"Of course she did," I muttered under my breath. "That's lucky," I said aloud.

"Or good planning," she informed me.

The double gates swung open. Claire pulled the car through and they closed behind us. We coasted thirty feet to the gatehouse. The small building looked dark and deserted. The weak morning sun did nothing to brighten its appearance.

A piece of bright yellow crime scene tape was tacked across the cottage's front door. Claire and I both pretended we didn't see it. She pulled around the back and parked in the same spot she'd used the other day.

"Too bad there's no place to hide the car," I said as we got out.

"Hide it from whom?" Claire asked. "Take a look around, Melanie. There's nobody here to see us."

So far, so good.

"Where's the window you were telling me about?"

"It's on the other side."

Claire began to beat her way through the underbrush that had grown up next to the house. Wearing thick boots, flannel-lined jeans, and an oilskin jacket, she was dressed for the job. My clothes were equally heavy, but I was all in black. Earlier that morning, that had struck me as the kind of outfit one ought to wear for housebreaking.

We didn't have to go far. And with Claire breaking a trail in front of me, all I had to do was follow behind. The window looked as though it opened into a storage room next to the kitchen.

As I drew closer, I could see a sliver of an opening between the window frame and the sill. Claire was already trying to wedge her fingers into the small gap. It wasn't working.

"Here," I said. "Let me try."

I started to move forward, but Claire held her place. "No, I have a better idea." She reached into a deep pocket on her jacket and pulled out a crowbar.

I shouldn't have been surprised. Claire was one of the best planners I knew. Of course she would have come prepared.

So instead I just shifted out of the way. "Be careful you don't break the window."

She gave me a withering look. "Really? Lila was always trying to get this place repaired, and nothing ever got fixed. Who's going to notice a little broken glass?"

Claire slipped the claw of the crowbar in beneath the window frame. When she levered the shaft downward, the window rose with a sharp squeal. The size of the chink quickly grew from one inch to six. Then Claire was able to get her hands in place and lift the window the rest of the way. That done, she stepped back.

"You're smaller," she told me. "You go first. If you can't get in through there, there's no hope that I will."

The opening wasn't big, but we were motivated. Three minutes later, we were both inside the gatehouse. It was just as cold inside the building as it was outside. I unzipped my jacket anyway, but I left my gloves on. Claire did the same.

The small room we found ourselves in had probably been a pantry once. Shelves, most of them empty, lined three of the four walls. Two steps took us from there into the kitchen.

I walked over to the table. There was no sign of the presents Claire had left piled there. I wondered where they'd gone.

"This is where you think your bracelet fell off?" I asked.

"Right." Claire was already down on her hands and knees, her gaze scanning the floor. "It has to be here somewhere."

Ten fruitless minutes later, we'd checked every inch of the kitchen. The bracelet was nowhere to be seen. I was ready to concede defeat. And eager for us to be on our way.

"Maybe it rolled into the living room," Claire said.

Our gazes shifted in that direction. Lila's body was long gone, but no one had cleaned the cottage since. Neither of us wanted to step into the next room.

I stood up and dusted off my knees. Claire was about to follow suit when the back door to the gatehouse suddenly flew open. I jumped out of the way just in time. The door bounced off the wall with a loud crash.

Claire screamed and leapt to her feet. She'd put the crowbar down on the kitchen table. I snatched it up and held it out in front of us like a weapon. The move was pure reflex. It wasn't like I was actually going to hit anyone with it.

Was I?

A man stood backlit in the open doorway. He was short, broad shouldered, and built like a tree stump. He had his feet braced wide apart and his hands fisted at his sides. A flat cap, pulled low over his forehead, put much of his face in shadow.

"Who the hell are you?" he demanded.

Adrenaline was coursing through me. Otherwise I might have behaved with more moderation. Instead I felt like I wanted to punch someone.

"Who the hell are you?" I shot right back.

"Hank Peebles. I'm the caretaker for this estate. And the two of you are trespassing." He motioned toward the crowbar. "Put that damn thing down before you hurt someone."

"How do I know you are who you say you are?" I asked.

The man grinned. His teeth were stained by tobacco juice. "Because—unlike you two—I have a key to let myself in here. Don't tell me you broke a window with that thing, or you'll be in even more trouble than you already are."

"We didn't have to break in," Claire said, her cheeks flushed. "The window was already open."

"Is that so?" He leaned back against the doorjamb. "And how would you have known that?"

"Because I was friends with the woman who lived here."

"The dead woman," Peebles spat out.

I'd started to lay down the crowbar. Now I lifted it again. Something about this man brought out the worst in me. Probably my suspicion that he'd had a hand in Lila's death.

"Did you kill her?" I asked.

Abruptly he straightened. "What kind of question is that? Of course I didn't kill her. Damn woman must have gotten someone all riled up, but it wasn't me. Is that why you're here? A couple of lookie-loos thinking it might be fun to check out the spot where it happened?"

"No, we came to look for something we lost."

"Oh yeah?" He looked skeptical. "And what would that be?"

"A bracelet," Claire told him. "I dropped it here a couple days ago. Melanie came to help me look for it."

"A bracelet," Peebles repeated with a smirk. "It must be something special to make you break the law for it. You two are trespassers. This is private property—and clearly marked as such. You got no right to be here. Especially not after what happened earlier in the week. I've called the police. They're already on their way."

Claire and I exchanged a look. That wasn't good.

"How did you know we were here?" I asked.

Peebles continued to stand in the open doorway. He was blocking the exit like he thought we might try to escape. It wasn't as if the idea hadn't crossed my mind.

"Not that it's any of your business, but I got a buzzer that lets me know anytime the gate opens," he said. "This is a big estate. I can't be everywhere at once. But I still gotta keep an eye out. Miss Mannerly, she's a very private lady. She doesn't like strangers—people like you—coming around where they don't belong."

He turned to glance outside. Moments later, I heard the sound of an approaching car. A patrol car pulled up beside the gatehouse. Two men got out. The first was a uniformed officer. The second man was Detective Hronis.

Oh joy.

Beside me, Claire uttered a small squeak of alarm. Yeah, that was helpful. She was the one whose powers of persuasion had gotten us into this mess. I could only hope that now she'd be persuasive enough to talk our way out.

"Hello, Hank," the officer said as he and the detective came inside through the open doorway. "What do you have here?"

"These two ladies want me to believe they came here looking for a lost bracelet," Peebles told him. "It sounds fishy to me."

Detective Hronis looked at us. His brow furrowed in a frown. "Ms. Travis," he said. "And Ms. Travis."

"Hello, Detective," I replied.

"You know them?" the officer asked.

"I'm afraid so. I can handle it from here."

Peebles and the officer dropped back. Together they stepped outside.

Hronis looked at me and held out his hand. For a moment, I was confused. Then I realized what he wanted. I handed over the crowbar.

"Any other weapons in your possession?" he asked.

Claire and I shook our heads.

"I'm guessing you didn't see the crime scene tape on the door?"

"We did," said Claire. "That's why we came in through the window."

"The window," he repeated.

"In the pantry," I told him. "It's warped."

He blinked, tipped his head to one side. "And that made it seem like a good idea for you to come back here and check things out? You realize this is a crime scene, right? There's a reason why it's secure."

The detective's gaze shifted to Claire. "So you were looking for something you left behind. Maybe some kind of evidence you didn't want me to find? Is that why we're all standing here in the cold?"

"No." Her voice squeaked. "That's not it at all."

I loved Claire, but she was a terrible liar. And the glare she sent my way clearly said, "I told you so!"

"Well, then." Hronis crossed his arms over his chest. "The two of you had better tell me what's going on before I decide to take you both down to the station to continue this conversation."

"That won't be necessary," I said quickly.

"I hope not. But so far, you haven't given me any reason to think differently."

"It's all my fault," Claire blurted. "Melanie had nothing to do with it."

She told him about the lost bracelet, given to her by her husband on their wedding day. She explained how it must have fallen off when she put down the parcels. She insisted that all we'd meant to do was retrieve it, then quickly leave.

"*After* you'd contaminated my crime scene," Hronis said.

Claire held up her hands. "We wore gloves."

He growled under his breath. "So I guess it didn't occur to you to call me and ask if we'd found it? Or if someone from the department could escort you over here to have a look?"

"Ummm," Claire said slowly. "No."

"Any particular reason why not?"

"Because I thought you'd say no," Claire admitted.

"You're not helping your case any, Ms. Travis," Hronis said forcefully. "I would have said no. Because you have no business being here. You're lucky I believe your story, cockeyed as it is, because otherwise I'd have to arrest you. And that would lead to a lot of unnecessary paperwork for everybody."

I hadn't realized until that moment that I'd been holding my breath. Now I exhaled slowly. A small puff of condensation blew out into the cold air.

"Thank you for believing us," I said.

Hronis shot me an aggrieved look. "I don't want your thanks. I just want you to stay out of my hair."

"We'll certainly try," I said with feeling.

"See that you do."

We followed him outside. He pulled the door shut behind us. I was ready to go. But now that the detective had released us, Claire chose that moment to decide to be helpful.

"I know something," she piped up.

"Is that so?" Hronis turned in her direction. He propped his hands on his hips. "Let's hear it."

"Lila Moran wasn't her real name."

The detective's expression didn't change. He still looked exasperated. "And you know that, how?"

"Because before I took her on as a client, I looked into her background." When his eyes narrowed, Claire quickly added, "I do it with all my clients. And I couldn't find any information about Lila that was more than five years old. It was as if she didn't exist before that."

The caretaker and the police officer had been standing off to one side, talking to each other. But now I saw Peebles abruptly fall silent. He appeared to be listening to what Claire had to say.

"Thank you, Ms. Travis," Hronis replied. "We are aware of that."

Claire smiled brightly, like a student trying to please a difficult teacher. "That could be a clue, right?"

"Maybe." His tone was noncommittal. "It would have been more helpful if you'd told me earlier. Before we'd already found out for ourselves. And speaking of things we found out, here's something else I know. You two ladies aren't sisters."

Oops.

I stopped staring at the caretaker and turned my attention back to the conversation in front of me. It seemed it had suddenly become more critical to my well-being than whatever Hank Peebles was up to.

"Claire and I aren't actual sisters," I told the detective. "But we're as close as sisters."

"That isn't what you told Officer Jenkins."

"Maybe he misunderstood," I said.

"He didn't." The detective frowned. Again. "Let me tell you something, Ms. Travis. Lying to the police is a dumb thing to do. Especially when we're investigating a murder."

"You're right," I agreed. "Absolutely."

"So bearing that in mind, is there anything else you might want to tell me?"

"Actually, there is." I lowered my voice. "But maybe not right here."

Detective Hronis wasn't stupid. He immediately caught on to what I meant. He cupped a hand around my upper arm and led me around to the other side of the gatehouse. When he was satisfied that he'd put enough distance between us and the others, he stopped and said, "What?"

"Hank Peebles, the guy who takes care of this property—I guess you know him?"

"We've met before today."

"Lila Moran was afraid of him."

"How do you know that?"

"She told a woman named Karen Clauson that Peebles was supposed to be making repairs on the cottage, but she was scared to let him inside. Lila thought he meant to take something from her."

"You have any idea what that item might have been?"

I shook my head.

"Clauson," the detective said. "Bit of an unusual name. Is she related to George Clauson, who worked with Ms. Moran at James and Brant?"

"Karen is his wife," I told him.

"I guess that means we'll have to have a chat with her." Hronis started to return to the others. Then he stopped and turned back. "Once I found out that you two weren't really sisters, I asked around about you."

He paused, waiting for me to comment. So help me, I couldn't think of a single useful thing to say.

"I heard you are the kind of person who likes to get herself involved in police business."

I cleared my throat softly. My gaze skittered away from his. "That might occasionally be true."

"I also heard you're the kind of person who sometimes comes up with good ideas."

I looked back at him. That sounded more promising.

"So let me tell you how this is going to work," he said. "I

think you should keep your nose to yourself. But if you should happen to find out something that pertains to this case, you bring it straight to me. Understand?"

And just like that, I felt chastised again.

"Yes, sir," I replied.

Hronis stopped just short of rolling his eyes.

"What was that private conversation about?" Claire asked when we were back in the car, making our escape.

"Mostly Detective Hronis wanted to warn me to stop asking questions."

"Yeah, right." Claire smirked and kept driving. "Like that's going to work."

Chapter 9

I was back home by 10:00 a.m. Sam wasn't there when Claire dropped me off, which was a relief. I had no desire to rehash the morning's ill-advised adventure in the conversation I knew would inevitably follow. At least Sam hadn't had to come up with bail money.

I'd already taken Chris Sanchez's advice and done an internet search for Lincoln Landry. It turned out she'd been mostly right about a couple of things. First, he wasn't hard to find. And second, Landry didn't work in a gas station, but close. He was a car mechanic.

I popped into the house and took the Poodle pack out for a quick play session in the backyard. Then, with apologies all around, I left the dogs again and drove back to New Canaan.

Fred's Fine Motor Repair was located on a side street near the downtown area. The business was housed in a squat brick building that was older than I was. A parking lot out front was littered with vehicles in various states of repair. Most appeared to be of foreign origin: BMWs and Mercedes rather than Toyotas and Mazdas. The garage next to the office had just two bays, but there were cars up on both lifts. Even so, there didn't seem to be much activity going on.

The office had a glass door. A buzzer sounded loudly enough to make me jump when I pushed it open. The small room must have also served as a waiting area because there were several tattered chairs pushed against one wall. A table between them held a stack of magazines that had been current the previous summer.

"Be right with you!" someone called from the garage.

Two minutes later, a door behind the counter swung open. A man wearing a jumpsuit with the name FRED stenciled on the pocket came inside. He was busy wiping his hands on a dirty rag, which gave me a few moments to study him.

He had dark, curly hair and the kind of chiseled features more likely to be seen on a fashion runway than sliding out from beneath a car. Even in the baggy jumpsuit, his body looked impressive. When I glanced up again, I was startled to find myself locking gazes with a pair of piercing brown eyes. The man had been assessing me with the same intensity with which I'd focused on him.

Now he favored me with a slow, sure, grin. We'd just met, and I already knew that the man was a player. And obviously he knew I'd liked what I'd seen. *Dammit.*

"Hello," I said. "I'm looking for Lincoln Landry."

"That's me."

I wasn't sure whether or not to believe him. Maybe he thought we were flirting, making a connection. If so, I was ready to shut him down.

I pointed toward his pocket. "Your name tag says Fred."

"That's right." He was still grinning.

"But that's not your name?"

"Fred's the owner. He hasn't worked in the garage for more than a decade. But customers don't know that. Fred, the owner, says that people like to deal with the man in charge. So we all wear name tags that say FRED on them. That way everybody's happy."

"Except maybe me," I muttered. "So you're really Lincoln Landry?"

"Linc, please. No one calls me by my full name except my mother." He extended a hand over the counter so we could shake. "And you are?"

"Melanie Travis."

"Well, Melanie Travis, what can I do for you? I see your Volvo out there. If you're having problems with it, you've come to the right place. Foreign cars are our specialty."

"No, my car is fine," I said. "I was hoping I could ask you a few questions about a friend of yours. Lila Moran?"

Linc screwed up his face in concentration. "Who?"

"Lila Moran," I tried again. "She worked at James and Brant in Stamford?"

He still looked blank.

Now what? I wondered. I'd never met Lila, so it wasn't as though I could describe her. Was it possible that Linc had so many girlfriends, he couldn't keep them all straight?

"She lived here in New Canaan on the Mannerly estate?"

Finally I saw a glimmer of recognition. "Oh. You mean Lily Mo."

Lila Moran . . . Lily Mo? I supposed that was close enough.

"Sure," I said. "Lily Mo. When was the last time you saw her?"

He thought back. "Maybe three, four, days ago when she dropped off her car." He pointed to a silver Kia that was sitting outside in the lot. "She's due back anytime to pick it up."

"She's due back . . . ?" I repeated slowly. Was it possible he didn't know? "Lila isn't coming back to get her car. I'm very sorry to have to tell you that she was killed in her home at the beginning of the week."

"Killed?" Linc sounded as though he didn't understand the word. "Like, she's dead?"

"Yes. I'm so sorry for your loss. I thought you would have already heard the news. The police are investigating what happened."

"My loss?" Linc shook his head, as if he was still having a hard time processing what I'd told him. "Wait a minute. What are you talking about?"

"Lila told her friends that you and she were a couple," I said. "Wasn't she your girlfriend?"

"No." It was the first definite thing he'd said since the conversation began. "No, Lily was *not* my girlfriend. She told you that?"

"She told several people," I confirmed.

"And now she's dead?"

"I'm afraid so."

He sagged back against the wall behind him. "I can hardly believe it."

"If Lila wasn't your girlfriend, what was the nature of your relationship?" I asked.

"I wouldn't call it a relationship." Abruptly Linc straightened. "Lily and I met at a bar a couple of months ago. We had a few drinks, spent a little time together . . ."

"How much time?"

"Two weeks, no more than that. She lived in an odd little house behind a big gate. The place was in the middle of a forest. And it was falling down around her ears. Going there gave me the willies. It was like visiting the witch's cottage in a Grimms' fairy tale."

"Is that why you stopped seeing her?" I was guessing that he'd been the one to end the relationship—or if he hadn't, he'd still remember it that way.

"Nah, that wasn't it. Lily was just too intense for me. Everything was guarded with her. She never said a single word without thinking about it first. Me, I'm more of a free spirit. I like to take things as they come. Life's too short to sweat the small stuff. And that wasn't her style at all."

"Was there anything inside the cottage—one of her possessions maybe—that Lila seemed particularly concerned about?"

"Not that I can think of." Linc was back to looking baffled. "Why?"

"I was wondering whether the person who killed her might have been looking for something."

"I wouldn't know about that." He stopped and frowned. Something had occurred to him. Linc didn't appear to be the brightest bulb. I figured I'd better grab the thought before he lost it again.

"What?" I asked.

"A couple times when I was with Lily, she got these phone calls. She'd look down at the number, drop whatever she was doing, and say, 'I have to take this.' Then she'd go into another room and shut the door. Like she wanted to make sure that I didn't hear what she was saying."

"Did you ask her about it?"

"No way. Why would I want to do that? It's not as if she was my *girlfriend* or anything. If Lily wanted to keep secrets, it was none of my business. Just like what I was up to on the side was none of hers. Plenty of fish in the sea, you know what I mean?"

Linc winked at me then. He actually winked. Was there a woman in the world who would find that juxtaposition endearing? I sincerely hoped not.

"Detective Hronis is the man in charge of the investigation into Lila's death," I said. "If you think of anything else, you should give him a call."

Maybe that would earn me some brownie points with the police, I thought.

"That's not going to happen," Linc told me. "But if you want to give me your number, I'll call you instead."

There I was, stuck between a rock and a hard place. On one

hand, I had no desire to give Linc my phone number. On the other, he might realize after I'd gone that he actually did know something useful.

Before I could think too much about the wisdom of the impulse, I scribbled the number down on a piece of paper and pushed it across the counter. Linc looked at it, then slipped it into his grimy pocket.

"You'll be hearing from me, Melanie Travis," he called after me as I let myself out.

I left New Canaan and drove straight to Graceland Nursery School to pick up Kevin. He wiggled back and forth as I was buckling him in his car seat.

"Where are we going now?" he asked. "Time to get a Christmas tree?"

I walked around the Volvo and slid into the driver's seat. "No, that's tomorrow."

"That's what you said yesterday." He pouted.

"No, that's what *you* said yesterday."

"I'm confused," Kev told me.

"So am I," I admitted. But it wasn't just Christmas that had my head spinning. For me, it was more of a cosmic "I have no idea what to do next" kind of thing.

I glanced back at him over my shoulder. "But you know who's a good person to talk to when you're confused?"

"Santa Claus?" Kev squealed happily.

"No. Aunt Peg."

"Oh." He slumped in his seat.

"She has puppies," I reminded him. "I bet she'll let you play with them."

He perked up a bit at that. "Puppies with funny names. Are they Poodles?"

"No, these three look like Australian Shepherds."

"Shepherds." Kevin turned the word over in his mind. "There were shepherds in the manger when Jesus was born."

I thought about explaining the difference. I truly did. But there was traffic on the Merritt Parkway, and I needed to keep my eyes on the road. So instead I said, "These will be just the same."

"Cool beans," Kev replied.

I'd called ahead, and Aunt Peg was expecting us. In fact, the front door to her house was open before we were even halfway down the driveway. There was an enormous pine cone- and cranberry-covered wreath on her door, but I noted that she had yet to rehang the Christmas stocking that had been on her mailbox.

Five Standard Poodles came spilling down the outside steps to greet us. Once I'd gotten Kevin out of the car, we took a minute to return their enthusiastic greeting. Still, it hardly took us any time to reach the house.

That wasn't fast enough for Aunt Peg, who was radiating impatience. She stood in the doorway with her arms crossed over her chest and her sneaker-clad foot tapping on the threshold. When we all reached the porch, Aunt Peg quickly ushered the Poodles inside the house, then turned to confront me.

"So," she said with relish, "I hear you almost got yourself arrested this morning."

"Shush!" I looked around for Kevin. Luckily, he'd followed the Poodles down the hallway. It looked as though the gang was heading toward the kitchen, where the puppies were stashed. "If you tell Kevin, he'll tell Sam."

"Meaning you don't intend to?"

"I'll own up to it eventually," I said, shrugging out of my coat. "I just want to make sure the incident has the right spin when he hears about it. Let's get Kev settled with the puppies. Then we can talk."

Kevin had shed his outerwear as he'd trotted down the hallway. I followed behind and gathered everything up. When

Aunt Peg and I reached the kitchen, my son was pressed against the baby gate that barred the doorway.

"How come they can't come out?" he asked.

"They're just babies, so it's safer to keep them confined," Aunt Peg told him. "But we can go in." She slipped her hands beneath his armpits and hoisted him over the waist-high gate. "Now sit down on the floor and give them a call."

The blue puppy was curled up, asleep, on a sheepskin mat. The two black males were wrestling over a stuffed toy. But when Kevin clapped his hands, all three fuzzy puppies came galloping across the floor.

The trio had grown and changed, even in the two days since I'd last seen them. The puppies were steadier on their feet now, and they liked to hear themselves bark. Their tiny ears flapped up and down as they ran. Kev giggled with delight as all three Aussies tried to climb up in his lap at the same time.

"Enjoy yourself," Aunt Peg told him. "Your mother and I are going to chat for a few minutes. While we're doing that, see if you can guess which name goes with which puppy."

She poured me a cup of instant coffee. Usually, I have to make my own, so I took that as a sign of her eagerness for updates. There was a plate of brownies on the counter, along with a mug of Earl Grey tea. Busy with the puppies, Kevin didn't even notice the sweets. I figured that meant we could speak with privacy.

I grabbed my coffee and the brownies and sat down at the kitchen table. Aunt Peg brought her tea and joined me.

"You've been talking to Claire," I said, nabbing a brownie from the plate between us.

"Of course I've been talking to Claire," she replied. "Somebody has to keep me apprised of what's going on. It sounds as though the two of you had quite an adventure."

"Not on purpose. The plan was to slip in and out before anyone noticed we were there."

"You can't seriously have believed that would be possible."

The snort that accompanied that statement was rather rude. "Josie Mannerly is a famous recluse, with enough money to ensure that people have to respect her wish for privacy. If anyone could come and go from that estate on a whim, the tabloids would be all over her. Especially now, after what happened there."

"You're right." I sighed. "It was an ill-conceived idea from the start. But Claire was determined and I didn't want her to go by herself."

"So she told me. She seemed to think that you should be absolved of blame. I'm withholding judgment myself." Aunt Peg paused for a large bite of her brownie. "Tell me everything. Start with the caretaker who waylaid you."

Despite her request, I couldn't start there. If I wanted the narrative to make sense, I had to backtrack. Aunt Peg had spoken with Claire about the morning's events, but she didn't know about the conversations I'd had the day before with Karen Clauson and Chris Sanchez. So I summarized those first. Then I jumped ahead to our encounter with Hank Peebles.

"I can understand why Lila was afraid of him," I said. "I know he scared the crap out of me."

"Do you suppose Karen Clauson was correct and there's something he wants inside that gatehouse?"

"Maybe." I stopped and frowned. "But apparently, he has a key to the place. So if he wanted to conduct a search, what would prevent him from entering anytime he wished?"

"Maybe the object he's after is new," Aunt Peg mused. "Or maybe he just found out about it. Perhaps he used the key to let himself inside the cottage the other day, not realizing that Lila was home at the time."

I nodded slowly. "You could be onto something. Because Lila's car was in the shop for repairs. So Peebles could have seen that it was gone, and figured he had free access to do whatever he wanted."

"Thereby precipitating the confrontation that led to her death," Aunt Peg said triumphantly.

I picked at my brownie. Chewy and oozing with chocolate, it tasted homemade, even though I knew it came from a bakery downtown.

"Except that Lila was shot," I pointed out. "If Peebles thought the cottage was empty, why would he have brought a gun with him?"

"Maybe that was Lila's gun." Aunt Peg played devil's advocate. "Maybe she accosted him, and he disarmed her. Have the police found the weapon that was used to kill her?"

I rolled my eyes until she got the message.

"You mean to tell me that even after your friendly chat this morning, Detective Hronis isn't keeping you informed of new developments?"

"I wouldn't exactly characterize our talk as friendly," I told her. "It was more like the good detective was advising me to stay out of his way."

"Oh pish. That's what the authorities always say. You know they don't mean it."

Earlier in the year, Aunt Peg had struck up a friendship with a detective from the Stamford Police Department. It had been the highlight of her summer. The two of them had become so chummy that she'd even added Detective Sturgill to her Christmas card list.

I didn't seem to have the same kind of luck with the police.

"They do mean it," I said.

She gave me a knowing smile. "Then it's a good thing you've never been particularly adept at following directions."

Chapter 10

"Hey!" Kevin suddenly looked up at us. "Nobody told me there were brownies."

"You didn't ask, you silly boy. Of course there are brownies," Aunt Peg said. "But if you want one, you have to come and join us at the table."

Kev's gaze dropped. Both male puppies were asleep in his lap. The blue girl was chewing on the tip of his shoe. He was clearly undecided. She'd given him a tough choice. "But the puppies are down here."

"It's a dilemma, isn't it?" she agreed. "Why don't you stay there and I'll pack a brownie for you to take with you when you leave?"

"Yes, please."

I was marveling at my son's polite answer when one of the black boys lifted his head and nipped at Kevin's finger. He giggled and pulled his hand away. Then he reached back and scratched under the puppy's chin. In the space of seconds, Kev had forgotten all about us.

"More for me," Aunt Peg said happily. She slid another

brownie onto her napkin. "Now go on. Surely that can't be all you've accomplished since the last time we saw each other."

"It isn't. I also had a chat this morning with Lila's supposed boyfriend."

"Supposed?" She glanced up. "What does that mean?"

"It means that he didn't think he was in a relationship with her. Linc Landry admitted to knowing Lila but said they'd just had a quick fling."

"He would say that, wouldn't he? The woman is dead. If he has something to hide, it only makes sense that he would want to disassociate himself from her."

"Linc was already having trouble remembering who she was before I told him that she'd been killed," I told her.

Aunt Peg looked surprised. "You mean he didn't know?"

"Apparently not."

"That's ridiculous. New Canaan is a small town. A murder there would be big news. I think your Mr. Landry was lying to you. Maybe he killed Lila, and this was his way of deflecting attention away from himself."

"He did say something else that was interesting."

"It's about time," Aunt Peg muttered under her breath.

I ignored that and pressed on. "Sometimes when they were together, Lila would get phone calls that were important enough for her to immediately stop what she was doing and go in another room to talk."

"Maybe she had a lover," Aunt Peg mused.

"She did," I pointed out. "Linc. And he was standing right there. Maybe she was talking to Josephine Mannerly. Do you think that's a possibility?"

The idea made her smile. "All I know is that if Josie were to call me out of the blue, I would drop everything to talk to her too."

"Josie was Lila's landlady," I said. "Maybe they had stuff to discuss."

"Like overdue rent?" Aunt Peg was skeptical.

"I was thinking more like why that creepy Hank Peebles was always hanging around the gatehouse." I grabbed a second brownie. Or possibly a third. It was hard to talk and keep count at the same time. "Or maybe the mystery caller was someone from Lila's dubious past."

"Ah, yes." Aunt Peg nodded. "Claire finally got around to mentioning that to me. That was quite a tantalizing tidbit for her to keep tucked away, don't you think?"

"I gather she felt we would think less of her if we knew she'd taken on a client with a questionable history."

"Less than if she took on a client who got herself killed?" She lifted a brow. "That's hard to credit."

"I'm ready for my brownie now," Kevin announced. The puppies had gone to sleep on the sheepskin bed. All three had cuddled together to form a small mound. "Is it time to go?"

"Just about," I told him.

"Not so fast." Aunt Peg pushed back her chair and stood. "You were going to guess the puppies' names, remember?"

"I know their names." Kev sounded very pleased with himself. "They're Black, Blue, and Ditto."

"Yes, but which is which? That's the hard part."

"Blue is the blue puppy," Kev told her. "Black is whichever one of the others comes over first. Then the last one is Ditto."

"That makes perfect sense to me," I said with a laugh.

Aunt Peg couldn't disagree. As she held out her hand, she looked like she wanted to laugh too. "Here, young man. You've earned yourself a brownie."

Saturday morning arrived faster than I'd anticipated. That probably had something to do with the fact that Kevin was out of bed and dressed before I even had my eyes open. And once he was up, that meant all the creatures in the house would be stirring too. As well as my husband and our older son. Everybody couldn't wait to go tramping around a forest on a cold winter day.

I was steaming in a hot shower when Sam opened the bathroom door. "Breakfast is on the table," he said.

I took that as my cue to turn off the stream of water. "What are we having?"

"Cereal. Lots of cereal. More cereal that you can imagine."

I peeked out from behind the shower curtain. Sam tossed me a towel. There was only one thing I could say next. "What did Kevin do now?"

"He decided to hurry us along by feeding the dogs himself. He also decided they must be tired of eating kibble. So he made them eight bowls of cereal. I got to the kitchen just in time to keep him from handing them out."

"Eight?" I wrapped the towel around me and stepped out of the shower. "Kev knows we only have six dogs."

Sam bit back a grin. "He thought Bud looked hungry, so he made him extra servings."

That little mutt was already shaped like a football. He needed fewer helpings, not additional ones. But Bud was a master at manipulation.

"Bud always looks hungry," I said.

"Kev and I had that conversation," Sam told me. "And we gave the dogs their kibble. Now all we have to do is eat eight bowls of cereal."

"And chop down a Christmas tree," I mentioned.

"Right," said Sam. "That's the fun part. Hurry up."

As he disappeared, I stared after him with a smile on my face. Was there a man in the world who didn't flex his muscles, suck in his gut, and grin with glee when he was handed a chain saw? If so, I wasn't married to him.

Haney's Holiday Home was a Christmas tree farm in northwest Wilton. Situated on ten acres of wooded land, it had been a popular holiday destination for decades, until its elderly owner died and the place was allowed to fall into disrepair. My brother, Frank, and my ex-husband, Bob, who also co-owned a bistro in Stamford, had purchased the property the previous December.

Then it had been a scramble to get the business up and running in time for Christmas. All able-bodied family members had found themselves pressed into service—either to help make repairs or serve as salespeople. This year Frank had been able to plan ahead and he'd hired college students to fill in for the season. After that, all Frank and Bob had had to do was open their doors and customers had come flooding back.

Sam parked his SUV in front of the clapboard office building. I hadn't been back to the tree farm in nearly a year. I could see that there had been additional improvements made in the meantime.

The outside of the structure was freshly painted and the parking lot had been resurfaced. A spruce wreath decorated with silver bells and sprigs of holly was hanging on the office door. Red and white ribbons were twined in a candy cane pattern around the banister that led to the porch. The place looked festive and inviting, and Kevin was already running on ahead to dash up the steps.

"I miss the snow." Davey came over and stood next to me. "Last year when we were here, the snow was up to my knees."

Last year we'd found a dead body half buried in the snow, I thought. I didn't miss anything about that.

"Snow's on the way," said Sam. "It won't be long now. We'll have six inches on the ground before Christmas."

Kev heard that. He'd been reaching for the doorknob, but now he spun around. "Promise?"

"Uh-oh," I said under my breath.

"Promise," Sam agreed.

I punched him in the arm. "What are you going to do if you're wrong?"

"That's easy." He followed his son up the steps. "I'll just blame the weather on you."

It took us half the morning to find the perfect Christmas tree. The cultivated forest around us had plenty of good options. But Davey and Kevin both wanted to have the deciding vote on which tree we brought home, and the two boys couldn't agree on which one to choose.

While they argued over the merits of height versus symmetry of branches, I just stood in the middle of the woods and inhaled deeply. All I wanted was a Christmas tree that smelled great. Fortunately, that part was easy.

It took another hour to cut the tall Douglas fir down, then get it back to the SUV. If the boys hadn't been helping, Sam and I probably could have accomplished those tasks in half the time. Not that it mattered. We had the rest of the day to get the tree up and decorated. It felt great just to kick back and enjoy family time for a change.

When we arrived home, the dogs met us at the door. It wasn't every day we brought a tree inside the house, and apparently, that was cause for canine mayhem.

"I know you remember this," I told Faith. The oldest and the wisest of the Poodles, she was the first to calm down. Tar, Augie, and Bud were still leaping and yapping and otherwise making fools of themselves. "Tell them everything is all right. This is only temporary."

Faith gave me a reproachful look. Just because she remembered didn't mean she thought a tree belonged in her living room.

While Sam and the boys got the Christmas tree set up in its stand, I put on holiday music and poured eggnog for everybody. I added a little kick to Sam's and mine.

That was a good thing, because when I returned to the living room the Poodles were adding to the party by zooming around the room. They bounced from couch to chairs, then back to the floor before racing circles around the tree. Kevin was giggling uncontrollably. He was also slipping Bud and Tar slivers of candy cane when he thought no one was looking.

I started unpacking the ornaments. Sam and Davey untangled the lights and strung them around the tree. Kevin was in charge of tinsel. The boys had chosen a towering Douglas fir, so it took us a while to decorate every inch. Finally everything was in place.

We all stood back to admire the effect.

"Wow," said Kevin.

Davey reached over to ruffle his brother's hair. "Now Santa Claus will know just where to find you. This tree is so big, I bet it's already on his radar."

Kev turned to him with wide eyes. "Do you think so?"

I didn't hear Davey's answer, because my cell phone began to ring. I'd left it in my bedroom earlier, so I had to make a mad dash for the stairs. Faith came racing behind me. She loved to talk on the phone, especially if Aunt Peg was calling.

I was slightly winded by the time I snatched the phone off the dresser and sank down on the bed. Faith jumped up beside me. I glanced at the screen, then held the device to my ear. Once again, it was Claire.

"You cost me a client," she said without preamble.

"Hi, Claire. Wait . . . *what*?" Abruptly my good mood vanished. "What did you say?"

"You cost me a client," she repeated slowly. "Karen Clauson. I just got off the phone with her. She's furious."

I reached over and pulled Faith into my lap. Dogs are a surefire stress reliever when things go wrong. And suddenly it sounded as though something had gone very wrong. I tangled my fingers in the Poodle's long ear hair.

"Claire, start at the beginning, please. Tell me what happened."

"I set it up so that you and Karen could meet."

"Yes, you did," I agreed. "And she and I had a perfectly pleasant conversation. She didn't seem unhappy when I left."

"Apparently, that was before she realized you were going to go running to the police with the information she gave you."

"Oh," I said. "Right."

In the spirit of sharing—and to take the sting out of the fact that Claire and I had just been discovered somewhere we definitely didn't belong—I'd related to Detective Hronis what Karen had said about the Mannerly estate caretaker. I'd given him Karen's name. I'd even confirmed that she was George Clauson's wife.

But wait a minute, I thought. What was wrong with that?

"That detective you talked to stopped by her house," said Claire. "This morning, on a Saturday. George was there. And her kids. And apparently a couple of the kids' friends. When a policeman parked right out front and marched into her house as if she'd done something wrong."

"But she hadn't done anything wrong," I sputtered. "He just needed to talk to her. He probably wanted to confirm what I'd told him."

"Yeah, well, I guess that wasn't how it looked to the neighbors. Then George got upset because he hadn't known Karen had previously talked to the police . . . and was she hiding things from him? And her kids got upset when they heard that someone their parents knew had been murdered." Claire stopped and sighed. "You can probably imagine how things snowballed from there."

"It was all a misunderstanding," I said. "Lots of people talk to the police about stuff, and nobody gets upset about it."

"No, Melanie, lots of people do not get involved with the police," Claire said firmly. "*You do*. And the rest of us probably would get upset about it, except that by now you've done it so many times that we just figure, 'What's the point?'"

I bit my lip between my teeth. My eyes blinked rapidly.

Suddenly it felt as though I'd been punched in the gut. That wasn't fair. Claire was the one who'd called me when she found Lila. She had asked me to become involved.

Faith sensed my change in mood. She snuggled her warm body closer to mine and laid her head down across my legs. But right now, even she couldn't make me feel better.

"So even though Karen was one of my oldest and best clients," Claire continued, "she has now severed her relationship with me."

"She can't do that," I said hotly.

"Of course she can. Karen is free to take her party planning business anywhere she wants to."

"She's the one who introduced you to Lila Moran. If it wasn't for Karen, you and I wouldn't even be mixed up in this."

"Good point." Claire sounded resigned. "And yet, I'm still fired."

"You can't be fired," I said. "It's not right. I'm going to fix this."

"Don't you dare call Karen. It will only make things worse."

"How can they be worse? You already lost her business. I won't call. I'll go see Karen in person. We'll have another friendly conversation. I'll remind her about all the great parties you've thrown for her. I'll tell her none of this is your fault. Don't worry, I'll get things smoothed over. You'll see."

She hung up without answering.

Chapter 11

Okay, so maybe I had an ulterior motive.

Of course I wanted to help Claire win back Karen's account. I hated being the cause of her lost business. But I also hadn't forgotten that Karen had promised to ask her husband about Lila Moran's résumé and the information about her past it might contain. Maybe I was being wildly optimistic, but this seemed like an opportunity to kill two birds with one stone.

Or then again, maybe not.

Karen wasn't amused when I texted her. Her reply came back quickly. **Don't contact me again.**

Fat chance of that, I thought. We needed to talk.

So that's what I told her. And that I was sorry for what had happened. I offered to come by and apologize in person.

Karen shot that idea down in a hurry.

Please just let me explain, I texted back.

Faith and I stared at the phone for two full minutes, waiting for a reply. Finally it chirped in my hand.

Not here. Meet me at West Beach in twenty minutes.

I picked Faith up and set her aside on the bed. "Sorry," I told the big Poodle. "I have to go."

West Beach was at the upper edge of the Shippan Point peninsula. On a Saturday before Christmas, it would take me at least twenty minutes just to drive there, which meant I was already in a hurry. Plus, it was a beach. So I definitely needed some warm clothing.

I explained to Sam where I was going while I pulled on boots and a coat in the front hall. I promised to be back soon. I stuffed some gloves in my pocket. Sam plopped a hat on my head and told me he'd entertain the kids with bloodthirsty video games while I was gone. I was pretty sure he was kidding about that.

Not surprisingly for a late afternoon in December, the beach at the park was nearly deserted. Long Island Sound looked gray and choppy. The sky above it was opaque. It wasn't hard to find Karen. She was sitting on a slatted bench, waiting for me.

Karen was bundled up against the weather, just like I was. Her puffy down coat covered her from neck to lower thigh, and her blond hair was tucked into a faux fur hat that was pulled low over her ears. Her hands were jammed in her pockets. She stood up as I approached.

"I'll give you five minutes," she said, heading across the sand to the water's edge. "Let's walk."

This close to the winter solstice, the sun went down early in Connecticut. Dusk was almost already upon us. My feet sank into the deep sand as I hurried to catch up. Karen had made it clear she wasn't going to wait.

"I'm sorry about what happened," I began. "I didn't realize you'd told me those things in confidence."

Not that that would have made a difference, I thought. But still.

Karen gave me a withering look. "George already talked to the detective at his office. It never occurred to me that the man would show up *at my house*, wanting to involve me in his investigation too."

"I'm sorry," I said again. I planned to keep repeating that until she accepted my apology. "But the important thing is that none of this is Claire's fault. If a mistake was made, I'm the one who made it. You shouldn't punish her for something I did."

"Claire isn't one of my children," Karen snapped. "She isn't being *punished*. She's simply having to learn that when you behave badly, your decisions have consequences."

"But that's the point. Claire did nothing wrong."

We'd reached the water. Froth-tipped waves were lapping against the shore. The sand was firmer here, and Karen followed a receding wave out. When a new ripple of water approached, she kicked a spray into the air.

"Claire asked me to talk to you," she said, without turning around. "She should have warned me that it might be a problem. Now George is furious, and that means I'm the one who will have to make amends. It was bad enough that the woman who died was employed by his firm. But to have the scandal intrude upon his personal life, too, is truly beyond the pale."

"I understand that you're upset." Karen continued to stare out over the Sound, so I was talking to her back. "But a crime was committed. And the police need to solve it. The fact that Lila worked for James and Brant means that your husband was already peripherally involved in their investigation."

Karen still said nothing, so I kept talking. "When we spoke before, you said you'd look into Lila Moran's résumé. What did you find out?"

Her head whipped around. "Why should I do anything to help you now?"

I shrugged. There wasn't anything I could say to convince her. She would either decide to help me or not.

Karen's shoulders were stiff. Her posture radiated annoy-

254 / *Laurien Berenson*

ance. As she turned to head back across the beach to the parking lot, she said, "There was virtually nothing on Lila's résumé. So I guess the joke's on you. There were only a few current items that didn't even fill up the page."

"That doesn't make sense," I said.

Now it was Karen's turn to shrug. It made no difference to her whether I found her answer satisfactory or not.

We'd almost reached the sidewalk. The parking lot was just beyond. I was running out of time. "How did Lila get a good job at James and Brant without a decent résumé?"

Abruptly Karen stopped. "How would I know that?"

"Because I'm guessing you asked. You're probably as curious as I am."

"Someone pulled strings," she replied shortly. "A big client asked Mr. Brant to hire her, and he did. That's all I know. Are we finished?"

"Almost."

Karen tossed her head. *"What?"*

"Once you get over being angry, you're going to remember that Claire is the best event planner in Fairfield County. And a great way to make amends would be to throw your husband the best party ever. Think about it."

"You gave me a splendid idea the other day," Aunt Peg told me the next morning. She and I were sitting on the ground in her backyard, watching the three Aussie puppies tumble around in the grass. Yes, I know it was December. Coming outside hadn't been my decision.

"Much better footing for puppies than that slippery kitchen floor," Aunt Peg had told me. So out we'd gone.

She and I were supposed to be having a super secret conversation about family Christmas presents. At least that was the pretext under which she'd invited me over. But I'd spent the past ten minutes telling her about my meeting with Karen. And since I couldn't remember any ideas I'd had recently—splendid or otherwise—that would help with Christmas shopping, I suspected the subject was about to be changed again.

I was chilly sitting on the hard ground, but the three wavy-coated puppies were loving the freedom to explore the enclosed yard. They were blossoming under Aunt Peg's care, growing bigger, brighter, and more adventuresome every day. Little Blue was the most spirited of the three. She matched her brothers stride for stride as they romped around us. If Sam wasn't careful, he might find her coming home with me.

I realized I'd been daydreaming when Aunt Peg abruptly stopped speaking. I also realized that I'd missed something important. "I'm sorry. What did you say?"

"We were talking about Josie Mannerly," she informed me. *We were?*

"You wondered if Lila's mystery caller might have been her landlady. Later, that got me to thinking about whether it might be possible to talk to Josie again after all these years. It occurred to me that perhaps I should try giving her a call."

I was torn between horror and delight. "Aunt Peg, you didn't!"

She smiled. Like the cat who'd had the canary and swallowed it whole. "First I waffled about it a bit—because who would be so rude as to invade the privacy of a famous recluse? But then I decided to do some nosing around, just to see how easy it would be to find a phone number."

"And?"

"It turned out that Josephine Mannerly has a listing in the New Canaan phone book. When I saw that, there was nothing left for me to do but dial it."

"*And?*" I demanded, when she paused again to rachet up the suspense.

"Josie didn't answer the phone, but I left a message. And she returned my call."

"She didn't!" I shrieked.

Aunt Peg chuckled at my response. "I was every bit as surprised as you are. I'd imagine she doesn't get too many phone calls. The people she knew in her heyday would have moved on with their lives after Josie left the social scene and went into seclusion."

"Did she remember you?" I asked breathlessly.

"Quite possibly not. After all, I was only one of many young debs who admired her in those days—but she was polite enough not to say so. Instead, she laughed and said, 'Nobody has called me Josie for years. Decades. Oh, that brings back such memories!'" Aunt Peg grinned. "After that, she and I got along splendidly."

The two black puppies went racing by. They'd found a small stick, and each was holding one end. Blue had her eye on her two brothers. I suspected she'd be stealing their prize from them shortly.

"Did you ask Josie what she knew about Lila Moran? And why the woman was living in her gatehouse?"

"I did not," Aunt Peg replied.

I stared at her in disbelief.

"Even better. I wangled an invitation for the two of us to visit her. At Josie's convenience, of course. Once we're there, I suspect we'll be able to ferret out all sorts of information."

I sighed happily. "Aunt Peg, you're a marvel."

"Yes, I know."

"Did she mention when a visit might be convenient?"

"Didn't I tell you that part?" Aunt Peg's eyes were twinkling. She knew perfectly well she hadn't. "We're expected this afternoon at four, for tea."

*   *   *

I spent the next several hours debating what one should wear to drink tea with a former Debutante of the Decade in the manor house of her posh estate. Nothing in my previous experience had prepared me to be able to answer that question. Google was no help either.

In the end, I put on a navy blue wool dress and knee-high leather boots. The outfit made me look reasonably presentable. Plus, in the event that the furnace in the main house worked as poorly as the one in the cottage, at least I would be warm. Faith, who'd observed my several changes of attire, seemed to approve. That was good enough for me.

Sam and the boys were out Christmas shopping when Aunt Peg came by to pick me up. I handed out peanut butter biscuits to the Poodles and Bud, then advised the wily little mutt to behave himself while I was gone. The previous year he'd waited until our Christmas tree was fully decorated, then scaled its branches like a cat.

Aunt Peg liked to drive fast and she made quick work of the trip to New Canaan. I directed her up Forest Glen Lane and saw her eyes widen as we continued along the tall wall that bordered the estate for a quarter mile before we arrived at the gate. Aunt Peg had the code—why was I not surprised?—and the majestic, iron-spiked barrier drew open before us.

When we came to the gatehouse, she braked the minivan and had a look. "That looks like the kind of place where something dire should have happened," she decided. "I don't think I've ever seen a gloomier home. It's a wonder anyone wanted to live in it at all."

"I'll be interested to hear how that came about," I agreed. "Let's hope Josephine Mannerly is in a chatty mood."

The driveway continued to wind its way through the dense forest. We'd driven for several more minutes before we suddenly emerged from the trees and a sweeping vista opened up before us.

A vast gently rolling lawn led to an enormous white stone mansion. Gleaming softly in the winter sunlight, the house was three stories tall. It had a mansard roof and an elegant double staircase that led to a wide front portico. There were more windows than I could count in the time it took us to approach.

"Wow," I said. "That's impressive. If I lived here, maybe I wouldn't want to leave either."

"I would," Aunt Peg retorted. "If only because leaving would offer me the pleasure of being able to return."

We climbed the steps to the front door and rang the doorbell. Moments later, the heavy door was opened by a maid in a severe black dress. She glanced at both of us briefly before her gaze settled on Aunt Peg.

"You must be Margaret Turnbull," she said. "Ms. Mannerly is expecting you. Please come inside."

"Margaret?" I said under my breath as we shed our coats. Nobody ever called Aunt Peg *Margaret*.

"A little formality seemed appropriate under the circumstances. Now mind your manners, or you'll make me wish I'd left you home."

That was enough to shut me up. We followed the maid down a spacious center hallway. When we reached the second set of double doors, the woman paused, her hands on the doorknobs.

"Ms. Mannerly has a degenerative condition. She will not stand to greet you. Instead she will expect you to cross the room and approach her. There are two chairs opposite her in front of the fireplace. Please make yourselves comfortable there."

The room Aunt Peg and I entered was a high-ceilinged library. Two of the walls were lined with bookshelves, and the floor was covered by a Savonnerie rug woven in vibrant jewel tones. Tall windows in the far wall provided a spectacular view of the panoramic park outside.

Josephine Mannerly was seated in an upholstered chair that faced the door. She had a book in her lap, but she carefully removed her reading glasses, then looked up and smiled as we approached. I knew she was just a few years older than Aunt Peg, but she appeared to be a much older woman.

Her white hair was gathered back off her face behind a wide headband, and her vividly colored Pucci dress would have been considered fashionable in the 1960s. Her legs, clad in support hose, were neatly crossed at the ankle. Josephine had a pale, heavily lined, face and clear blue eyes. Her hand trembled slightly as she extended it to Aunt Peg.

"You'll pardon me if I don't get up," she said. "Mildred will have explained why. You must be Margaret. Despite our snippet of shared history, you don't look familiar. After all these years, I dare say you probably wouldn't have recognized me either."

"Your eyes are exactly the same as I remember them," Aunt Peg replied diplomatically. "Didn't a society columnist once say they were the shade of a summer bluebird on the wing?"

"Oh my." Josephine laughed. "Your memory exceeds mine. Although if someone actually did say that, perhaps it's better off forgotten. Who is this young woman?"

"I'd like to introduce you to my niece, Melanie."

I stepped forward and shook her hand. It felt dry and weightless in mine. "I'm very pleased to meet you," I said.

"Yes, well, we'll see about that, won't we? Have a seat, both of you. Mildred will be in shortly with refreshments."

Josephine set her book and glasses down on a nearby table. She waited until we were seated before her gaze settled on Aunt Peg. "I agreed to see you because I was curious. And because for the first time in my very long life, I now find my name attached to a source of scandal. You were maddeningly indirect about your intentions on the phone. I suppose that was intentional—and it obviously worked, because here you are."

Aunt Peg nodded. She could probably be forgiven for looking rather pleased with herself.

"I don't see many people, and I don't suffer fools lightly," Josephine continued. "So let's get down to brass tacks. I'd like to hear what sort of information you think I might possess. And perhaps more importantly—should I choose to share what I know—what you intend to do with what I tell you."

Chapter 12

There was a discreet knock on the door. Mildred entered the room, pushing a wooden trolley cart holding our tea. She set out delicate china cups and saucers on a low table between our chairs. A plate of wafer-thin vanilla cookies followed. The tea pot was large and looked heavy. It was made of Edwardian silver and there were teaspoons to match.

"I'll pour," Aunt Peg offered as Josephine dismissed the maid.

Mildred withdrew and we addressed ourselves to the food. The tea was Earl Grey, Aunt Peg's favorite. I preferred coffee, but I was willing to make do, especially since the vanilla cookies were divine.

After a minute had passed, Josephine looked up from her tea. "I'm waiting," she said pointedly.

"I was just gathering my thoughts," Aunt Peg said. She set down her teacup. "We've come today because a member of my extended family was acquainted with your tenant, Lila Moran. Claire had the misfortune to be the one who discovered her body and called the police. That chain of events led to Melanie's subsequent involvement in the investigation."

"Oh?" Josephine lifted a brow delicately. She turned in my direction. "I wasn't aware that you were a policewoman."

I swallowed a gulp of very hot tea. "I'm not. But Claire called me that morning. She asked me to come to your gatehouse for moral support."

"And yet your involvement lingers?"

"Melanie has a talent for solving mysteries," Aunt Peg told her.

Josephine's lips pursed. She did not look impressed. "What an unusual gift."

"I like asking questions," I said. "And taking bits of information—clues, you might call them—and weaving them together to form a pattern that tells a story."

"Whether or not you are talented at what you do remains to be seen," Josephine replied. "Ask your questions, and we will see if I choose to answer them."

All righty then. She'd gotten straight to the point. I would do the same.

"The woman who was living in your gatehouse was not who she said she was. There is no information about Lila Moran's past life that goes back more than five years. Before that, she appeared not to exist."

I watched the older woman's face as I spoke. Her composure never wavered. I'd expected the news to surprise her. Instead, Josephine Mannerly surprised me.

"You already knew that," I said.

"Of course I did," she replied calmly. "I knew everything about Lila. Otherwise she never would have been allowed on my property."

Aunt Peg and I shared a startled look.

"How did Lila come to be living in your gatehouse?" she asked.

"That's a long story. Much of it is old history now."

"I like old history," I said.

"I *lived* old history," Aunt Peg added drily.

"So you wish me to continue?"

Aunt Peg and I both nodded.

"Many years ago, when I was young, I had a suitor. This was before your time, Melanie, but Margaret will understand what I'm saying. In those days, very few women thought about having a career. We were expected to find a husband and start a family. That was what my parents wanted for me. It was what girls of my set aspired to."

Thank goodness times had changed, I thought.

"I met a man named William Schiff. He was five years older than me, very handsome, and terribly sophisticated." Josephine paused for a private smile. "Those things mattered to me. What mattered to my mother was that he came from a good family, had an Ivy League education, and was well employed in his father's business. All the pieces seemed to fit together perfectly. I thought we were a match made in heaven."

"It sounds as though things didn't turn out that way," I said.

"No, they did not. What I didn't know was that Billy was being pressured by his parents to court me. They wanted the prestige—and, of course, the money—that would come from having their son marry Joshua Mannerly's daughter."

"That could have been a problem with many of your suitors," Aunt Peg mentioned.

"Yes, although usually I was able to ferret out such ulterior motives. But with Billy, it was different. I fell head over heels in love."

"What happened?" I asked.

"Once we were engaged, Billy became moody and distant. I still had stars in my eyes, however. I thought everything would be fine once we were married. That was what I'd been brought up to believe."

"But you didn't get married, did you?" said Aunt Peg.

"No. A week before the wedding, Billy broke off our engagement. One day I thought we were blissfully happy. The next, everything I'd imagined we had together was gone. Billy asked for the ring back. It had been in his family for generations. For some reason, at the time that seemed like the worst blow of all."

"I remember there was a broken engagement." Aunt Peg thought back. "But I thought you were the one who ended it?"

"That was the story we told everyone. My mother insisted upon it. She sat Billy's father down and told him how things were going to be, and Mr. Schiff didn't dare say no."

Josephine hadn't been kidding when she said it was a long story. It seemed to me that we were still several decades away from Lila Moran and the mysterious gaps in her life. On the other hand, the vanilla wafers were superb. I helped myself to another and settled back in my chair.

"I was very young, and very naive, in those days," Josephine said.

"We all were," Aunt Peg agreed.

"I pictured myself as the spurned heroine in one of the romance novels I loved to read. Billy had been my knight in shining armor—or so I thought. I waited for him to come riding back to me on a white horse."

Good luck with that, I thought.

"A year later, Billy married someone else. A girl who had neither the class nor the connections that I possessed. By that time, my mother had died and I was on my own. I had come into my inheritance, but my family was gone. I was all alone. Up until that point, I had led rather a sheltered life. I wasn't accustomed to making my own decisions. And there was no one left who might have provided me with proper guidance."

"There hadn't been any other suitors?" Aunt Peg asked.

"Of course there were." The older woman waved a hand dismissively. "There were plenty of men who professed to be interested in me. But I'd grown cynical, and I never gave them a chance. I didn't have to, you see. By then I'd realized that I didn't need a man to take care of me."

"What does this have to do with Lila Moran?" I asked.

Aunt Peg shot me an annoyed look as Josephine frowned.

"I told you this was going to be a long story," she said. "You must let me tell it my way. Either that or you can finish your tea and go home."

"Yes, ma'am," I replied meekly. It looked as though we were going to be here awhile.

"Looking back now it seems foolish, but even after Billy married I kept tabs on what he was doing. I knew about his life with his new wife and their young daughter. I knew when his father died, and how Billy stepped up to take over the family business in his stead."

Josephine abruptly stopped speaking. She sipped her tea, then picked up a cookie and absently broke it into small pieces before setting it aside. This time I knew better than to try to hurry her along.

"Mind you, I'm not proud of what happened next," she said when she finally spoke. "In my own defense, I can only plead the arrogance of youth. Just when Billy thought he had everything—a successful career, a lovely child, and a wife who was wearing a ring that I thought belonged on *my* finger—I set about quite methodically to ruin him."

I sucked in a breath and slowly let it out. For a moment, the silence in the room was so complete that I could hear the ticking of a grandfather clock by the window.

"I assume you mean financially," Aunt Peg said.

"Of course that's what I mean," Josephine snapped. In her case, confession didn't appear to be good for the soul. "That was the instrument I had at my disposal. I put my father's money to use in aid of my own selfish cause. What I did was wrong, but I'm not going to apologize for it. I was headstrong and foolish, and I lashed out. It was a poor decision, but it was one I made years ago."

"Let me guess," Aunt Peg ventured. "Was Lila Moran Billy Schiff's daughter?"

"You're quite smart, aren't you?" Josephine regarded her with admiration. "Yes, that's exactly it."

"I still don't get it," I said. "How did Lila end up here?"

"I suspect that all these years later, Josephine set out to make amends," Aunt Peg told me.

The older woman nodded, then continued her story. "After Billy lost his company, he began to drink. After alcohol, he turned to drugs. Things spiraled downward from there. Billy and his wife were divorced, so he lost his family too. My revenge was complete and I expected to feel satisfaction—but instead my intemperate actions led only to a crushing sense of remorse."

"I should hope so," I muttered. Aunt Peg kicked me under the table.

I jumped slightly in my seat as Josephine trained a beady gaze on me. "Have you never made a mistake?" she demanded.

"I've made many," I admitted. "Although not one of that magnitude."

"Then you're lucky," she shot back. "But you're still young. It may yet happen."

I hoped not. I couldn't imagine wanting to manipulate someone else's life like that.

"Billy's wife married two more times," Josephine said. "Lila had a difficult upbringing. She was arrested for the first time when she was still in high school. Shoplifting became petty theft, then grand theft. She seemed to have a hard time keeping her hands off of other people's possessions. Eventually she served a year in jail. When she got out, her past missteps had made her virtually unemployable."

"That would have been five years ago," I guessed.

"Precisely. At that point I decided to step in and see if I could use my considerable resources to turn things around for her. Lila had already built herself a new identity by the time I contacted her. That sort of subterfuge certainly wouldn't have been *my* idea, though it did smooth things along. After that, I made sure that Lila always had a decent job and a place to live. It hasn't been easy. There have been several setbacks along the way, but I've done my best to keep nudging her in the right direction."

"So eventually you found her a job nearby and moved her into your gatehouse."

"I'm not as young as I used to be," Josephine pointed out unnecessarily. "Nor as healthy. After Lila had been let go from her previous place of employment, I decided it made sense to put her somewhere close, where I could keep an eye on her. I thought it would be easier to keep her out of trouble that way."

"And yet this is where she ended up dead," Aunt Peg pointed out.

Josephine nodded but didn't reply.

"Do you have any thoughts about that?" I prompted.

"I most certainly do not," she said sharply. "Peebles, the man who looks after the estate, has been in contact with the local police. He assures me they are doing everything they can to solve this horrible crime."

"But you haven't spoken to them?"

"No, of course not. Why would I do that? Peebles is handling everything. That's his job."

"Mr. Peebles was also supposed to be taking care of Lila's cottage," I mentioned.

"Yes. What of it?"

"When was the last time you saw the place?" Aunt Peg asked. "It looks as though it was falling down around her ears."

"That can't be right." Josephine stared at the two of us.

"I'm afraid it is," I told her. "A friend of Lila's told me she was afraid of your caretaker."

"Afraid? That's preposterous. Peebles wouldn't hurt a fly."

"I also heard that he wanted something from Lila," I said. "Do you have any idea what that might have been?"

"None whatsoever," Josephine stated firmly. "Peebles has been with me a long time. He thinks he knows what's best for me. Perhaps that leads him to be a bit overprotective when it comes to looking out for my interests."

"Territorial sounds more like it," Aunt Peg muttered.

"The gatehouse had been empty for years. After all, it's not as though I have many visitors. But Peebles assured me that he'd fixed the place up properly before Lila moved in. I don't know how it could be in such a state of disrepair."

It sounded as though Peebles was often quick to assure the older woman that all was well. I wondered how often Josephine had checked to see whether or not he was telling her the truth. When I asked her that, she stiffened in her seat. Intrusive as our earlier questions had been, this time I'd gone too far.

"Peebles isn't just an employee. He's also a relative. Distant, to be sure, but one of the very few that I have left," she said in a tight voice. "I am quite certain he wouldn't do anything to undermine my wishes."

Even with the fire blazing beside us, the atmosphere in the room had suddenly cooled. Aunt Peg took that as her cue. She rose to her feet.

"Thank you for allowing us to visit this afternoon. We've taken up enough of your time," she said, taking the woman's hand in both of hers. "It's been lovely to see you. I hope we'll have another opportunity to get together soon."

"I'd like that," Josephine replied, her good manners as ingrained as Aunt Peg's.

"If there's ever anything you need . . . ," Aunt Peg offered.

Josephine shook her head. "No, there wouldn't be. I'm aware

that those in the outside world who remember me are puzzled by my lifestyle. But I'm not a prisoner in this house. I live this way by choice. Why would I ever need to leave when everything I want is right here?"

Mildred showed us out. Aunt Peg and I waited until we were back in her minivan before speaking again.

"Imagine ruining someone's life out of spite," I said.

"To have that much money and choose to use it in such a destructive way." Aunt Peg sounded shaken as she turned the key and put the van into gear. "I don't suppose I'll ever understand *that*. But at least we solved the mystery of Lila's past."

"But unfortunately that doesn't lead us any closer to knowing who killed her," I said. "Or why."

Chapter 13

On Monday Sam had meetings in the city all day. That made it my turn to get everybody up and fed, and to make sure that both Davey and his homework got on the school bus. Then I dropped Kevin off at preschool.

After that, all I had to do was wait an hour for the stores to open. Then it was time for some serious Christmas shopping. Due to extenuating circumstances, I was way behind on my gift buying. Today was my day to remedy that deficit. Since I had time to kill before I could go wear out my credit cards, I decided to take the dogs for a run.

That idea went out the window when the doorbell rang. I wasn't expecting anybody. I'm almost never expecting anyone. But that never seems to stop random people from showing up at my door at all hours.

This visitor was a real surprise. And not necessarily a good one. I opened the door anyway.

"Mr. Peebles," I said. "What are you doing here?"

Before he could answer, all five Standard Poodles came swarming out the open doorway. Only Bud was missing. He doesn't usually pass up anything of interest, so I wondered what kind of trouble the little miscreant was getting into elsewhere.

There was no opportunity to look for him now, however, because Hank Peebles had thrown up his hands and gone stumbling backward off my front step. A strangled sound came out of his mouth. Judging by the expression on his face, he thought death was possibly imminent.

Karma's a bitch, isn't it?

"Don't like dogs?" I inquired pleasantly.

"Those aren't dogs," he growled. "They look like bears."

Maybe the Poodles' freshly blown-out coats did make them look bigger than they actually were. But not *that* big. Definitely not bears.

"Nope," I told him. "They're Poodles. And this is their house."

I added that last part in case it might discourage him from prolonging this encounter. And also because I didn't exactly trust him. If Peebles had stopped by with something stupid in mind, I wanted him to be clear about the fact that my peeps and I had him outnumbered.

"We need to talk," he said. "Can I come in?" He gazed around at the Poodles, as though he wasn't entirely sure that was a wise idea.

Good, I thought. That made two of us.

"I guess so." It wasn't an invitation.

Peebles stepped past me through the doorway. The Standard Poodles followed him inside. As he stood in the hallway, the dogs continued to crowd around his legs. I continued not to discourage them from doing so. The dogs were only being friendly, but apparently Peebles didn't know that. And I had no desire to enlighten him.

I closed the door behind us and asked, "What do you want?"

Peebles was wearing the same tweed cap he'd had on the last time I saw him. Once inside the house, he reached up and swept it off his head. When his hand returned to his side, Augie stepped in close to sniff the cloth cap. Peebles cringed away from the big black dog.

Darn it. I wanted him to be intimidated. But the guy actually looked afraid.

"They won't hurt you," I said reluctantly.

"How do you know that?"

"Because they're my dogs and I trained them. They only attack on command."

Just kidding. But Peebles paled slightly. The cap twisted in his hands. Clearly the man had never met a Standard Poodle before.

"Look Ms. Travis," he said. "I'm not your enemy."

"Are you sure?" My brow lifted. "Because that's not what it seemed like the last time we met."

"Yeah, well, that wasn't the best of circumstances, considering that you and your friend had just broken into a house that's in my care."

"I wouldn't admit that so freely if I were you. That gatehouse doesn't look like it's been in anybody's care for years. Lila said she could never get you to come and fix things."

"Lila said a lot of things." Peebles smirked. "I wouldn't take her word as gospel on any of them."

"The police must have questioned you about her murder," I said.

"They did," he grumbled. "Not that there was a need. It's not like I knew anything about it."

"I knew something." I stared at him across the small space. "I told the police that Lila was afraid of you. That she had something you wanted."

"What?" I'd expected Peebles to react angrily. Instead he looked perplexed. "I don't know what you're talking about. Who told you that?"

"A woman named Karen Clauson. Her husband worked with Lila."

He shook his head. "I never met that woman. I have no idea where she'd come up with an idea like that. The only thing I wanted from Lila Moran was for her to go away and leave Ms. Mannerly in peace."

"And now she has," I pointed out.

"I had nothing to do with Lila's death," Peebles snarled. "Don't go trying to pin that on me. I didn't do anything to her."

The Poodles had grown bored listening to us talk. They'd laid down on the wooden floor around us. But now, hearing the menace in Peebles' tone, Tar and Faith jumped to their feet. The two Poodles looked at me questioningly. I patted my thigh, and both big dogs moved to stand between me and the caretaker.

Good dogs.

Peebles' eyes tracked the Poodles' movements. When they took up their new positions, he backed as far away from me as he could. The length of his body pressed against the wall behind him.

"It doesn't sound as though you did anything to help Lila either," I said.

"That woman didn't need my help." Peebles was still angry. But when Tar shifted his stance, the man glanced down at the male dog and moderated his tone. "Lila knew all about how to look out for herself. Which is more than you can say for Ms. M. The boss is a great lady, but she's led a secluded life. She doesn't always understand how the real world works. All I was trying to do was protect her."

Right. I crossed my arms over my chest and waited for further explanation.

"Okay, maybe I didn't always get around to making repairs," he admitted. "Maybe it occurred to me that if the furnace was smoking and the roof leaked, Lila might decide to pick up and move on to someone else's cushier digs. That's what her kind does. They're users, always on the lookout for someone to take care of them."

"How would you know that?"

"I've got eyes and ears, don't I? I pay attention to what goes on around me, especially when it concerns Ms. M or the estate. So I've seen the kind of people who come and go at that gatehouse since Lila moved in and made herself at home. Bunch of lowlifes, if you ask me."

Pot meet kettle, I thought.

Peebles frowned. "Except the one guy. Drove a red Ferrari, for Pete's sake. Classic midlife crisis car. I had to admire his taste in wheels, even if he was stooping to boink the help."

"The help?" I was confused. "What help?"

"It's my job to know what's happening on the estate so I looked up his license plate. The guy was Lila's boss. He's been showing up at the gatehouse once or twice a week for the past six months. The guys she hung out with before him didn't have much staying power, but this one sure did."

"Who are you talking about?" I asked. "What boss?"

"You know him," Peebles told me. "You were talking about his wife earlier. Guy named Clauson, George Clauson."

My stomach dropped. "He was having an affair with Lila?"

"I just said that, didn't I? That woman, she had him wrapped around her little finger. Probably thought he was going to be her ticket to a better life. And who knows? Maybe he would have been. Guy must have really been into her."

Damn, I thought. How had I missed that?

"Did you tell Detective Hronis about that?" I asked.

"Sure." Peebles shrugged. "Last week. I answered every question he had. He said he'd look into what I'd told him, along with everything else."

"Someone needs to tell him again," I said.

"Not me." With an eye on the Poodles, Peebles stepped away from the wall. In two steps he was back at the door. He reached for the knob and turned it. "But if you think it matters, go ahead."

"I will."

I'd call the detective just as soon as Peebles left. But meanwhile, I still had no idea what he was doing at my house. And now he was about to go. He'd drawn the door open and was ready to walk out.

"Wait," I said. "Why did you come?"

Peebles stopped and turned back. "Oh yeah. With your dogs attacking me like that, I almost forgot."

He reached a hand inside his jacket and my breath caught. I hoped he didn't have a weapon in there. Then he withdrew his hand and held it out to me. I couldn't see what he was holding, but I found myself reaching for it anyway.

Something cool and lightweight dropped into my palm. I looked down at it and blinked in surprise. Claire's gold bangle.

"I found it on the ground near where your friend parked her car," Peebles told me. "I know she wanted it back. I figured you could give it to her."

I looked up at him and swallowed. Maybe I needed to re-assess a few things. "Thank you for returning the bracelet. Claire will be thrilled to have it back."

"It's nothing. Like I said, Ms. Travis, I'm not your enemy."

No, I supposed not.

I waited until Peebles had driven away before I grabbed my phone and called Detective Hronis. I had to wait two minutes for someone to find him. Or for him to decide whether or not he wanted to speak to me. Either one was possible. By the time the detective picked up, I was drumming my fingers on the banister impatiently.

"Detective Hronis," he barked. "Ms. Travis?"

"Yes, I'm here," I said. "I was just talking to Hank Peebles. You know, the caretaker at the Mannerly estate?"

"Yes, I'm familiar with Mr. Peebles." He waited for me to continue.

"He told me that Lila Moran was having an affair with George Clauson."

"We're aware of that."

"Did you ask him about it?"

"Ms. Travis, I'm not required to keep you informed of police activity."

"No, of course not." I walked around the newel post and sat down on a step. The Poodles were spread out on the floor, listening as I talked. They probably understood me better than Detective Hronis did. "But George Clauson's wife, Karen—"

"We talked to her too, Ms. Travis." He was beginning to sound bored.

"Karen's position as George's wife and her standing in the community mean everything to her. If his relationship with Lila put those things at risk, or if she was afraid that George might leave her . . ."

My voice trailed away. I was waiting for Detective Hronis to connect the dots, just as I had. Several long seconds ticked by in silence.

"We've considered that, Ms. Travis, and we're looking into it," Hronis replied finally. "But right now, all we have is speculation. Mrs. Clauson told us she was aware of her husband's extramarital activities. And both of them told us that he had already ended the affair before Lila Moran was killed."

"And you believed them?" I asked skeptically.

"Let's just say I'm keeping an open mind. But as I said, this is all just conjecture. We would need some kind of proof before pursuing this line of inquiry further."

"I could talk to Chris Sanchez again," I said. "Maybe she knows something."

There was another pause before the detective spoke. "I'll repeat what I told you before, Ms. Travis. This is police business.

The best thing would be for you to put it out of your mind. I wouldn't want you to do anything stupid."

"Nor would I," I replied. But that didn't mean I wasn't going to talk to Chris again.

"He didn't care about what I had to say," I told the dogs glumly when we'd severed the connection. "Thank goodness for you guys. You always pay attention to me."

Faith and Eve hopped up. Augie was already on his feet. The Poodle group was ready to play. I still had time to get in a run before heading out to shop. But first I needed to find Bud. What the heck could he be up to that was more interesting than a visitor in the front hall? No doubt it was something nefarious.

Since it was Bud we were talking about, it probably involved food. So I headed to the kitchen first. The pantry door was standing open. Suspicious noises were coming from within. I walked around and had a look.

Bud was lying on the floor next to a forty pound bag of kibble. He'd managed to chew a small hole in the bottom of the bag. Now he was using his tongue to pull out the kibble piece by piece. You know, because we never fed him, poor thing.

"Bud, cut that out!" I said.

He looked up at me and wagged his tail. *Happy! Happy!*

"You are not happy," I said firmly. "You're in trouble."

Happy! Happy!

Dammit, it was a good thing he was so cute.

I dragged him out of the pantry. Then I went back and taped up the bottom of the bag. It wasn't a perfect patch, but it would do.

Five minutes later I was finally getting ready to go for that run when my phone rang. I snatched it up. Maybe it was Detective Hronis calling back to tell me I was brilliant.

No such luck. It was Claire.

"Hey," I said. "Good news! I've got your missing bracelet."

"That's nice," she replied. *Nice?* "But I don't care about that right now. Can we talk?"

"Sure. What's up?"

"Not on the phone." Her voice sounded shaky. "In person."

"I guess so," I said slowly. There went my run. And my Christmas shopping. But something didn't feel right. "Claire, are you okay?"

"Yes," she replied. I wasn't reassured. "But I need to see you. Now."

"I can do that. Where are you?"

"I'm at the gatehouse."

"What?" Thoughts whirling, I nearly tripped over Bud. "What are you doing there?"

"I can't explain. I just need you to come."

I was already dodging around Poodles as I hurried from the kitchen. "Claire, what's going on?"

"Just come."

Luckily I had the phone pressed tight against my ear. Because that meant I heard her slip out the word "not" in a breathy whisper before saying out loud, "Alone."

Oh crap, I thought.

"Claire, talk to me!" I cried.

She didn't reply. The connection had already ended.

Chapter 14

If I took the back roads between North Stamford and New Canaan, I could be at the Mannerly estate in ten minutes. I called Detective Hronis on the way. This time, it took even longer for him to come on the line.

"Pick up, pick up, pick up!" I muttered, my fingers tapping on the steering wheel.

By the time he finally did, I was so stressed that I wasted another couple of minutes trying to make him understand the urgency of the matter.

"I thought I told you the gatehouse was off-limits," he said.

"That's not the point," I almost yelled. "Claire isn't there by choice. I know something's wrong. I'm on my way there right now to find out what."

"If you think there's trouble, the last thing you should do is go running toward it," the detective told me.

How could he remain so calm when what I wanted to do was scream in frustration?

"Somebody has to!" I snapped.

I tossed the phone on the other seat and drove. The Volvo's

tires squealed as I made the turn onto Forest Glen. Not much farther now.

As I flew along beside the Mannerly estate's high wall, a car came up behind me. A plain sedan with an angry detective at the wheel. Beggars couldn't be choosers. I'd have preferred a happy detective, but at least he'd come.

I skidded to a stop in front of the iron gate. It was closed.

Detective Hronis pulled up behind me. He rolled down his window. "You drive like a maniac," he said. "Move your car out of the way and get in. I have the gate code."

I hurried to obey and was already seated beside him before the gate began to swing open.

"If this is a false alarm, I'm going to give you a speeding ticket," Hronis informed me.

"It isn't."

He glanced at me across the seat as we rolled up beside the gatehouse. "How can you be so sure?"

I pointed to a black Mercedes coupe parked behind the cottage. "Because that isn't Claire's car. Whatever she's doing here, she didn't come because she wanted to."

"Wait in the car," said Hronis.

Fat chance of that. I had jumped out and was heading toward the gatehouse before he had his seat belt unfastened. Apparently, once motivated, the detective could move quickly. When I reached the door, he was right beside me. Hronis held out an arm to bar my way.

"I'll go in first." He slanted a glare my way. "Or are you going to argue with that too?"

I stepped to one side. The detective lifted a hand and knocked on the wooden door. "Ms. Travis, it's Detective Hronis. Are you in there?"

For a moment, there was no response. The detective and I shared an uneasy look. He raised his hand to knock again.

Abruptly a shriek rent the air. The hair on the back of my neck lifted. A chill slipped down my spine. I froze in place but the detective's reflexes were quicker. He shoved me away, then leapt sideways himself.

We landed on the hard ground together just as I heard a loud roar. The sound was so unexpected that it took me a moment to realize what it was. A gunshot. A hole blasted through the wooden door above us. Shards of splintered wood came raining down.

"Claire!" I screamed. I started to scramble up. All I knew was that I had to get inside the cottage.

Detective Hronis had a different idea. He grabbed my arm in a viselike grip, dragged me back to the car, and shoved me down behind it. "Don't move," he said. When I nodded, he crawled inside the sedan and called for backup.

"Claire's in there," I said when he was finished.

"Who's she with?" he demanded.

"I don't know. She didn't say." My voice wobbled. "She probably couldn't say."

The detective's radio came on. He talked some more. I could already hear the sound of sirens in the distance. He turned back to me and said, "They ran the plate. It's Karen Clauson."

"She has Claire," I said. "And a gun. We have to do something."

"We are doing something, Ms. Travis. We're doing everything we can, as quickly as we can. In just a few minutes, we'll have the gatehouse surrounded. A hostage negotiator is on the way."

A phalanx of cars came flying up the driveway toward us. They stopped a short distance away. Doors slammed. Officers got out. They were wearing body armor and they were armed.

My body shook uncontrollably as I sat on the ground behind the detective's sedan. I wasn't just cold; I was in shock. Things like this didn't happen in suburban Connecticut. It was like watching a scene from a movie. How had things escalated so quickly?

Detective Hronis rose to his knees and gazed at the gatehouse through the windows of the car. All was quiet. Nothing moved. "Stay here," he said.

He went to confer with the other police, who'd assembled behind us. I received a few curious glances. Other than that, they all ignored me. I supposed that was fair. I was the one who'd gotten them into this mess.

Several of the officers left the group. I watched as they fanned out around the gatehouse. While they were doing that, Detective Hronis donned protective body armor. Someone handed him a bullhorn. He lifted it to his lips.

"Karen Clauson," he said. "We know you're in there. We need you to open the door and come out now with your hands up."

There was no response. Detective Hronis didn't look perturbed. He calmly repeated his message. I chewed on my lip, waiting with the others.

A minute later, Hronis tried again. "We have the gatehouse surrounded," he announced. "The only way out is through that door, with your hands up. You're only making things worse for yourself, Karen. Let's end this peacefully before something happens that we all regret."

Several regrettable things had already happened, I thought. Of course, it wouldn't help to remind anyone of that. All I could do was keep my head down, stay out of the way, and pray for Claire's safety.

I was still sitting with my back against the sedan, so when I heard the sound of a door scraping open, it came from behind me. What *was* in my line of vision were half a dozen police officers who immediately snapped to attention. I spun around, got up on my knees, and peered through the car window.

Karen Clauson was standing silhouetted in the doorway. "I'm coming out," she said.

Detective Hronis nodded. He still looked remarkably calm. As if he'd never expected any other outcome.

"Put down your weapon," he said. "And raise your hands in the air."

Karen complied.

"Now slowly walk toward us."

After that, everything that happened felt like one long blur of frantic activity. Karen was quickly taken into custody. As several officers moved to surround her, I was already up and running. When Detective Hronis entered the gatehouse, I was right behind him.

Claire was in the kitchen, lying slumped on the floor. Her eyes were closed; her face was pale as milk. My stomach plummeted—and then I realized that I didn't see any blood. She hadn't been shot.

Instead, there was a purpling bruise on Claire's forehead. A knot the size of a golf ball was already forming. Hronis knelt down beside her and felt for a pulse. "Strong and steady," he said, looking up at me. "Although I'm sure she'll have a nasty headache when she wakes up."

The ambulance was at the end of the driveway. By the time the paramedics reached the cottage, Claire was starting to regain consciousness. Against the detective's wishes, she wanted to sit up. As I held her steady, she looked around in confusion.

Her hand lifted to touch the bump on her head. "Where's Karen? What did she do to me?"

"It looks like she knocked you out," I said.

Claire blinked slowly. "She must have hit me when I tried to warn you not to come inside. Karen made me call you. She had a gun."

"We know all about that," Detective Hronis told her. "You can relax now, Ms. Travis. She doesn't have the gun anymore. My men have taken her into custody."

I took her cold hand in mine and squeezed hard. "Claire, tell us what happened."

She frowned, as though it hurt to think back. "Karen called

me this morning. She said she'd made a mistake when she'd told me she didn't need my services anymore. She wanted to talk to me about an upcoming event. And dummy that I was, I fell for that."

"You couldn't have known," I told her.

"All Karen really wanted to do was pump me for information about how much you knew," Claire said. I was glad to see that her color was starting to return. "I told her you were good at solving mysteries. And that I was sure you'd get to the bottom of things, because you always do. That must have made her panic, because she took out a gun. She brought me here and made me call you."

There was a sudden commotion in the doorway. We all looked up. Karen was standing there. Her hands were cuffed behind her back, and there was an officer on either side of her. She wasn't wearing a coat and she was shivering from the cold. Ask me if I cared. I curled an arm around Claire's shoulders protectively.

Hronis lifted a brow at the interruption.

"She said she had something to say," Office Jenkins told him.

"Go ahead," the detective told her.

Karen ignored him. Instead, she looked at me. "This is all your fault," she spat out.

"How do you figure that?"

"If you hadn't kept coming around, asking your stupid questions, and sticking your nose where it didn't belong, everything would have been fine."

I snuck a glance at Detective Hronis. He looked like a man who'd just swallowed something distasteful. But he had the sense to remain silent and let the conversation play out.

"Except that Lila Moran would have been dead," I said mildly.

"That bitch was sleeping with my husband. Always telling him how handsome he was, and how smart." Karen's face was mottled red with rage. "She wouldn't leave George alone. She told him that just like his car, he needed a newer model woman. She said I was *too old* for him, can you imagine?"

A gesture of solidarity seemed necessary, so I shook my head. "After all the work you'd done to keep yourself in shape for him too."

My sarcasm must have gone right over Karen's head, because she nodded in agreement.

"I guess Lila deserved what happened to her," I said.

"Damn right she did," Karen swore. Then she glared at me. "Except that you got in the way. When you wanted to meet with me for a *second* time, I realized I was in trouble. You pretended the conversation was about Claire, but I knew you knew."

She was giving me more credit than I deserved, I thought sadly. If only I'd been that quick on the uptake, this whole crazy episode could have been avoided.

"I haven't been able to sleep since," she snapped. "I knew I had to fix things *again*. I had to fix you."

"Why drag Claire into it?" I asked.

Karen's gaze dropped. She looked at Claire without remorse. "I knew you two were close," she said with a shrug. "I figured you'd do whatever she asked."

"You're right," I replied. "I would."

I heard Claire sigh. She reached out and wrapped an arm around my waist in a sideways hug. But I had one more question for Karen.

"Why here?"

She looked surprised. "Are you kidding me? Why *not* here? This cottage is a dump. It looks like the kind of place where people would die. Besides, I thought if two more women came to grief in the same place Lila did, the police would devote their resources to checking out this weird abandoned property."

Karen glanced at Detective Hronis dismissively. "And that would direct their attention away from me."

The property wasn't abandoned, but I didn't think Josephine Mannerly would appreciate my issuing a correction. Plus, only an idiot would be dumb enough to insult the police while she was standing there wearing their handcuffs. Detective Hronis obviously felt the same way.

"That's enough," he told the officers. "Get her out of here."

He and I helped Claire to her feet. She was examined by the paramedics and told she had a probable concussion. They recommended that she see her personal physician, and I assured them I would take her myself. I felt incredibly lucky that the injury wasn't worse.

Epilogue

After all that excitement died down, I finally got a chance to finish my Christmas shopping. Claire bounced back quickly. Over her objections, I also helped her complete her remaining holiday shopping assignments. Under the circumstances, it seemed like the least I could do.

Aunt Peg invited our family to her house for Christmas dinner. I knew she didn't cook, so I wondered what kind of alternative plan she'd come up with. I hoped it didn't involve me and an apron. But when we arrived, the table in her dining room was set with polished silver and a linen tablecloth, and the heavenly smell of roasting turkey filled the air.

There were more presents under Aunt Peg's Christmas tree for both Kevin and Davey. After they were opened and admired, the three Aussie puppies were brought into the living room to be played with. Meanwhile, we grown-ups relaxed in front of the fireplace with mugs of heavily spiked eggnog.

"I asked Josie Mannerly to join us for dinner," Aunt Peg mentioned.

Sam and I stared at each other in surprise.

"Is she coming?" I asked eagerly.

Aunt Peg laughed. "Gracious, no. The woman's a recluse. She never leaves her house. I just couldn't resist asking, to see what she'd say."

"After everything she went through with Lila Moran, she's probably relieved to be finished dealing with outsiders," Sam said.

"As it turns out, she's not entirely finished," Aunt Peg told us. "I happened to remember that Josie was a dog lover. Years ago she and her mother had a pair of Pekingese they took everywhere. The dogs became nearly as famous as their owners. Of course, on an estate that size, she might want a larger dog."

My head swiveled her way. "Aunt Peg, what did you do?"

"I merely made the obvious suggestion."

I glanced down at the puppies, who were rolling around on the floor with Kevin. They'd grown again since the last time I saw them. An adult Australian Shepherd would be tall enough to rest its head comfortably in Josie's lap while she sat in her chair.

"Did she want a male or female?" Sam asked with a smile. "A black puppy or a blue?"

"Josie's always been a bit spoiled," Aunt Peg said. "She isn't used to having to make choices. So there was no need for her to start now. Once those puppies are old enough to be inoculated and have their training started, the two boys will be going to live in the former carriage house with Hank Peebles. Blue will reside in the mansion with Josie."

"That sounds like a wonderful solution all the way around," said Sam.

"I thought so," Aunt Peg agreed with satisfaction. "Now, who's ready to eat?"

Davey looked up from his seat on the floor. "Who cooked?"

"Shush," I told him. "That isn't polite."

"But a sensible inquiry nonetheless." Aunt Peg slipped him a wink. "Village Catering did the honors. Does that meet with your approval?"

Davey and Kevin both nodded. Even Sam looked relieved.

"Everything you do meets with our approval," he said.

"Don't tell her that." I laughed. "She'll get a big head."

"Bigger than I already have?" Aunt Peg was amused. "That hardly seems possible. Now hurry up, you lot. Last one to the table doesn't get a drumstick."

The boys each picked up a puppy. Aunt Peg nabbed the third. The three of them left the room together, moving like people on a mission.

Sam and I stood up to follow. Aunt Peg had lowered the lights and the decorations on her Christmas tree glistened in the firelight. Their soft glow was reflected in the windows. It all looked so beautiful that I just wanted to pause briefly to appreciate the moment.

Sam felt the same way. He stepped closer and slipped an arm around my shoulders.

"It's been a great year," I said.

"We've been very lucky." He leaned down and kissed the top of my head. "And next year will be even better."

Author's Note

The background for this book was partially inspired by the story of Huguette Clark, a woman of immense wealth who shut herself away in her New York City apartment after the deaths of her sister and her parents. She spent the remainder of her life—nearly fifty years—speaking to very few people and seeing almost no one. Among the grand properties Huguette owned (and never visited again) were Bellosguardo, a twenty-three-acre beachfront estate in Santa Barbara, California, and Le Beau Chateau, a secluded mansion on fifty acres of wooded land in New Canaan, Connecticut.

Dear Readers,

For years Melanie Travis has starred in her own mystery series, with Aunt Peg hovering—not altogether quietly—in the background. Eager to share her opinions and dispense advice, Peg has always grabbed center stage whenever she's had the chance. Now I'm delighted to announce that she'll have the opportunity to be totally in charge when she gets her own mystery to solve.

At long last, Peg will have everything her own way. Or will she?

Rose Donovan is Peg's sister-in-law. She's been a thorn in Peg's side for forty years. But somehow, when Rose decides to join a local bridge club, she can't think of anyone she'd rather have as her partner than Peg. Apart, these two women can be difficult. Together, they're more trouble than a sack of cats. Perhaps it's no surprise that when a member of the bridge club is murdered, Peg and Rose are named as suspects.

I had a great time writing *Peg and Rose Solve a Murder*, which is now available wherever print and e-books are sold. Peg has been a voice inside my head for so long that I loved being able to finally let her out to do her own thing. I hope you'll give her book a try. Otherwise Peg will never let you hear the end of it—and trust me, nobody wants that.

Happy reading!
Laurien

Chapter 1

Peg Turnbull was standing in the hot sun on a plot of hard-packed grass, staring at a row of Standard Poodles that was lined up along one side of her show ring. She'd been hired to judge a dozen breeds at the Rowayton Kennel Club Dog Show, and she couldn't imagine a better way to spend a clear summer day. Judging dogs involved three of her favorite things: telling people what to do; airing her own opinions; and of course, interacting with the dogs themselves.

A tall woman in her early seventies, Peg had a discerning eye and a wicked sense of humor. In this job, she needed both. Aware that she'd be on her feet for most of the day, she had dressed that morning with comfort in mind. A cotton shirt-waist dress swirled around her legs. A broad brimmed straw hat shaded her face and neck. Her feet wore rubber-soled sneakers, size ten.

Though her career as a dog show judge had taken her around the world, today's show was local to her home in Greenwich, Connecticut. Peg had arrived at the showground early. She'd begun her assignment at nine o'clock with a selection of breeds from the Toy Group. Now, two and half hours later, she finally found herself facing her beloved Standard Poodles.

As she gazed at the beautifully coiffed entrants in front of her, Peg knew exactly what she was looking for—a sound, elegant, typey dog displaying the exuberant Poodle temperament. Having devoted her life to the betterment of the Poodle breed, and spent the previous decade judging numerous dog shows, Peg was well aware there were days when those coveted canine attributes could be in short supply. Thankfully, this first glimpse of her Open Dog class had already indicated that this wasn't going to be one of them.

Peg flexed her fingers happily. She couldn't wait to get her hands on the Poodles. She was eager to delve through their copious, hair-sprayed coats to assess the muscle and structure that lay beneath. It was time to get to work.

A throat cleared behind her. "Peg?"

Marnie Clark was Peg's ring steward for the day. While Peg evaluated her entries and picked the winners and losers, it was Marnie's job to keep things running smoothly. That was no small feat. To the uninitiated, the arrangement of classes, record keeping, and points awarded could appear to rival a Rubik's Cube in complexity.

Marnie was an officer of the show-sponsoring kennel club. She was bright, vivacious, and two decades younger than Peg. Peg's Poodles and Marnie's Tibetan Terriers were both Non-Sporting Group breeds. The two women had known and competed against each other for years.

Reluctantly, Peg turned away from the four appealing Open dogs to see what Marnie wanted. The woman was holding up an unclaimed armband. The fifth Standard Poodle entered in the class had yet to arrive.

Absent? Peg wondered. *Or merely late?*

Each exhibitor was responsible for being at the ring on schedule. However, busy professional handlers with numerous breeds to show could sometimes find their presence required in more than one ring at the same time. In those cases, it was up to the judge to decide whether or not a concession would be made.

Peg glanced at the armband and lifted a brow.

Marnie wasn't supposed to tell her the missing exhibitor's name—a nod to impartiality that didn't fool anyone. The dog show world wasn't large. As soon as the handler arrived, Peg would recognize him or her, just as she knew the other exhibitors currently in her ring. As long as a judge remembered to evaluate the dogs on their merits and not their connections, that didn't have to be a problem.

Marnie obviously agreed. "It's Harvey," she said under her breath.

The steward nodded toward a big, black Poodle waiting just outside the gate with the handler's harried-looking assistant. Peg hadn't seen the young man before. He must be new. He was casting frantic glances toward the Lhasa Apso ring farther down the row of enclosures.

Peg took a quick look herself. Yes, indeed, there was Harvey—standing in the middle of a class of Lhasas that he very clearly wasn't winning. The handler was glaring at the indecisive judge as if he wanted to throttle her.

Peg felt much the same way. In her opinion, anyone who didn't want to have to make tough choices shouldn't apply for a judging license. Peg presided over her ring with the deft precision of a general inspecting troops. People might not agree with every decision she made, but they all respected her ability to get the job done.

Peg turned back to Marnie. "Give the young man the armband. Tell him to bring the dog in the ring and take him to the end of the line. You can switch Harvey in when he gets here."

"I already tried that," Marnie told her with a sidelong smirk. "The poor guy looked like he might faint. I wouldn't be surprised if this was his first dog show."

"And possibly his last." Peg felt an unwanted twinge of sympathy. It was no wonder that Harvey's assistants always looked stressed. The handler had entirely too many clients to do each one justice.

On the other hand, she was well aware that Harvey's Open dog was a handsome Standard Poodle who compared favorably with the others now in the ring. Unless she was mistaken, the dog only needed to win today's major to finish his championship. Harvey would be devastated if he missed this chance.

Peg sighed. Time was a valuable commodity for a dog show judge. And now hers was passing. She was done dithering.

"I'll start the class but take things slow," she said to Marnie. "Harvey has my permission to enter the ring when he gets here. But for pity's sake, do try to hurry him along."

Ten minutes later, Harvey made it to the ring in time, but only just. Peg leveled a beady-eyed glare in the handler's direction as he took possession of the big Poodle at the end of the line. Her meaning was clear to everyone in the vicinity. She'd granted Harvey leniency this time, but he shouldn't make a habit of needing it.

After weighing the merits and flaws of her male Standard Poodle entry, Peg was further annoyed when her earlier speculation proved to be true. She ended up awarding Harvey's dog the title of Winners Dog and the coveted three point major that went with it. With an outcome like that, Harvey would never learn better manners. But darn it, the dog had deserved the win. So what else was she supposed to do?

Peg hated it when her principles found themselves at odds with each other.

It didn't help that Marnie was laughing behind her hand as she called the Standard puppy bitch class into the ring.

"Wait until you get approved to judge," Peg said as they crossed paths at the judge's table. "Then I'll come and make fun of you."

"As if you'd stoop to stewarding," Marnie sniffed. Then

winked. Stewarding was a difficult and often thankless job and they both knew it.

The Standard Poodle bitch classes passed without incident. Peg took the time to reassure a nervous novice handler whose lively puppy couldn't keep all four feet on the ground. The woman left the ring delighted with her red second-place ribbon in a class of just two.

In the Open class, Peg purposely paid scant attention to a local handler who'd brought her a black Standard bitch that wasn't at all her type. The man had shown under Peg on many previous occasions. He would have known that she preferred a more refined Poodle, not to mention one with a correct bite. He would also have been aware, however, that Peg and the Poodle's owner were friends.

No doubt he was hoping to capitalize on that relationship.

The implication made Peg steam. If the handler had the nerve to think that would sway her decision, he deserved the rebuke she was about to deliver. With a dismissive flick of her hand, Peg sent the pair to cool their heels at the back of the line. Then she awarded the class, and subsequently the purple Winners Bitch ribbon, to a charming apricot bitch she hadn't previously had the pleasure of judging.

After that, Best of Variety was an easy decision. It went to a gorgeous Standard who was currently the top winning Poodle on the East Coast. The apricot bitch was Best of Winners, which meant she shared the three-point major from the dog classes. Her elated owner-handler pumped Peg's hand energetically when she handed him his ribbon.

"You certainly made someone happy," Marnie commented as she turned the pages of her catalog to the next breed on the schedule.

"Yes, and my fingers may never recover." Peg smiled. "He was so excited by the win, I was afraid for a moment that he might burst into tears. Were we ever that young and enthusiastic?"

"Of course we were. It's just that it was so long ago, we're too old to remember what it was like."

Peg turned away and surveyed her table. If Marnie was old, what did that make her? Perhaps it was better not to think about that.

She grabbed a sip of water from her bottle, then flipped her judge's book to a new page. Miniature Poodles were up next, and they'd drawn a big entry. Dogs and handlers were already beginning to gather outside the ring.

More fun coming right up.

"I wonder what that lady's story is," Marnie said. "Even in beautiful weather like this, dog shows hardly ever draw spectators anymore."

Not like in the good old days, Peg thought. She was arranging her ribbons and had yet to look up. "What lady?"

"Over there." Marnie gestured discreetly. "She's sat through four different breeds. There's a catalog in her lap but she looks like she hasn't the slightest idea how to read it."

"Maybe she just loves dogs," Peg said happily. *Welcome to the club.* She straightened to have a look, then abruptly went still. "Oh dear."

Marnie was heading to the in-gate. It was time to start handing out numbered armbands. She glanced back at Peg over her shoulder. "What?"

"That's my sister-in-law, Rose."

"Okay. Then that makes sense."

"Not to me," Peg muttered.

Marnie returned to her side. "She's really a relative of yours?"

Peg nodded.

"And you hadn't noticed she's been sitting there for an hour?"

"Apparently not." Why would she waste time perusing the ringside when she had all those lovely dogs in her ring?

"Right." Marnie didn't sound convinced.

Now that Marnie and Peg were both looking in her direction, Rose lifted a slender hand in a tentative wave. Her pleasant features were framed by a firm jaw and a cap of short gray hair was brushed back off her forehead. She was perched on the seat of a folding chair with her head up and her back straight. Rose had always had excellent posture.

Marnie smiled and waved back. Peg remained still.

Marnie gave Peg a little push. "Go say hello to her."

"I think not."

"Don't be silly. You have plenty of time."

Peg drew herself up to her full height. Even in sneakers, she neared six feet. "Not now. I have Minis to judge—"

"You're running early. I won't call the puppy dogs into the ring for at least two minutes."

"Rose can wait. I have a lunch break after Minis. She and I will talk then. Or maybe we won't." Peg pulled her gaze away. "Her choice."

"I see." Marnie bit her lip. It suddenly sounded as though this had ceased to be any of her business. "Then let me just finish handing out these armbands and we can get started."

Peg refused to let herself be distracted by her sister-in-law's presence as the first class of Miniature Poodle dogs filed into the ring. She had a job to do. Numerous exhibitors had honored her with an entry, and each of them deserved her complete attention.

Still, it was hard not to sneak a peek in Rose's direction every so often. What on earth was she doing here? As far as Peg knew, Rose didn't like dogs. Nor did she like Peg.

That feeling was mutual.

Animosity had sizzled between the two women since Peg became engaged to her beloved, and now dearly departed husband, Max, more than four decades earlier. In all the intervening years, neither Rose nor Peg had managed to put the things that were said during that rocky time entirely behind them. Max was Rose's older brother—and a man for whom Peg would have done anything. Yet even he had never succeeded in forging a friendship between the two most important women in his life.

Peg plucked a stunning white youngster from the Puppy class and awarded him the points over the older dogs. She suspected once she'd seen the rest of her Mini entry, he would win Best of Variety too. That would be a bold move on her part. People would take notice. There was bound to be talk.

As she waited for the first bitches to enter the ring, Peg allowed herself a small smile of satisfaction. The white puppy was a star in the making. He would finish his championship handily, and she would be known as the judge who'd discovered him.

Buoyed by the prospect of that success, she allowed her gaze to flicker briefly in Rose's direction. It aggravated Peg that she felt compelled to gauge her sister-in-law's reaction. It aggravated her even more than to see that there was none.

Rose had set aside her catalog. Now her hands were folded demurely in her lap. Her expression was bland, her features arranged in a mask of resigned complacency that Peg knew infuriatingly well.

Of course Rose hadn't noticed anything unusual. She probably couldn't tell the difference between a Miniature Poodle and a hamster.

That brought Peg back to her earlier thought.

It was never good news when Rose appeared. Peg wondered what the woman wanted now.

Chapter 2

Peg finished her Mini Poodle judging by making the handsome white puppy her Best of Variety winner. Since she put the dog up over two finished champions, her selection caused some minor grumbling among the other exhibitors. Not that anyone would dare say anything to her face, of course.

"Don't worry," Marnie told her. The show photographer had been called to the ring so they could take pictures of the morning's winners before the lunch break. They were waiting for the man to appear. "I've got your back."

"Thank you," Peg replied. "I wasn't worried, however. Should I be?"

"You didn't hear what Dan Fogel said as he left the ring."

Fogel was a busy and successful professional handler with a very high opinion of himself and his dogs. He clearly hadn't been pleased when Peg moved the white puppy up from the middle of the line and placed it in front of his special dog.

"And I don't want to either," Peg said firmly. "Considering all the breeds he handles, Dan shows under me frequently. If a momentary lapse in judgment caused him to say something unfortunate, I'm better off not knowing about it. I'd hate for it to taint my opinion of him in the future."

"Your loss. He used some rather colorful language." Marnie grinned. "For what it's worth, I'd have done the same thing you did. There wasn't a better moving dog in the variety ring than that puppy."

Once the photographer arrived, a dozen pictures were taken in quick succession. Everybody knew the drill. Pose the dog, hold up the ribbon, smile, flash! Done, and on to the next.

"Lunchtime," Marnie said happily when they were finished. "I can't wait to get off my feet for a few minutes."

"You go ahead." Peg glanced toward the side of the ring. "I'll catch up."

Apparently the extra time Peg had spent taking photographs had been the last straw for Rose. Now she was squirming in her seat. Peg didn't blame her. Those folding chairs weren't meant for long-term use.

"Sounds good." Marnie followed the direction of Peg's gaze. "I'll save you a place."

The two women exited the show ring together. Marnie headed toward the hospitality tent. Peg went the other way, striding around the low, slatted barrier that formed the sides of the enclosure. She stopped in front of Rose, who looked up and smiled.

"Good morning, Peg."

"Afternoon, now," Peg replied smartly. There was another chair nearby. She dragged it over and sat down. "Imagine my surprise to find you sitting outside my ring. What are you doing here?"

"I was curious. I came to see what you do for a living."

Peg wasn't buying that for a moment. But she was willing to play along. "And?"

"It's rather boring, isn't it?"

"Not to me." Peg's smile had a wolflike quality, more a matter of bared teeth than shared humor.

"Perhaps not. I'm sure you know more about these things than I do."

Having been immersed in the sport of purebred dogs for the majority of her adult life, Peg knew more about *these things* than ninety-nine percent of the world's population. She might have been tempted to point that out except it sounded as though Rose was trying to be agreeable. And that immediately made Peg suspicious.

"If you found the judging boring, why did you stay?" she asked pleasantly.

Rose shifted sideways in her seat. Now she and Peg were face-to-face.

"I think it's time you and I got to know each other better."

Peg's mouth opened. Then closed. She could have sworn she already knew more about Rose than any sane person would ever want to know.

"Why would we want to do that?"

"Because despite our differences, we're family."

Family. Huh. As if that was a good excuse.

Peg's eyes narrowed. "What are you up to?"

"What do you mean?" Rose's reply was all innocence.

Abruptly, Peg was reminded that her sister-in-law had found a vocation early in life. She'd entered the convent straight out of high school and spent most of the intervening years as Sister Anne Marie of the Order of Divine Mercy. Rose had perfected that serenely guileless look during her time in the convent. She still used it to great effect on occasion.

Peg wasn't fooled. Having been called both a heathen and a sinner by Rose in the past, she disdainfully thought of the expression as Rose's *nun face.*

"As entertaining as it is to spar with you," she said, "I'm sure you can see that I'm quite busy today. If you have something to say to me, please do so. If not, it's time for my lunch."

The other woman sighed heavily. That was Peg's cue to stand up. Somewhere on the showgrounds there was a rubbery prewrapped sandwich calling her name. And a trip to the porta-potty wouldn't go amiss either.

"Wait," Rose said. "Give me a minute."

"I've already given you three."

"Sit back down. Please?"

It was the novelty of hearing the word *please* that did it. Peg thought that might be the first time she'd ever heard Rose voice such an appeal. She swished the skirt of her shirtwaist dress to one side and sat.

"Go on," she said.

"I want to join a bridge club. And I want you to join with me as my partner."

"You're joking."

"No." Rose frowned. "Why would I joke about something like that?"

"Because it's funny?"

It was funny, wasn't it? Any moment now, the two of them would dissolve into laughter. Not that they'd ever done so before. Belatedly it occurred to Peg that it didn't appear to be happening this time either.

Instead, Rose was simply sitting there, staring at her. Her calm manner was almost unnerving.

"A bridge club," Peg repeated. Apparently it wasn't a joke. "I would think you'd be too busy for a frivolous pastime like that."

"Of course I'm busy. But I can't spend all my time doing good works." Rose managed to deliver that statement with a straight face. "Besides, bridge isn't a frivolous game. You should know that. You used to play."

Yes, she had. But how did Rose know that?

"You mentioned it once." Rose answered the unspoken question. "You were talking about living in a dorm when you were in college. You said every night after dinner, you and your friends would go down to the living room for demitasse and bridge."

Peg was slightly stunned. "That was fifty years ago."

"Even so. You talked about it."

Peg shook her head. She barely remembered playing bridge, much less having a conversation about it later. And with Rose of all people. How had that come about? She had no idea.

"I never went to college," Rose said in a small voice.

"No. You left home to become a nun instead."

"I had a vocation."

Even Peg wasn't mean enough to point out that Rose's vocation had apparently vanished like a puff of smoke when—after more than three decades in the convent—she had met a priest and fallen in love. Peter and Rose had recently celebrated their tenth wedding anniversary, however. So there was that.

"I realize now that there are many things I missed out on in my youth," Rose said.

"That was your choice," Peg pointed out.

"I didn't know that then. I was young enough and naive enough to think that God had made the choice for me. Now that I'm older, I realize that there are many paths to eternal salvation."

"And one of them includes playing bridge?" Peg regretted the words as soon as they'd left her mouth. In all the years she and Rose had known each other, they'd never had a conversation quite like this. All at once, Peg didn't want to be the one responsible for shutting it down. "I'm sorry. That was uncalled for."

"No, I get it. You're skeptical. I probably deserve that."

"Yes, you do."

"That goes both ways."

Peg snorted. "Don't tell me you're waiting for an apology."

"Of course not." A small smile played around the corners of Rose's mouth. "I know better than that. But I didn't come here today to fight with you."

After a pause, Peg shrugged. "It wasn't on my calendar either."

The two women shared a look of mild accord. It wasn't quite rapprochement, but perhaps a small step in that direction.

"I gather you're missing lunch on my account," Rose said. "I passed a food concession on my way in. Maybe I could buy you a salad?"

Peg nearly laughed. "Thank you, but no. Obviously you've never had dog show food."

"That bad?"

"Probably even worse than you're imagining."

"All right, then." Rose reached down into a canvas tote beside her chair and pulled out a shiny red orb. "Apple?"

Peg accepted the piece of fruit. She studied the apple from all angles, then took her first bite. "Maybe you should tell me something about your bridge club. I haven't played the game in years. I may not be up to their standards." She cocked a brow in Rose's direction. "Or yours."

"You don't have to worry about that. My friend, Carrie, belongs to the group. From what she's told me, the members enjoy getting together to play bridge, but they aren't seriously dedicated to the game. They don't play duplicate or anything like that. Just plain old rubber bridge, and it's mostly for fun and socializing."

"What about Peter?" Peg asked. "I would think you'd want to play with him."

"His game is chess, not bridge," Rose told her. "Besides, just because he and I are married doesn't mean we have to do everything together."

Peg helped herself to another bite of the apple and stared off into the distance. She and Max had done everything together. Their relationship had been one of moving in tandem toward shared goals and accomplishments. They'd created a family of renowned Standard Poodles, while building a life that suited each of them perfectly. Max had been the other half of Peg's whole. Even a decade after his death, she still felt incomplete without him. Peg would have given anything to have those days to live over again.

"Plus, I like to win," Rose was saying. "So I'd prefer to have a partner who's competitive. Someone cutthroat like you."

Peg blinked, yanking her thoughts back to the present. "Cutthroat?"

"You know what I mean. You make Genghis Khan look like a sissy."

Peg suspected she was meant to be offended. In truth, she didn't mind the comparison. Strength was a virtue in her eyes. Speaking of which, Rose wasn't giving in and going away like she usually did whenever the two of them crossed paths. Maybe she possessed more backbone than Peg knew about.

"Apparently you're not as mild-mannered as you'd like people to believe," she said.

"Then perhaps we'd make a good team."

"We'd probably end up fighting with one another."

Rose shrugged. "We fight now, so what's the difference? Who knows? Maybe after all these years, we could become friends."

Peg nearly choked on her last bite of the apple. "I highly doubt that."

"Now you sound like a quitter."

"I do *not*."

"A coward, then?"

"I see what you're doing," Peg said mildly. "You think if you back me into a corner, I will give you what you want."

"Not at all," Rose replied. "It seems to me this should be something we both want."

"How do you figure that?"

"Neither of us is getting any younger."

"So?"

"At our ages, life is all about personal connections. It's inevitable that we'll start losing people from our lives. Doesn't that make it even more important to appreciate the friends and family we have with us?"

Family. This was the second time Rose had referenced that relationship. As if things were really that simple. Unfortunately, where the Turnbull family was concerned, complications had always been a way of life.

Peg's heart squeezed painfully in her chest. Rose did have a point about losing loved ones, however. Peg hadn't needed to reach the age of seventy-two before realizing that.

Still, she hated having to admit that Rose might be right about something. So instead she said, "I'll think about your offer and get back to you."

"Don't wait too long." Rose picked up her tote and stood. "This isn't an open-ended invitation. If you dawdle, I might find someone better."

Someone better. Peg blew out a breath. *Right.* Like that was going to happen.

Visit our website at
KensingtonBooks.com
to sign up for our newsletters, read
more from your favorite authors, see
books by series, view reading group
guides, and more!

Become a Part of Our
Between the Chapters Book Club
Community and Join the Conversation

Submit your book review for a chance to win exclusive
Between the Chapters swag you can't get anywhere else!
https://www.kensingtonbooks.com/pages/review/